YOURS,
JEAN

YOURS, JEAN

— A NOVEL —

LEE MARTIN

DZANC BOOKS

5220 Dexter Ann Arbor Rd.
Ann Arbor, MI 48103
www.dzancbooks.org

First Edition: May 2020
Cover design by Matt Revert
Interior design byMichelle Dotter

ISBN: 9781950539147

Printed in the United States of America

10   9   8   7   6   5   4   3   2   1

In memory of Georgine Lyon, 1928-1952

"...she will not be alone.
She will have a book to open
and open and open.
Her life starts here."

—Naomi Shihab Nye,
"Because of Libraries We Can Say These Things"

"What is there sadd'ning in the Autumn leaves?"

—William Cullen Bryant,
"The Indian Summer"

1

Jean woke just before dawn to the sound of birds singing in the maple tree outside her window.

Cheer, cheer, cheer, they seemed to be saying.

The cardinals' song, the sweet call of daybreak. A perfect accompaniment to the gladness rising in her heart.

She'd lain awake long into the night, too excited to sleep, and had finally dozed off in the wee hours. Now the sky was brightening. She gave the window shade a tug and let it retract on its roller. Here at the end of summer, the nights were still warm enough to sleep with the window up, and she felt the morning breeze move over her legs, bare below the hem of the rayon nightgown she'd let the lady at Delzell's sell her when she'd gone shopping for the sorts of clothes she imagined a woman might wear if indeed that woman were her, Miss Jean De Belle, the new librarian and English teacher at Lawrenceville High—a woman setting out on her own.

"Rayon will wash and dry much faster than cotton," the clerk told her, "and I know how important time will be to a busy gal like you." The clerk was a tall, angular woman who wore cat-eye glasses with silver flowers etched onto the black frames. "Sweetie, just feel it. Now isn't that soft? Imagine how that'll feel against your skin. Ooh la lah."

Why not, Jean thought. Why not ditch the kid pajamas and wear something more womanly.

The clerk's name was Mildred. "But most folks call me Midge. Sweetie, I'm going to take good care of you. I'm going to set you up with exactly what you need."

Jean let Midge guide her through the purchase of dresses and skirts and blouses and sweaters—even stockings and shoes and gloves and scarves, and a winter coat she didn't really need, but it was a swing coat, Midge said. "Very chic, sweetie." And like that, it was hers.

Her new wardrobe was now carefully hung and folded in the closet and the dresser drawers inside her rented room at 115 Dubois Street, the home of Mrs. Mary Ellen McVeigh, an English teacher at the high school. A widow with a daughter, Robbie, who was starting her senior year and reminded Jean of herself at that age, when she was impatient for her grown-up life to begin.

Now here it was—at long last, the start of things for her. Soon Mary Ellen and Robbie would be up, and then the shared bath in the hall would be in demand. She grabbed her robe.

"Better shake a leg," she said aloud, and then grimaced at the sound of those words, something her former fiancé, Charlie, had said time and time again. She'd done her best to forget it—and him. Even her parents, who'd liked him at first, finally saw what she'd been trying to tell them. She had to let him go.

She felt a bit of gloom move over her. Then she laughed it away. The birds were still singing; the sun was up. It was a glorious day at the start of September, and she was ready—more than ready—to step into it.

"Oh, my," Mary Ellen said when Jean came downstairs for breakfast. Mary Ellen was untying her apron, and she paused a moment, her hands behind her back, as Jean took careful steps down the stairs. "You look like a million bucks. Doesn't she, Robbie? Doesn't Jean…I mean, Miss De Belle…doesn't Miss De Belle look grand?"

Robbie sat at the dining table eating a piece of toast. She was wearing the sort of pajamas Jean had worn just a month ago—striped pants and shirt—and she had a head full of rag curlers. She let her toast drop to her saucer and gave Jean an appraising eye. Robbie was a pretty girl with blond hair and a fair complexion, marred this morning by a single pimple on her chin. Jean would wonder later if that was what had her in a snit—a pimple on the first day of school, the first day of her senior year to boot. *Hell's bells and buckets of blood!*

That was the saying among the kiddos that summer. Jean heard it at the drive-in theater, the city pool, the county fair—the teenagers' cry of anger and exasperation. *Hell's bells and little catfish, hell's bells and shotgun shells, hell's bells and buckets of blood!* Ever since Jean had moved in and Mary Ellen had latched onto her—*We'll be best friends, Jean. Just you wait and see.*—Robbie had seemed to hold her in contempt.

Now she said, "I suppose. If you like that sort of look." She brushed toast crumbs from the tips of her fingers and pushed her chair back from the table. "It's a little too severe for my taste." She drew a square, her two forefingers coming apart and then meeting again at the bottom. "But I'm sure Miss De Belle wants to make a good impression, this being her first job and all. If she wants to look like an old maid, I'd say she's certainly turned the trick."

"Robbie Sue McVeigh!" Mary Ellen whipped off her apron and threw it at Robbie, but the girl was already running up the stairs, her arm knocking against Jean's. "I'm so sorry," Mary Ellen said. "Ever since her father died, she's been impossible."

"No need to apologize." Jean stooped and retrieved the apron and held it out to Mary Ellen. The apron was organdy with hand-painted red roses. So sheer and pretty, Jean thought, something Mr. McVeigh must have liked seeing his wife wear in the kitchen. "It can't have been easy for her."

"Oh, you know how it is with teenage girls." Mary Ellen took the apron and folded it nicely. "Nothing's ever easy with them."

"No, I suppose not," Jean said, uncomfortably aware that only a few years ago, she'd been one of those difficult teenage girls. *You'd bite off your nose to spite your face,* her mother always told her. *Jean Georgine De Belle! You need to grow up.* That's what she was trying to do. That's exactly what she intended—to grow up and make something of her life that would matter.

"Sometimes," she said to Mary Ellen, "I get the feeling that Robbie has no use for me."

"Welcome to the club." Mary Ellen laughed. "You know she blames me for Mr. McVeigh's death."

Jean looked down at her new shoes—a pair of two-eyelet oxfords, red leather, trimmed with blonde. She liked the sturdy heels and the noise they made on the hardwood floor. A smart shoe that would wear well, Midge at Delzells's had assured her. A shoe for someone whose steps were sure. A shoe that her mother would have chosen. Jean looked down at her shoes to remind herself that she'd need to be confident and strong with the people her life was about to make room for—her students and colleagues. She looked down at her shoes because she hadn't known Mary Ellen long enough to be comfortable with the intimacy she was about to share.

For whatever reason, folks with hard-luck stories always felt they could confide in her. Her mother said it was because she had such a friendly smile, but Jean believed people like Mary Ellen could sense that there was a sadness, an inclination toward melancholy, just beneath her friendly smile. It was true; she was a sucker for a sad story, but she was trying to steel herself against sharing too much. She was trying to stiffen her backbone to face all the ways her students would try to take advantage of her.

"I really don't need to know that," she said to Mary Ellen, and then moved quickly to take a seat at the table where a glass of orange juice had already been set out for her. "Really, I have no business in your affairs."

Mary Ellen sat down next to Jean and took her hand. "Aren't we best friends?" she said. She leaned forward, a sad grin on her face. Jean could tell she'd never felt she had a friend with whom she could share the details of her life. Mary Ellen was a woman just past forty, with a streak of gray hair showing in the roll that she backcombed from her forehead, a style Jean remembered her mother favoring a decade before. Now everyone sported shorter cuts with curls and waves. *Oh,*

Mother, Jean had heard Robbie say. *You really need to do something with your hair.* Not that Jean was any movie star, but she agreed that Mary Ellen could spiff herself up some. That streak of gray? A shorter cut and a box of Miss Clairol would fix that right up.

Jean withdrew her hand from Mary Ellen's, with just the slightest difficulty, and looked at her wristwatch.

Mary Ellen said, "Mr. McVeigh…"

Jean interrupted her. "Geez, would you look at the time. Wouldn't want to be late the first day, now would we?"

There was a flurry of activity: a rumble of a car engine, a series of loud horn honks, a boy's voice calling out, "Robbie. Hey, Robbie. Shake a leg, will ya?"

"It's that boy," Mary Ellen said. "Tom Heath and his jalopy. I wish Robbie had never taken up with him."

Then Robbie was running down the stairs, the rag curlers out of her hair now—that soft bob—and the pajamas traded for a red circle skirt and a white blouse with puff sleeves.

"Coming," she said. "Hold your horses."

She was out the door with a slam, and then Tom Heath's jalopy was roaring away. Mary Ellen said time was wasting and she was yet to finish dressing, and Jean had a few blessed minutes of silence to drink her juice and find some coffee and toast in the kitchen and to gather herself for whatever might find its way to her that day.

Then Mary Ellen was back with her pocketbook and her car keys, a sweater over her shoulders. Somehow she looked just right. Jean suddenly felt out of place in her new clothes and shoes. Those shoes that were already pinching her toes, a navy blue dress with a Peter Pan collar and a red fabric belt, a Parker 51 fountain pen—a college graduation gift from Charlie that she couldn't bring herself to throw away—clipped to her breast pocket. She felt like she was playing teacher the way she'd done when she was a little girl.

"Ready?" Mary Ellen asked.

"You bet," said Jean.

"Well, all right then. Here we go."

Jean had looked forward to this moment ever since she arrived in Lawrenceville at the beginning of August and moved into her room at Mary Ellen's house—this moment when she unlocked the door to the library and stepped inside. She loved the quiet. Soon the hallways would fill with students on their way to assembly. She loved the way the morning sun came through the windows and slanted over the wooden tables. That and the slight crackle of the fluorescent lights as she flipped the switches. There was the card catalog, the brass pulls of its drawers worn smooth and slightly tarnished from years of use. There was the globe in its floor stand, ready to be spun, and there were the shelves and shelves of books, all in their proper place, all of them the domain of Miss Jean De Belle, who took a few steps into her library on this beautiful morning in September and stood there, more convinced than ever that she'd done the right thing when she'd broken off her engagement to Charlie Camplain.

She'd loved the month she spent learning her new town, even if Mary Ellen had seemed a bit too desperate for her company. She loved the way the sunlight came into her room and the sound of the courthouse clock chiming the hour. She loved the lazy days. Often, she and Mary Ellen whiled away the afternoons swaying back and forth in the porch swing. Or maybe Mary Ellen would say, "How about an ice cream?" and off they'd go to George's on the square for chocolate sundaes. Afterward, they'd stroll around the square, window shopping, and later they'd drop into the Candle Lite restaurant for dinner.

"Just a couple of gals," Mary Ellen often said. "A couple of gals out on the town."

There were movies to see at the Avalon Theatre, and some days they went to the city pool and sunned themselves on chaise lounges in their modest one-piece bathing suits. Sometimes they took books to read, and time drifted by, neither of them saying a word.

One day, Mary Ellen read a short poem to her.

Without warning
as a whirlwind
swoops on an oak
Love shakes my heart

"Isn't it lovely?" Mary Ellen said.

It was. Jean felt it inside her, that shaking, the way she'd felt when she first fell in love with Charlie. And then, just as in the poem, without warning she was crying. A silent crying, the sort most people wouldn't notice, but Mary Ellen did.

"My dear girl."

She closed the book and reached out and took Jean's hand. A group of teenage girls were chattering nearby, and Jean noticed they stopped when Mary Ellen took her hand. They looked on in silence for a moment and then exploded into giggles. They put their heads close together and whispered.

"My dear Jean," Mary Ellen said. "You're crying."

"It's just so beautiful," Jean said, and as much as she wanted to pull her hand away she couldn't. She squeezed Mary Ellen's hand. She held tight. "You know that, don't you?" she said.

Mary Ellen nodded. "Sometimes the world is so marvelous it takes us by the throat."

"Yes, that's it exactly," Jean said.

That was the moment, Mary Ellen said later, when she knew the two of them were simpatico. "We understand, you and I," she said. "We know the beauty and the pain."

Now, in the library, Jean opened her purse to get a handkerchief, and she saw a sheet of folded paper. On it was the poem in Mary Ellen's handwriting. A sweet gift on the first day of school. A reminder of how swiftly love can come.

"It's all yours." Mary Ellen's voice startled her, and Jean turned quickly to see her standing in the doorway. "Your own library, dear. I wish you years and years."

Jean folded the sheet of paper and slipped it into her skirt pocket. "Thank you," she said. "Thank you for the poem. Thank you for giving me a home. Thank you for this last month. You've made me feel so welcome."

Mary Ellen smiled. "And you, my dear, have brought me such joy."

"I only hope the students like me," Jean said. "I hope I can help them along."

"Don't let Robbie trouble you." So Mary Ellen knew what Jean had been thinking. "She's a hard nut." Mary Ellen came into the room and stood close to Jean and lowered her voice. "She's got senior-itis, not to mention Tom Heath-itis." Mary Ellen grinned, her lips twitchy, and then a single loud "Ha!" exploded from her. She put her hand to her mouth. Then she took it away and said, in a much calmer tone, "You know how it is with girls."

Jean *did* know. Hadn't she been smitten with Charlie, so much so that she'd agreed to marry him, had worn his engagement ring, had set a date that had now come and gone, had ignored what troubled her about him—his drinking, his temper—because her mother told her no man was perfect and a marriage would always hit a few rough patches along the way, but nothing two people who loved each other couldn't work through.

"You do love him, don't you?" her mother asked.

"Yes, I think so," Jean said. Then she added in a whisper, "I guess."

"Young girls shouldn't get all wrapped up in a boy," she said now to Mary Ellen. "They have their whole lives ahead of them."

"Try telling that to Robbie." Mary Ellen laughed again. "She thinks her whole life is right now."

Jean could hear locker doors opening and closing in the hallway. Mary Ellen glanced behind her. "I better get to my homeroom," she said. "The heathens will be upon us soon. I'll see you at assembly, Jean. You know the principal will expect you to say a few words after he introduces you to the students, right?"

"Yes, he informed me."

"Okay, then." Mary Ellen gave Jean a quick kiss on the cheek. "A kiss for luck. I know you'll do just fine."

She squeezed her hand, and then she was gone. Jean felt a wave of panic come over her. The thought of standing in front of the student body at assembly and coming up with something to say about herself momentarily shook her confidence.

Standing there in the library, her new life about to begin in earnest, she was surprised to feel a twinge of sadness for everything she'd been about to have with Charlie before she decided to let it go. Would she do it differently if she could? She really couldn't say, and what was the use of the question now? She'd made her decision, and now here it was—the first day of school, the day that in her mind marked the end of one stage of her life and the true beginning of another.

She turned around once more to take in the splendor of the library—*her* library—and then she heard a small voice behind her. "Oh, my," that voice said.

Jean turned and saw a young girl taking a few hesitant steps into the library. A freshman, if Jean was any judge. She clutched a loose-leaf notebook to her chest. Her hair was raggedly cut into a bob, and she wore rimless glasses. A blond girl with pale skin. Her clothes were out of style—a plain print housedress, a pair of worn oxford shoes—and Jean thought she might be one of those who rode the bus in from the country. Someone who came from one of the two-room township schools, maybe Birds or Pinkstaff. "I just wanted to see," the girl said in a trembling voice. "Oh, gosh. I just wanted to see all the books."

"So you like to read," Jean said. "You like to learn, yes?"

The girl pushed her glasses up on her nose. "My old school didn't have many books."

"Well, you can come in here anytime and check out all the books you want." Jean held out her hand to the girl. "What's your name, dear?"

"Etta." The girl let Jean take her hand. "Etta Lawless."

"It's very nice to meet you, Etta." Jean smiled. "I'm Miss De Belle."

"I like the way books smell," Etta said. "I like the way they sound when I open them and the way the pages feel. Oh, golly. Just listen to me. I'm so embarrassed."

"I know exactly what you mean." Jean squeezed her hand. "No one should ever be embarrassed about the things they love."

"I'm a freshman," Etta said. "This is my first day."

"It's my first day, too. I have a feeling it's going to be a good one. For both of us."

"Thank you, Miss De Belle." The bell was ringing, calling the students to assembly. "Goodness, I have to go. I'm so nervous. This school is so big, and I hardly know a soul."

"Well, you know me. You come back and see me, okay?"

"I will," Etta said, and then she eased her hand from Jean's and took a few reluctant steps backward, as if she could barely bring herself to leave. "I like it here," she said, taking a final look around the library. "You're so lucky."

"You don't want to be late," Jean said, trying not to show how pleased she was that Etta had a schoolgirl crush on her. "Go on now."

Etta lifted a hand to wave goodbye. Then she went out into the hallway that was loud and crowded now with students, and Jean watched her get swallowed up in their number. Jean stood there, feeling her heart go out to the girl, and to herself, both of them about to make their way.

2

Eleven miles to the east of Lawrenceville, the night clerk at the Grand Hotel in Vincennes, Indiana, heard the rattle of a key being tossed onto the counter and a man's voice saying, "Checking out, bub."

The man—a Mr. Charles Camplain—drummed his fingers on the counter. He rocked up on his toes and then back on his heels as if he could barely make himself stand in one place long enough for the clerk, Norville Rich, to attend to him.

Norville turned the page on the desk calendar from September 2 to September 3. Then he made a note in the private ledger he liked to keep: *Wednesday, September 3, 1952: Sunny and clear with temps approaching 83 degrees. First day of school. A perfect day to begin.*

"I trust everything was to your liking," he said, making sure to raise his voice a tad. The night before, he'd taken note of the wire threading discreetly up from Mr. Camplain's collar to the hearing aid in his left ear. "Your room, Mr. Camplain. I trust you spent a comfortable night?"

Mr. Camplain dipped a finger into the left side pocket of his suit coat, a gray flannel. Norville noticed the rectangular shape there, the one he'd first assumed to be a cigarette pack when Mr. Camplain checked in. Then he'd spotted the wire and the earpiece. Now he figured Mr. Camplain was fiddling with the volume on his hearing aid.

"Ducky," Mr. Camplain finally said. "Aces all the way around."

The Arrow Coach had brought him from Evansville to Vincennes, and Norville had watched him walk across Second Street and into the lobby of the Grand Hotel. He was smartly dressed, and he carried an oxblood leatherette suitcase, a Samonsite with brass latches and a monogram in gold flourish on a brass plate underneath the handle: *C C E*. His black hair was combed in a forward brush Ivy League cut. He wore a gray flannel suit, the flat edge of a maroon pocket square peeking up from his breast pocket. His black wingtips were polished and neatly laced. He carried himself with more confidence than his diminutive stature suggested he deserved. He was someone who had prospects.

The suitcase was sitting on the floor now, as Mr. Camplain removed a money clip from his trouser pocket and slid out a ten and four ones and tossed them onto the counter. The money clip was gold with a gleaming reddish-brown tiger's eye. Norville noticed that Mr. Camplain wore a matching tie clip. It held a maroon necktie to his white shirt, a tie unlike any Norville had ever seen, with a geometric design of white circles overlaid with a white grid, the lines and circles intersecting like a game of tic-tac-toe gone mad. To look at it too long was dizzying.

"Say, that's a snazzy tie," Norville said. His own tie was narrow and striped, the knot loosened from his unbuttoned collar. "Yes, sir," he said. "Catches the eye, if you know what I mean."

"It's imported," said Mr. Camplain. "It's from Italy. Silk."

"You must have been around."

"What's that?" Again, he reached into his pocket to adjust the volume on his hearing aid. "I was in the Army. Demo unit. I've got nerve damage in this ear."

Norville started to repeat what he'd said, but then something fell from Mr. Camplain's money clip and landed on the counter. It was a wallet-sized photograph of a girl. A pretty girl. Not movie-star glamorous—her chin was too long, her nose too much of a bulb— but a pretty girl all the same, a girl with a great smile and her wavy brown hair just a little frizzy. She looked like she was full of pep. She was looking right at the camera, which made Norville feel like she was looking at him.

"Who's the dish?" he asked.

"Careful, Mac," said Mr. Camplain. "That *dish* is going to be my wife."

"Fiancée, huh?"

He patted the right side pocket of his sport coat. "Got the ring right here."

"Well, that's fine. Mind if I have a look?"

Mr. Camplain had some trouble getting the ring box out of his pocket, and when he gave it a tug, the barrel of what appeared to be a snub-nosed .38 poked up for just an instant before he pushed it back down.

Norville took a step back from the counter. He'd always worried that someday someone might catch onto the fact that there was a small safe under the counter, and it held a healthy amount of cash before the day clerk carried it to the bank. Norville had wondered what he would do if some thief held a gun on him and told him to open it.

"I'm a traveling man." Mr. Camplain smoothed the flap of the pocket as best he could. "A traveling man can't be too careful. Savvy?"

Norville felt his shoulders relax. "What's your line?"

"Insurance. I'm with the State Security Life Insurance Company." He opened the ring box and held it out to Norville. "How about you, bub? Will your loved ones be provided for after you're gone?"

The truth was, Norville had no loved ones. No wife. No children. His mother had died a year ago and left him alone. He did have a friend, Miss Lorene Deveraux, whom he secretly took a fancy to, but he was fifty-three years old—too old, he thought, to wish for anything more than friendship.

The engagement ring was a thin platinum band with a modest diamond solitaire, the sort of ring Norville could imagine saving up his money to buy. The simplicity of the ring—its near homeliness— endeared Mr. Camplain to him. He thought he saw scratches on the band, but before he could be sure, Mr. Camplain closed the box with a snap and returned it to his pocket.

"I'm not married," Norville said.

"What's keeping you?" Mr. Camplain snatched up the girl's photograph and slid it back into the money clip. "Nothing like the company of a good woman. I can tell you that."

"What's her name? Your girl."

"Jean De Belle," Mr. Camplain said. "Now, can I get a taxi? Gotta make hay while the sun shines." He gave Norville a wink. "Lucky gal. She doesn't know I'm about to change her life."

3

ON THE DRIVE TO SCHOOL, Robbie asked Tom whether he'd given any more thought to what she'd insisted he consider, namely going to work in his father's paint store after graduation instead of going off to college. Why waste those four years if, at the end of them, he was only going to come back to Lawrenceville and take over Heath Paints? Hell's bells. Why not get married right away?

"Geez, Robbie." Tom cranked the wheel of his jalopy—a gold Chevy Fleetline, a fastback with fat whitewalls and tons of chrome—and punched the gas. The 350 engine responded, and the air rushed in and pushed her hair into her face as they raced down Lexington toward Tenth Street. "It's the first day of school," he said. "Senior year. Can't we just enjoy it?"

They were heading up Tenth now, climbing the hill toward State Street. Kids, underclassmen most of them, were walking along in their new school clothes—the boys in sharply creased chinos or cuffed blue jeans that would never be that blue again; the girls in new blouses and plaid skirts and freshly shined penny loafers and bobby sox that were white against the summer tan of their shins. Poor dopes, Robbie thought. Having to hoof it to school. It was grand being a senior. It was even grander still to imagine being Tom's wife.

"Don't you want to marry me?" She laid her hand on Tom's leg and stroked her finger along the inseam of his jeans. From time to time, she liked to tease him like that, to feel the power she held over him, but that was as far as it went. A touch here or there once in a while. Never anything more than that. She had to save something for him to look forward to. Like her mother always told her, no boy will buy the cow if he can get the milk for free.

Not that her mother had known a thing about how to keep a man. Look at what had happened with Robbie's father. He'd been so miserable he'd up and died just to get away from her mother. The doctor said he died from a ruptured aortic artery, but Robbie knew better. She knew he died of a broken heart, and it was all her mother's fault.

"Sometimes, Tom." Robbie took her hand away from his leg. "Honestly. If I didn't know better, I'd think you didn't love me."

Tom came to a stop at the top of the hill and let the Fleetline idle as he waited for cars to pass on State Street. Some women were going into the Clock Café for breakfast. One of them, a redhead with big teeth, tossed her head back and laughed, and Robbie thought how wonderful that would be. Tom off to work at the paint store and her off to breakfast with her girlfriends.

He wasn't the most handsome boy in their class, but she found him attractive enough. He had a rugged, square jaw and brown eyes that made her melt every time he looked at her. So what if his ears stuck out just a tad too far, or one of those gorgeous eyes seemed to droop at the corner, or that he had to wear eyeglasses that made him look like an old man to read the blackboard at school? He was her man, now and forever. She knew that for sure.

Then he looked over at her, and she saw the pain in those beautiful eyes, and she knew something was about to change.

"Robbie," he said, and his voice broke.

"Go," she said.

Tom did what she told him to do. The traffic had cleared, and he eased on through the intersection. At the crest of the hill, the flagpole in front of the school came into view, and then the roofline and the red brick building, and then they were coasting down the hill, not saying a word, just letting the air rush in and the sun warm them on this beautiful day in September, the first day of school, their senior year and all that lay ahead of them.

◦◦◦◦

Tom told her in the school parking lot, as soon as he shut off the engine and the quiet settled around them. Later, she would think if only she had gotten out of the car before he had a chance to speak—if she'd stepped into the stream of students passing by—he wouldn't have dared tell her when someone might hear, and then, if the terrible thing didn't get said, it would be like it hadn't happened at all.

"Robbie, you've got to listen to me," he said. "I'm not who you think I am."

She knew exactly who he was. Tom Heath, the boy she'd gone with since their freshman year, the boy who always treated her with kindness, the one her father had proclaimed "a keeper." He was an Eagle Scout, editor of the *Toma Talk,* president of the senior class. He ran high hurdles for the track team, belonged to the Library Club. On Saturdays and over holidays, he worked in his father's paint store. He was a straight arrow, a steady Freddy, earthbound. But he was no wet rag. He could get goofy and make her laugh and laugh, and he was all boy—hadn't she felt him hard against her hand often enough to know that? When she was with him, she was just gone. That's all she knew. There was something about him that just made her flip, and that was something she meant to hold onto. He was Tom Heath, the boy she intended to marry.

"You're talking crazy," she said.

She had her hand on the door handle. She was about to pull it back and push her way out of the car. Then he blurted it out: "Robbie, there's this girl."

"Girl?" She let the handle slip from her fingers and turned to face him. "What girl?"

Her name, he said, was Millie Haines, and she was from Vincennes. He kept his hands in his lap, his head bowed. Robbie watched his fingers tremble when he lifted his right hand to touch the strip of cashmere that he'd tied to his rearview. She'd cut the strip from one of her sweaters and given it to him—a mirror warmer to announce their love. He touched the cashmere, and she felt her heart go out to him while at the same time she braced herself for what was to come. She'd cut that strip of pink cashmere and given it to him the day he gave her his class ring. She wore it on a chain around her neck. She'd grown accustomed to feeling its weight tapping her breastbone when she walked. Now she put her hand on it as if she were having trouble getting a breath. Although the morning air through the open windows was cool, the sun was hot on her face and she felt as if she might break out in a sweat. A boy in a group passing by shouted, "Hey, Tom. How's the boy?" Tom just touched two fingers to his brow in a salute.

"What's this mean, Tom?" Robbie said. "Are you in love with someone else?"

"In love? Gosh, no. Not even close."

"What is it, then? What's the story with this girl? How do you know her?"

"She's just a girl." Tom's voice was nearly a whisper. "I met her one night in Westport."

"Westport?" She knew there were boys who managed to do some drinking in the bars by the river. "Does your father know you've been spending time there?"

"He's about to know a lot more than that. I guess you are, too."

Then he told her. He told her everything.

"One thing led to another," he said.

Robbie felt an ache in her throat and knew she was about to cry. "Pregnant," she said.

"Robbie, I'm scared. I don't know what to do."

Now she was pushing her way out of the car. The last bell was ringing, calling everyone to assembly. "I guess you should have thought about that," she said just before she slammed the door and started walking toward the school. She heard Tom calling after her.

"Robbie, don't," he said. "Robbie, you know I love you."

4

Norville carried Charlie Camplain's suitcase out to the taxi and let the driver, Bert Haines, stow it in the trunk. Norville knew him as Grinny. He was a toothless man who favored wearing porkpie hats. Didn't have a tooth in his head, but he didn't care. He was always showing folks his gums, always smiling. "Life's too short not to enjoy it," he said to Norville once. "Got to love it. Got to love it to death."

Nights when he didn't have many fares, he often came by the Grand and shot the breeze with Norville, and over time the two of them became friendly.

One night, Norville had to get some money out of the safe for the cash drawer, and Grinny whistled. "Whoo-ee," he said. "Just listen to those tumblers click. I'd be afraid to be here at night with all that cash."

Norville felt a rush of relief flood through him when he admitted he was indeed frightened. "I think about it all the time," he said. "How easy it would be for someone to come in here with a gun."

"Don't worry, I'll keep it to myself. I know what it's like." Grinny patted his pants pocket. "Some nights I end up with a wad from fares. I'm not ashamed to say I'm scared, too." He winked at Norville. "You and me, we're working men."

Norville had thought kindly of Grinny since then. This morning, he was glad to hand him this fare.

"Where to?" Grinny asked.

"Lawrenceville," Charlie said.

Grinny pushed his hat back on his head and studied Charlie. "That's eleven miles."

Charlie pulled out his money clip. "Don't worry, bub. I'm good for it. I'm Charlie Camplain."

Grinny smiled, showing his gums. "All right, then. Yes, sir. You just say where."

Norville offered Charlie his hand. He didn't know why, but he felt it was something he should do. It had taken a while to get the taxi, over an hour, and Norville had felt Charlie's frustration. The least he could do now was to wish him well.

"Good luck to you," he said.

Charlie shook his hand and said, "Thanks, but I won't need it."

Then he was gone, and Norville was left with the picture of that girl in his head—the girl from the photograph. He wondered if Lorene had looked that way when she'd been that age.

Lorene Devereux. A never-married woman who lived in a box house near the Old Cathedral. A sewing woman who did alterations for Gimbels Department Store, kept her flower gardens in bloom spring to winter, enjoyed a single glass of Schlitz beer each Saturday night while watching Championship Wrestling on WTVW out of Evansville, and went for walks with Norville along the Wabash River evenings toward dusk when swallows cut through the twilight and the lights along the river bridge came on. Sometimes he thought about taking her hand or kissing her in the dark, but he could never quite work up the courage to try either one. "This is nice," she often said, and he let that be enough.

There he was, a man who had almost given up on love, and now look at him. He had an early lunch date with Lorene—it was her day off—and he was surprised to find himself thinking about trying out a proposal. Charlie Camplain had given him the idea. Why not today? Why couldn't Norville say to Lorene, "Now look here. You're a woman of a certain age, and I'm a man of like years, and, well, heck, we seem to enjoy each other's company. Why not make it a permanent arrangement?"

Why couldn't he say something like that? It was a delightful day in early September, but before long full autumn would set in and then make the turn toward winter. Norville wanted to be ready. He couldn't bear the thought of the cold and the early dark and being all alone in his house. But today—ah, today!—the sun was shining and the muggy air had let go. A blue sky with a few high clouds, puffs and wisps of white just floating by. He stood in front of the hotel and tipped back his head to look at that sky. He felt his spirits lift, and he determined today would be the day. He'd speak his heart to Miss Lorene Devereux, and he'd give her the chance to speak hers back to him.

But first he had some business to attend to. Mr. Raymond Hardy, the man who'd also been keeping time with Lorene, needed to know what Norville had in mind. Why not pay him a visit, tell him what was what, get him out of the picture. That was exactly what Norville meant to do, just as soon as the day clerk arrived to relieve him.

∽✐〜

Grinny was usually the happy-go-lucky sort, but on the morning he picked up Charlie Camplain at the Grand, he was inching toward an unusual and unwelcome gloom. His daughter, Millie, was a splinter under his skin. She'd told him just before he went to work that she was going to have a baby, a piece of news that might have been cause for celebration had it come some years in the future. The daddy was a high school boy from Lawrenceville, a boy named Tom Heath, who'd met Millie one night at the Showboat in Westport—both of them underage, but when did that ever matter at the bars on the other side of the river. One thing led to another. That's what she told Grinny. "One thing led to another, Daddy, and, well, you know…"

Now she was with child. His sweet Millie, the surprise that had come to him and his wife after they'd given up on ever having that blessing. Peg was forty-five when she got pregnant. Grinny was forty-seven. A miracle, one that filled them with so much happiness even

Grinny's smile couldn't hold it all. Now here they were, sixteen years later, and Millie was going to have a baby.

"What in the world are we going to do about that?" Grinny said to her that morning.

"Well, Daddy, I just don't know."

For some reason, when he saw Charlie Camplain flash that money clip, he got the idea that something good might be just around the bend. Maybe his luck was going to change. He didn't know how, but as he pointed his cab toward Lawrenceville, he felt something he'd always relied on: an intuition, a presentiment, a suspicion that everything would be dandy.

"A beautiful day." He glanced in his rearview mirror and saw that Charlie Camplain had his elbow on the door handle, his hand propping up his head and covering his right ear. He looked forlorn as he watched the city flash by, the Old Cathedral, the river bridge, and then they were in Illinois—in Westport, a smattering of clubs and bars along the river bottoms. "Why the long face, chum?" Grinny asked.

He didn't know that Charlie had turned off his hearing aid so he could be alone with the thought of what he was about to do. Then he turned his head a bit and Grinny caught his eye. He gave him that smile, and sure enough, Charlie couldn't resist. He smiled back.

"That's the ticket," Grinny said. "Life's too short."

Charlie asked him to make a stop at the Showboat in Westport. "Just for a sec, bub. I need to talk to a man."

The man turned out to be Dick Dollahan, the proprietor, barrel-chested with a thick head of curly black hair, a man who always had a cigar stub screwed into the corner of his mouth. Later, he would say he didn't know Charlie Camplain from Adam. "This Joe," he said. "He just waltzed right in. Said he needed a favor. Asked me if I'd mind if he left his grip with me. I said, 'Who the hell are you, mister?' and he said, 'Bub, I'm Charlie Camplain. By the time you see me later today, I'll be on my way.' 'On your way where?' I asked him. 'Easy Street,' he said, 'or straight to hell. Right now, I'd say it's a toss-up.'"

Charlie set the oxblood suitcase on the floor. This early in the morning, the Showboat was nearly empty. Chairs were still turned upside down on a few tables. The day cook was just heating up the grill.

The night janitor was mopping the floor. He was a skinny man with high-waisted work pants. His shirt pockets nearly touched his belt. He was whistling a tune, Charlie could tell, but he couldn't hear it well enough to make it out. Something slow and dreamy. That's all he could tell. Something he imagined Jean would like. Something the two of them would have danced to at the Broadway Hotel in Madison only a few months ago. Something she would have hummed into his good ear, her cheek laid against his chest—something he would have hummed to himself over and over after he took her home.

He saw Dick Dollahan behind the bar at the Showboat and immediately knew he was the owner. He could tell from the way he had the newspaper spread out on the bar, the way he was eating olives from a tumbler, the way he glanced at his wristwatch and shouted to the janitor, "Clancy, hey, Clancy. Shake a leg for Christ's sake."

Shake a leg. How many times had Charlie said that to Jean? *Shake a leg, sweets. We've got things to do, places to go, people to see.*

One day, she said to him, "Jesus, Charlie, if I have to hear you say that one more time, I'll lose my mind."

He knew she was joking him. How could that saying possibly get on her last nerve? "Don't cuss," he told her. He didn't like it when she used coarse language. A lady should be a lady.

He'd run across enough rough talk in the Army. Language that made him blush every time. Soon his bunk mates caught on. Charlie was a bit of a prig. He read books each night before lights out—real books, not dime-store novels like the Mickey Spillane books the other boys favored, but books by Oscar Wilde, Ernest Hemingway, Thoreau, for Pete's sake—and he wrote his mother long letters each Sunday, and he never used bad language. "Wouldn't say shit if he had a mouthful," one of the boys in his barracks finally proclaimed. That was Charlie Camplain—a thinker, a mama's boy.

"Bub," he said to Dick Dollahan, "I need you to do me a favor."

Then he gave Dick that smile of his, the one Jean could never resist, the one that made men want to be his best friend. Just enough of a smirk in it to suggest that something fun or exciting was around the corner. Just enough to make people think he was a wise guy, a smartass, but he wasn't, not really. Just ask the boys in his platoon at Camp Dix. He was a pushover, a bookworm. Charlie knew what they thought of him, and he let them think it. He just gave them that smile. It was like he knew something they didn't, something that would knock them over when they finally figured it out.

"I just need to leave this bag here this morning. I'll be back for it later. Would that be okey-doke?"

Dick popped an olive into his mouth and held it there, squinting his eye at Charlie. "You're no customer of mine. I've never even seen you before."

"We can fix that. How about a shot of Old Grand-Dad?"

"Sort of early in the day, ain't it?"

"It's a special day." Charlie put his foot up on the rail and puffed out his chest. "I need to travel light. I'm about to be engaged."

Again, he gave Dick that grin, and Dick grinned back, his cigar stub rising toward his eye. "That calls for a toast," he said. "It's not every day a man lays claim to his sweetheart. Who's the lucky girl?"

"Jean," Charlie said. "Jean De Belle."

Grinny waited for Charlie Camplain to come out of the Showboat. As he did, he stared at the huge sign that rose up above the long, squat building. Below the word SHOWBOAT were three women in evening gowns next to a bottle of Sterling beer. DANCING, ENTERTAINMENT, the sign said, and Grinny thought this was what had lured his daughter here, this promise of excitement. He gave some thought to Millie's situation. He knew a man, Raymond Hardy, who said there was a certain doctor on Busseron Street who, for the right price, was able to make a baby disappear before it got born. The doctor's name came up one evening around a poker table in the back room of Alice and Woody's Cocktail Bar.

"I've had occasion to make use of the good doctor's services," Raymond Hardy said. He tipped up his glass and drained the last of his beer. Bottles of Drewrys and Falstaff littered the table. Heavy glass ashtrays overflowed with butts from packages of Chesterfields and Pall Malls and Lucky Strikes. A haze of blue smoke hung over the table. The payphone on the wall rang, but no one answered it. Finally, Raymond Hardy said, "More than one occasion." He winked. "If you get what I'm talking about."

Grinny did indeed get what he was talking about, but he thought Raymond Hardy was just talking big, as he was apt to do, particularly when he was drinking at a poker table.

"What nonsense," Grinny said to Peg when he got home and told her about Raymond Hardy's boast. "That man rubs me the wrong way."

Peg sat up in bed and snapped on the table lamp. It was winter time, and she had on her flannel nightgown. Her hair was in curlers; she'd scrubbed off her makeup, and her face was pale and marked with worry lines. Even so, Grinny felt that little fall in his stomach, as he had all the years they'd been together when he first saw her after they'd been apart. She was still his sweet Peg, the love of his life. He could still see the girl she'd been, the one who'd set him into a swoon. Every time he looked in her clear brown eyes, he fell in love all over again. He knew men who got tired of their wives and started shopping around, but he didn't think that would ever happen to him. He couldn't imagine a day when he wouldn't be crazy about Peg.

Raymond Hardy, though, was a different sort of man. He was a bounder, a tomcat, a cad.

"He's always had a reputation," Peg said. "I couldn't count the number of women he's had an eye for."

Grinny sat down on the edge of the bed and began pulling off his shoes. The hardwood floor was cold. Outside, it was starting to snow. He could see the flakes coming down under the streetlight. The storm window rattled in its frame.

"Do you really think a doctor would offer an abortion?" he asked Peg.

"*That* doctor?" She let Grinny think about it.

"Really, Peg?"

"Yes," she said. "Yes, I do."

Grinny considered it. He watched the snow come down. He could see the light inside the spire of the Old Cathedral.

"It'd be a sin," he finally said. "A mortal sin, Peg."

She shrugged her shoulders. "I guess some people just don't care."

Grinny was thinking about all of this now as he sat in his cab at the Showboat, watching the waters of the Wabash River ripple past. A buzzard circled high above the river. On the far bank, the paper-white trunks of the sycamores were bright in the sunlight. He heard the putt-putt-putt of the motor on a jon boat somewhere in the distance. All of this ordinarily would have pleased him, but how could it now, in light of what he was facing? He and Peg were too old to raise another baby, and Millie was too young to get married, even if Tom Heath agreed to it. Grinny wondered what the boy's parents thought—if they even knew. His father owned a paint store in Lawrenceville; Millie had said that much. Grinny imagined Mr. Heath as a man of privilege, someone who wouldn't encourage his son to take responsibility for his actions, but maybe that wasn't true. Maybe Mr. Heath would be just as disappointed and angry as Grinny. Maybe if the two of them sat down and talked things out, maybe then an answer would appear.

But what would that answer be? To send Millie to one of those homes for unwed mothers and then put the baby up for adoption? To let her have the baby, and then give it to the Heaths to raise? Or would Mr. Heath turn Grinny away, make him feel like a beggar, someone not worth his time.

The only thing Grinny knew for sure was that there were two kinds of people in the world, the ones who had money and the ones who didn't, and life was always so much easier for the ones who did.

Like this fella, Charlie Camplain, who was coming out of the Showboat now in his gray flannel suit and his shiny black wingtip shoes and a necktie unlike any Grinny had ever seen. He'd left his suitcase inside the tavern, and Grinny wondered why a man would leave a case of such fine leather behind. That was the way with the ones who had the money. They could be careless and never expect to have to pay.

"What about your grip?" Grinny said when Charlie was once again in the backseat of the cab.

"Say what?" Charlie reached into the left side pocket of his suit coat. "Damn hearing aid goes haywire from time to time."

"Your suitcase," Grinny said.

"Don't worry about that. I'll be back for it. Now let's hit the road."

"You sure you can trust it to be there?"

"Forget that case," Charlie said. "I've got bigger fish to fry."

Still, Grinny let the motor idle, hesitant to leave that beautiful suitcase behind. "If it was mine," he said, "I wouldn't let it out of my sight, let alone leave it in a tavern where anyone might walk off with it."

That's when Charlie got sore. He grabbed the top of the seat near Grinny's head and raised himself forward until he was so close Grinny could smell the soap he'd used for his morning shower.

"Am I paying you for advice?" Charlie said in a low voice that had just enough bite to it to set Grinny on edge. "No, I'm paying you to drive, and you better be doing it soon, or else." "Are you threatening me?" Grinny asked.

"No threat, bub. Just a fact. You might not think it to look at me, but I'm a dangerous man."

So Grinny did what he was told. He pulled the gearshift lever into low and rolled out of the parking lot and pointed the cab toward Lawrenceville. Although it shamed him to do so, he said, "Yes, sir," because somehow he knew that Charlie Camplain was telling the truth on himself. He *was* a dangerous man.

"That's it." Charlie eased back in his seat. "Like you said, it's a beautiful day."

5

RAYMOND HARDY RAN THE PANTHEON Theatre at Fifth and Main Street and lived in an apartment above it. It would be a quick walk for Norville from the Grand Hotel.

"You look like someone set a fire in your britches," the day clerk, a widow named Zelma Partridge, said when she finally arrived with a tale about an alarm clock that didn't go off. Norville knew she was lying. He knew she'd stopped at the Beauty College for an eight o'clock appointment. He could smell the permanent solution and the Aqua Net. She gave her hair a little pat and smiled at him. Then she took her time settling her pocketbook behind the counter. "Mercy, what's the rush?"

He was shrugging on his suit coat and buttoning his collar as he came out from behind the front desk. She always tried to get him to linger and talk a little, maybe even offer him a little something she'd baked at home, but this morning he was in a hurry. She'd made it plain that she was sweet on him, but Norville wasn't interested. He only had eyes for Lorene.

"Got to see a man about a horse?" Zelma asked.

"Something like that," Norville said, and with that he pushed through the revolving glass door and out into the morning. The clock at the Old Cathedral was chiming. He glanced at his wristwatch. Nine already. He was burning daylight.

So off he went on this splendid morning. *Get ready, Raymond Hardy*, he thought to himself. *I'm coming to tell you what's what.*

It was half a block to Main Street and then three blocks to the Pantheon. It pleased Norville to hear his heels clacking along on the sidewalk as he passed Gimbels Department Store and made quick work of the Woolworth's and the Ft. Sackville Bowling Lanes. He crossed the street at Fourth and angled between two cars parked at the curb in front of Breyfogle's Shoe Store. He hopped up onto the curb with a spring to his step, and he was so satisfied with that motion that he snapped his fingers and said "Yes, sir" right out loud.

The planter boxes along the street were filled with petunias, the birds were singing, bells chimed from the stores that were just opening their doors. The smell of donuts came to Norville as he passed the Tip-Top Café. A light breeze, so welcome after the long heat spell, lifted the end of his necktie and made him walk even faster.

A doorway along the street led up to the apartment above the Pantheon. *Cyrano* was playing. Norville paused a moment to look at the poster—Jose Ferrer with that ridiculous nose, lunging forward with his sword; the beautiful Mala Powers looking quite fetching in the upper left-hand corner. Norville took heart, slipped through the door, and bounded up the stairs.

"Raymond, here's the story," he said, when Raymond Hardy answered the knock at his door. Norville could see a half-empty bottle of Jack Daniel's on the coffee table inside, two drink glasses, a package of Chesterfield cigarettes, one of them still burning in the ashtray. "There's something you should know," Norville said.

Raymond Hardy was a red-faced man with broken veins in his nose and cheeks. His sleeveless undershirt was tucked into his gabardine trousers and was stretched tight across his chest. He smelled like Aqua Velva aftershave and cigarette smoke. He held the door a quarter of the way open with his left hand and leaned against the jamb with his right. His bulk filled the doorway.

"Norville," he said. "What brings you here so early?"

He was just about to tell him. A few seconds more, and he'd start in. He took a breath. Then, before he could find his voice, he heard a woman's voice call out from somewhere in the apartment. He realized, then, that the shower had been running and now it wasn't.

"Ray," the woman said. "Ray, baby. Fetch me a towel, will you?"

And Norville knew he was listening to the voice of Lorene Devereux.

Raymond Hardy winked at him, his lips set in a smirk.

"You savvy?" he said.

Then he closed the door.

Norville started walking. He walked past the Old Cathedral and thought for a moment about going in, but it'd been so long since he'd been inside a church he thought he had no right. He walked across the river bridge into Westport and stopped at the Showboat. The grill was hot now, and the joint was full with the breakfast crowd. Norville was surprised to discover he was famished. He sat down at a table and ordered eggs over easy, and hash browns, and a short stack of pancakes. "And coffee," he told the waitress. He wanted it black and strong.

"You got it, sugar," she said. She was a woman near to his age with thick black hair and elegant hands, long-fingered and neatly manicured. He imagined what it would be like to hold one of them, to feel her fingers intertwine with his. He wanted to ask her name, but before he could screw up his courage, she said, "You work at the Grand Hotel, don't you?"

"That's right. Do I know you?"

"You wouldn't have any reason to know me." She finished writing out his order and then stuck her pencil into that thick black hair just above her left ear. He knew she was busy, and yet she lingered. "But I've seen you sometimes when I come past the Grand on my way to work. I saw you this morning out in front, helping a man with his suitcase. You looked chipper. You looked like you were ready to take on the world."

Just a short time ago, the morning had seemed fresh and clear to him, and the day was full of possibilities. Then he bounded up the stairs to Raymond Hardy's, and in an instant everything changed. Now here was this woman who had taken notice of him. What about that?

"It's going to be sunny and clear today," he said to her, "with temps approaching eighty-three degrees."

"Summer's stretching on, isn't it?" The waitress smiled at him. "I'm Ruth," she said. "I'll get that order right in for you."

"Norville," he said. "My name is Norville."

"Sure it is, sugar." Ruth gave him a wink. "I already knew that."

He watched her walk away, swiveling her hips to squeeze between the tables. She had on a pair of black and white plaid pedal pushers and a white sleeveless blouse. Her arms were thin and tanned. Her name was Ruth. And she knew his name.

He ate like a thresher. He shoveled in eggs and potatoes and pancakes. He asked for toast with lots of butter and jelly. He ate like a man who'd nearly forgotten how to eat, a man who'd long been missing the goodness of food.

"Look at you go," Ruth said with a laugh. "You must have been starved."

"I was," he said. "I surely was."

He was thinking of the long years of his bachelorhood. Night after night alone, picking at meager meals cooked for one, opening a can of Campbell's soup, perhaps, or frying a single pork chop. He ate slowly trying to delay the end of the meal, when he would have to rise and face the rest of the evening. Off to work at eleven in the general quiet of the Grand. On occasion, he had a few words of conversation with late-arriving guests or ones checking out early, like he had today with Charlie Camplain. His closest human interactions were with people he'd never again see, people just passing through his life.

Even his time with Lorene had its restrictions. They might have supper together and a quick walk before she was off to bed and he had to go to work. Mornings, she was getting ready for work when he was leaving the Grand, or, as he'd found out this morning, waking up in the bed of Raymond Hardy. He could see her at lunch if he didn't mind sacrificing his sleep. He remembered they had a lunch date scheduled on this very day. Would she be there? Would Raymond Hardy have told her how he showed up at the apartment this morning? What if Norville were to keep that lunch date and not let on that he knew about her and Raymond. That was something to chew on.

Finally, Norville laid down his knife and fork. His gut strained against the belt of his trousers. He dabbed his sweaty forehead with his napkin.

Ruth brought him his ticket. "Can I get you anything else?"

He shook his head. "I'm afraid I've been a bit of a glutton."

"I just love to see a man eat the way you do." She leaned over the table and started stacking saucers and plates. She smelled of hot grease from the kitchen, but underneath that scent was a sweeter one, a perfume of flowers—just a faint aroma, but enough to make Norville want to press his face to her hair. "You come back and see us anytime," she said.

"Oh, I will," he said. "You can count on that."

At the cash register, Dick Dollahan was chewing on a cigar. Norville knew him because on occasion Dick booked "special guests" into the Grand. Rumor had it they were young ladies meant to provide companionship for VIP gamblers who came from out of town to play in private high-stakes poker games in the Showboat's back room.

"Are these girls prostitutes?" Norville asked him one night. Dick gave him a grin. He put his arm across Norville's shoulders and pulled him in so close he could smell cigar smoke and whisky and Old Spice.

"Don't you know prostitution is illegal in Indiana?"

Now Dick asked him if his breakfast had been to his liking.

"Very much so," Norville said. "Your waitress, Ruth, she's top-notch."

"You like her, do you?"

"She treated me fine."

"Ruth has a way about her. I've known her a long time."

Norville fished a few ones out of his billfold. "Local gal, is she?"

Dick punched the total into the cash register and the change drawer sprang open with a bing. "Lives on Second Street, two blocks down from the Grand. Little bungalow with a blue gazing ball in the yard. You musta been by it a million times."

He had indeed, and never once had he known a thing about who lived there. Norville held out his hand for his change. That's when he saw it resting against the wall behind Dick—the oxblood leatherette suitcase, the one with the brass latches and the monogram that told him it was the same case that belonged to Charlie Camplain.

"How'd you come to have that case?" Norville asked.

Dick glanced back at it. "Fella brought it in early this morning. Said he needed someplace to leave it, said he'd be back for it later. A real spiffy fella."

"Maroon necktie?"

"A crazy pattern on it." Dick rubbed his eyes. "Circles in circles. Enough to make me dizzy."

Norville nodded. "I checked him out of the Grand this morning."

"He said it was a special day. Sorta gave me a boost just to be around him."

"I know what you mean, but there's something fishy about that guy. He had a gun in his pocket. A snub-nosed .38."

"What's he carrying a gun for?"

"Said he was a traveling man and he couldn't take a chance."

Dick took the cigar out of his mouth and studied it. "A real friendly fella."

As he took his change from Dick Dollahan, Norville felt a heavy hand clamp down on his shoulder.

"Looks like you'll serve anyone these days, Dick."

Norville knew without turning around that the voice belonged to Raymond Hardy.

"Anyone with cash," Dick said with a laugh.

Raymond Hardy slapped Norville on the back. "I guess that's one thing Norville's got. Probably got the first dollar he ever made."

Norville opened his billfold and slipped the two ones that Dick Dollahan had given him in with his other cash.

"I think I just saw a moth fly out," Raymond Hardy said. "Did you see it, too, Dick?"

"Flew right past my ear," Dick Dollahan said.

Ruth was passing by with a fresh pot of coffee. She was chuckling, and Norville imagined she thought she was overhearing some good-natured ribbing. She didn't know Raymond Hardy had no intention of being friendly.

He swatted her on the fanny as she passed. She turned back and waved her free hand at him. "Oh, you," she said in a way that pretended to be angry, but Norville could tell she was secretly pleased.

He said to Raymond Hardy, "I hear you like to play fast and loose with your money. Word is you're a careless man."

The smile faded from Raymond Hardy's face. His nostrils flared, and he closed his hands into fists. The conversation had taken a sharp turn. It wasn't about joking and ribbing any longer. It was personal and pointed, and Norville knew it would be clear to anyone who was nearby that they each disliked the other.

"What's that supposed to mean?" Raymond Hardy said.

"It would be ungentlemanly for me to say." Norville put his billfold in his hip pocket. "But I understand that you've had reason to pay for the services of a certain doctor. More than once, or so I've heard. Perhaps you also play fast and loose with your affections."

Raymond Hardy smirked. "You don't know a thing. You're trying to make something out of nothing."

"I don't imagine it was nothing to the women involved. I suspect it was very much something to them."

"Some people make mistakes." Raymond Hardy gave Dick Dollahan a wink. "Other people make mistakes go away."

Ruth was passing by again. "What are you boys talking about?"

Raymond Hardy glared at Norville, daring him to say something more, but Norville didn't.

Finally, just as the silence was starting to get uncomfortable, Raymond said, "We're just gassing. That's all. Just pulling each other's leg. Right, Norville?"

Norville nodded. Immediately he hated himself for doing that, and by so doing, sanctioning Raymond Hardy's behavior. "I'll be seeing you," Norville said to Dick Dollahan.

"Leaving so soon?" Raymond Hardy said. "Slipping away just when things are starting to get interesting. What are you? Some sort of wet blanket?"

Ruth laughed again. "Don't be a wet blanket, Norville."

It was at that moment that Norville made up his mind. He'd go to Gimbels. He'd keep his lunch date with Lorene. He'd promised her he'd be there, and so he would. He'd keep his word. He'd try to be a man to whom that still meant something.

"I've got a clear conscience," he said.

6

THE RADIO TOWER CAME INTO view, and that was when Charlie knew he was close. WAKO in big red letters. The cab was still running through the river-bottom farmland—fields of corn and pumpkins—but there was that radio tower and the town beyond it and the high school, and the love of his life, who would soon be his, as she was meant to be since they'd fallen for each other when they were both students at Eastern Illinois University.

"That's Lawrenceville, right?" Charlie pointed at the radio tower.

"Yes, sir," said Grinny. He'd kept his yap shut ever since Charlie had to get firm with him in the parking lot of the Showboat. "That's where you want to go, right?"

"Oh, yes, my friend. That is indeed where I want to go."

Because her name was De Belle and his was Camplain, they ended up sitting next to each other in an English Literature class at Eastern in the autumn of 1948. Their seats were near the tall windows on the west side of Old Main, a castle-like building with wide marble halls and doors with transoms and an auditorium for assembly each morning, where the student body heard inspirational speeches, learned about world events, and received lessons on decorum. Little by little in the classroom, as the afternoon lengthened, the sun slanted first across him and then across her, and in the warmth he started to imagine a life for them. He even said to himself, though he knew how corny it would sound if he heard someone else say it, "Charlie, old pal, you're going to marry that girl someday."

One afternoon, as the prof, an ancient man with a humped back and a pink face, droned on about Robert Gray's "Elegy Written in a Country Churchyard," she leaned toward him and whispered, "It's nice, isn't it? The sun?"

He could smell her perfume, a flowery scent that reminded him of the gardens outside Walter Reed, where he'd liked to sit while he waited to see what the doctors might do for the nerve damage in his ear, until they finally gave up and fitted him with a hearing aid and sent him home. In those first weeks, when he moved through the world of muted tones, it was practically a relief after the noise of the war and his work on the demolition crew. He liked to sit in the sunlit gardens and close his eyes and take in the scents of freshly cut grass and roses and to dream of moments like this: a girl who smelled of flowers, and whose hair fell in waves over her collar, and who smiled at him, the way Miss Jean De Belle was doing now.

Was it his imagination, or had she said something to him? He wished his good ear was turned toward her. He reached for the volume control of his hearing aid, but it was too late. She'd already turned her attention back to the prof, and to Charlie it now seemed that her lips were set in a tight line. He feared he'd ruined his chance. He waited until the class was over, meaning to say something to her—something charming and maybe a bit flirtatious—but he couldn't think of the right words, and, much to his regret, he watched Miss Jean De Belle gather up her books and walk out of the room, leaving him all the more enchanted with her.

Then one evening, when he was walking across the quad from the library to the student union, he saw her standing alone in the light cast by one of the lamps that lined the walkway. She was just standing there, her books cradled to her chest, her face tipped down as if she were studying her loafers or her white ankle socks. She had on a long wool coat and a head scarf tied under her chin. The first cold snap of autumn had come in, and most of the students were skittering along in a hurry to be somewhere warm. She looked so forlorn standing there alone. Charlie felt his heart go out to her.

"Waiting for someone?" he said.

She lifted her head and looked at him, and that's when he saw that she'd been crying. Her eyes were red, and her cheekbones were damp with tears.

"Cold, isn't it?" he said. "My eyes always water in the cold."

She gave him a hesitant smile. "It's not the cold," she said. "It's just…" She bit her lip, unable to continue, and then the tears came in earnest, and before Charlie could think what to do, she said, "I have to go." She turned and hurried on up the walkway, her hand pressed to her mouth, her steps growing longer until she was practically running.

Charlie stood there in the cold and watched her go. He felt all alive inside his skin, the way he had when he worked demo in the Army and he hit that moment of pause just before the detonation, that silence when he anticipated the explosion. Like then, he knew that something was going to happen. He didn't know what it might be, but he was fairly certain that something was going to happen between him and Jean De Belle.

So he wasn't surprised when, the next day in their English Literature class, she passed him a note. She stared straight ahead at the prof while Charlie unfolded the piece of notebook paper and began to read. She didn't look at him then, or when he was finished. She didn't look at him the entire class. At the end of it, she gathered up her books and left the room without a word, leaving him to read the note again and again, although really there was no need since he'd already memorized it:

You must think me a silly goose for the way I acted last night. Please forgive my rudeness. Meet me at the pond tonight at 7, and I'll explain. That is, if you want me to. If you don't show, I'll understand. Probably the last thing you need is a silly goose like me. Yours, Jean.

Would he show? Boy, howdy! Over and over, he read the words *Yours, Jean.* Then he got a move on. He needed a haircut. He needed to iron a shirt and press his trousers. Should he wear a coat and tie? He had to polish his shoes. And here it was nearly four thirty. Time to shake a leg, because he had a date tonight with the girl who had long visited his dreams. She was his. She'd said so. *Yours, Jean.*

The pond was on the other side of Fourth Street, on the west edge of the campus. Charlie followed the path that countless students had worn into the grass. He checked his wristwatch and saw that he'd been overanxious. It was only six thirty. A half an hour to kill before Jean arrived. He should have stayed a bit longer in the room he rented in a house on Seventh Street, but geez, it was so hard to sit still. He'd shaved and dressed by six, and then he paced back and forth, stopping at the dormer window that looked out onto the street. He could see the turrets at Old Main and students passing through the glow of the streetlamps on campus. The girls had scarves tied under their chins and car coats buttoned to their throats. Some of the boys wore earmuffs and kept their hands jammed into the pockets of their jackets. They all hurried along as if they had somewhere to go and short time to get there.

Well, Charlie had somewhere to go, too, and the longer he waited, the smaller his room seemed to get. How many nights had he opened a can of soup and warmed it in a pan on his hotplate and eaten it with saltine crackers and sardines in that room while listening to the distant sound of music playing on radios in other rooms, and the chummy yackety-yak-yak of the other boys who lived in the house? Just gassing about anything—a Trig exam, the basketball team, the girls they'd like to… But then someone called out a name—maybe it was Bill, or Peanut, or Harry or Dale. "You wanna come along? Hey, you wanna come, too?" Then it was a madhouse: fists knocking on doors, those doors opening and closing, feet pounding down the stairway, calls of "Hey, wait up. Wait for me."

No one ever knocked on Charlie's door. Sometimes he turned off his hearing aid so the noise would be more distant, so it would be noise and nothing more than that.

They were all kids, full of piss and vinegar but barely dry behind the ears. What did they know—what did any of them know—about what it was to be him? "The Old Man," they called him under the guise of good-humored camaraderie. But Charlie knew what they really thought of him. He'd heard them call him another name. "Maybe we ought to ask the dummy if he wants to come along." "What? What say?" "Exactly. Who wants to have to shout all night."

So he sat in his room and ate his soup and sardines and then went out to the library to study. Sometimes on his way home, he stopped at the beer joint across from Old Main, Ike's, to have one or two, maybe something stronger if he thought he might have trouble falling asleep. But not tonight. Tonight, while his housemates were wherever they were, not giving him a thought, he'd be here at the pond, thinking nothing of them in return, because here she was walking toward him. Here was Jean, the girl who had said she was his.

"You're early," he said, and then thought it was bad manners to point that out. He'd been so surprised to see her, he'd blurted out the first thing that came to him. Then he said, "Time's a funny thing, right? Never enough of it until there's too much."

Another dopey thing to say. Charlie curled his hands into fists deep inside the pockets of his overcoat and felt his fingernails dig into his palms.

But if Jean thought him stupid, she gave no sign. She even smiled at him. A full moon had risen over the pond, and there was enough light for him to see that her cheeks were red from the cold.

"Jeepers," she said. "It's wicked out here tonight."

He took her arm. That's what he felt like doing, so he did it. He took her at the crook of her elbow and said, "Come on. Let's get somewhere warm."

And like that, they started to walk back across the field, neither of them saying a word, their heads down to keep the wind out of their faces, the feel of their hips occasionally brushing against each other a most wonderful thing to Charlie Camplain.

That's what he was remembering as Grinny drove the cab past the WAKO radio station and on across the Embarras River into Lawrenceville—the way she'd gone with him when he'd taken her by the elbow, the way she'd let him lead her.

"What's the name of this river?" he said now to Grinny.

"We call it the Ambraw."

"The way it's spelled, it looks like embarrass."

"It's French," said Grinny.

"French, heh? What does it mean?"

"I used to know, but now I can't recall. Where do you want to go, mister?"

"The high school, bub." Charlie patted the side pocket of his suit coat. "I've got a surprise here for someone special."

The sun was warm on his face. He wasn't thinking about the turn toward autumn and the long winter days to follow. He was only thinking about this day and what was about to happen. He felt his heart quicken the way it had that night, when finally he was in the coffee shop of the Student Union with Jean and they were sitting in a booth by themselves, warming their hands with their coffee mugs, and Jean reached across the table and touched his wrist.

"Sometimes," she said, "I get so sad. I bet you know what I mean."

"What makes you sad, Jean?"

She pulled her hand away and looked down at her coffee mug. "Nothing I can say. Nothing and everything all at once. Sometimes I just feel all empty inside."

He wanted to tell her he knew exactly what she meant, but he was afraid to admit as much, afraid to let her know that he felt it, too—that gloom—because so much of the time he wondered whether he was meant to always be alone. He was the "old man," the "dummy." A war veteran with a hearing aid. A short man that other men looked down on.

And now here was Jean, telling him she felt the loneliness, too.

"I'm not pretty," she said. "Not really. My nose, my chin. And I don't have much confidence. My father says I have to have gumption. He says he's not paying for my education just so I can be a coward all my life. That's what he wrote to me in a letter after I told him I'd turned down my prof's invitation to nominate me for Beta Phi Mu. That's the honorary society for library studies. Sometimes I guess I'm just too shy for my own good. I read my father's letter just before you found me crying the other day. Such a silly goose."

She wouldn't look at him, so he reached across the table and put his finger beneath her chin—just the lightest touch to bring her face up. Then he looked into her eyes. He looked and looked before he said, in what was practically a whisper, "What do you love, Jean? What makes you happy?"

"I love books." She tried to duck her head again, but he wouldn't let her. "Sometimes," she said, "I'm afraid I love them more than people."

"I love them too," he said, and then he told her about what had happened to him during the war and the time he'd spent at Walter Reed. "The only thing that got me through was books," he said. "Novels, mostly." He'd read the classics. He'd read Tolstoy and Flaubert and Fitzgerald, and, of course, Hemingway. "I love being in someone else's life," he said. "That way, I don't have to feel so alone."

She gave him a tremulous smile, and he let go of her chin. "I knew I could tell you," she said. "I watch you in class. You really listen."

He pointed to the hearing aid in his ear and chuckled. "I sorta have to," he said.

"No, it's not that. You and me, we're alike. I know we are."

She touched his wrist again, and this time he took her hand and she let him. He wished some of the boys from his house would come by and see him there. What would they think of him then? The old man, holding hands with his girl.

Now, in the cab, Grinny said, "Say, I happened to remember how the river got its name. It's a crooked river, all tangled up. The word in French means something about that."

"Nothing tangled in me this morning," Charlie said. "I'm a straight arrow. I've got a date with my best girl. Step on it."

❧

At the high school, Grinny said, "Here you go. You sure you don't want me to wait?"

Charlie straightened the knot of his necktie, tugged at his shirt cuffs, brushed a piece of lint off his lapel. "How do I look?"

"You look like a million bucks," Grinny said.

"That's right." Charlie winked at him. "I'm aces."

He gave Grinny a two-finger salute. He patted the breast pocket of his suit coat. Then he turned and went up the walkway to the school.

"He walked in there just as big as day," Grinny would say later, when there would be a reason to say it. "He walked in there like he owned the place."

So the hell with that nice suitcase he left at the Showboat. And the hell with how he intended to get back to Vincennes. Grinny figured that was all his business. Grinny had his own matters to attend to, namely a visit to Tom Heath's father.

I'm going to walk in there just as big as day, Grinny told himself. *I'm going to walk in there like I own the place.*

And he did. He opened the door to the paint store and closed it so hard the bell that hung from it fell to the floor.

Grinny knew everyone's eyes were on him. He felt foolish now and almost turned around and walked out of the place. Then a man in a white shirt, his sleeves rolled to his elbows, gave him a broad smile and said, "Holy cow, mister, you must want something in a hurry. What can I do you for?"

"Are you Mr. Heath?"

"Guilty as charged."

"Tom Heath your son?"

"Guilty again. And who might you be?"

Two women at the counter were giving him the once-over. He could tell they were proper women, each of them in a lady's suit, the kind with a jacket that was tapered at the waist. Each with a strand of pearls around her neck. One of them had on a pair of glasses. She adjusted them to take a better look at him. The other woman wore white gloves. She held a paint sample between her fingers, and she looked peeved that Grinny's noisy entrance had interrupted her.

Suddenly, fixed by these women's stares, Grinny was ashamed of his clothes—his wrinkled khaki work suit, his bowtie that sagged at the ends, his scuffed shoes with the heels run down, his porkpie hat.

He said to Mr. Heath. "What I have to say won't take long."

"Well then say it." Mr. Heath wasn't smiling now. He crossed his arms over his chest and waited for Grinny to go on.

But Grinny couldn't, not with those two ladies listening. He stopped and picked up the bell from the floor. He leaned in close to Mr. Heath, offering him the bell. When Mr. Heath unfolded his arms to take it, Grinny whispered, "It's something private, something about your son. It's not the kind of thing you'd want me to say where other people might hear."

Mr. Heath glanced back at the two ladies who were still staring. "All right, then," he said. "Come with me." He gave a little bow to the ladies. "Take your time with those samples," he said. "I'll be back in two shakes of a lamb's tail."

Grinny followed him to the rear of the store into a dimly lit room where paint cans were stacked.

"What did you say your name was?" Mr. Heath asked.

"My name's Bert Haines." He wouldn't tell Mr. Heath his nickname. He wouldn't say that folks called him Grinny. Grinny sounded like what someone would call an idiot. He knew Mr. Heath might not respect him, but he wanted to make by God certain that he heard what he had to say. He wanted him to feel it—the weight of it—the way he had when Millie had given him the news. "I've got a girl, just now sixteen."

"What does this have to do with my son?"

"Your son and my girl." Grinny hesitated, choking back the memory of Millie telling him she was pregnant. Her fingers had trembled. She hadn't been able to look at him. She kept her head down, and he saw a vein pulsing behind her eyelid. His baby girl. He wanted to take all of this away from her, but he couldn't. It was real. He knew this, and he knew he had to tell Mr. Heath what was what. "My girl," he said, "she's going to have a baby. She's going to have your son's baby."

Mr. Heath laid the bell on top of a paint can. The room smelled of turpentine and dust, and the wooden floor sagged and creaked under Mr. Heath's weight as he took a step toward Grinny.

"I don't know who you are," he said. "I don't know why you think you can come in here spreading lies."

"It's not a lie. Mister, it's the God's truth."

"Says who?"

"My daughter. She told me this morning."

Mr. Heath studied him a good long while. Then he laughed. He put his hands on his hips, rocked back on his heels and laughed.

"My son has a girl," he said. "A *good* girl. Why in the world would he be running around with the likes of your daughter?"

Grinny narrowed his eyes. He remembered how Charlie Camplain had gotten testy about leaving his suitcase at the Showboat. "You should be careful," Grinny said to Mr. Heath. "You don't know who you're dealing with."

Mr. Heath took a step back. "Is that a threat? Is this about money? Is that what you're after?"

Grinny didn't say anything. He let Mr. Heath believe just a minute longer that he'd come looking for hush money, or worse yet, that he meant to hurt him, or maybe his son. A lifetime of letting people tell him where to go, and now he took pleasure in being the one calling the shots.

Then he saw the worry on Mr. Heath's face, and he knew exactly what he must be thinking—the same thing Grinny had thought when Millie told him she'd let Tom Heath get too close to her. What in the world would they do now? How would anything ever be the same?

"No, it's not about money," he said. "It's about your son and my daughter. It's about you and me. It's about your wife and my wife. It's about all of us." Grinny waved his hand in the air, toward the doorway, toward the front of the store, out through the bell-less door that would now open so quietly to the world beyond. "It's about how we're going to choose to treat one another now that trouble's come."

Mr. Heath nodded once. His shoulders sagged, and he let out a sigh. "My Tom," he said.

"And my Millie," said Grinny.

One of the ladies in the store was calling for him. "Mr. Heath. Oh, Mr. Heath."

Mr. Heath reached out then and clasped him by his shoulder. "Wait here," he said. "I've got a clerk coming in just a few minutes. Then we'll talk. All right?"

"I'm not after anything," Grinny said. "I just don't want to be alone with this."

"You won't be," said Mr. Heath. "I promise you that."

7

JEAN SAT ON THE STAGE in the auditorium, a handkerchief twisted in her hand. Perspiration dripped down her arms, but she told herself to remember to smile, to be pleasant, to pretend to be assured. Though the high windows were open, the day was warm, and she was antsy about having to address the assembly. What in the world would she say that anyone would be interested to hear?

"You'll do fine, honey." Mary Ellen, who was seated next to her, leaned over and patted her arm. "Just remember. You're not a student anymore."

Jean nodded and tried to sit up straighter on her wooden folding chair. Her mother had always told her to keep her shoulders back. "Don't slouch," she said. "Mercy, you look like you've got no backbone at all."

Well, she'd stood up to Charlie, hadn't she? She'd told him exactly what was what and had stepped into this new life, knowing that as she did, she said goodbye to a version of herself she'd always liked—the happy-go-lucky girl with stars in her eyes, swept up and carried away by love.

She *had* loved him. She'd never denied that and couldn't even now. There was a part of her that loved him still, but there was another, stronger part of her that knew she'd done the right thing when she broke off the engagement.

"Oh, there you go again," her father said when she told him the marriage was off. "Afraid of your own shadow. What the hell is wrong with Charlie Camplain?"

She told her father he drank too much. It got to the point that she'd been afraid to get in the car with him.

"A man enjoys a drink now and then," her father said. "Doesn't he have a right?"

Charlie would never do anything to hurt her, he said. Charlie worshipped the ground beneath her feet. And he had a good job with the State Security Life Insurance Company. "He insures lives," her father said. "And you think he's going to hurt you?"

It wasn't just the drinking. That was just what she could bring herself to tell her father. The rest of it was too hard to say.

The truth was this: there was a tendency in men like Charlie and her father, men who had lost too much, to hold on too tightly to everything that they loved. She'd seen it happen with her father, this safeguarding to the point of suffocation. She'd felt its effects on her, and because she had, she came to know what her mother was surely feeling, afraid that the very fabric of who she was might unravel. Sometimes she came upon her mother sitting alone in the darkened living room, her hand to her chest as if to assure herself her heart was still beating. It was the closest Jean ever felt to her, this woman who was unaware of how they connected in those moments of silence. Jean knew exactly what her mother was feeling because she had begun to feel it herself.

It was maddening, really, the way her father—and her mother, too—told her to be stronger, bolder, in this house filled with fear. Her mother, the sweet woman she'd once been, had disappeared. She'd given herself over to the life her husband had made for her, a life of mistrust. "No one's going to give you anything, missy," she told Jean. "You have to take it."

Jean's father knew what it was to claw for something. He'd been a young father during the heart of the Great Depression, a teller at the Farmers Mercantile Bank when the bottom fell out of the stock market and just like that, everyone lost most, if not all, of what they'd put back for a rainy day. Jean was too young to recall the worst of it, but she grew up with the specter looming over her—the sense that in the wink of an eye, everything you held dear could be gone.

Her father insisted on thrifty habits. If Jean left a light on in a room, he was all over her about being penny-wise. If she complained about having to work in the summer sun hoeing weeds out of their enormous garden plot, or having to sweat in the kitchen helping her mother can vegetables, he told her come winter she'd be happy to have the food they'd grown and preserved. "I've seen people go hungry, girlie. I've gone hungry myself. Plenty of times."

When the market recovered, he gradually regained what he'd lost. He went from being a teller to being a loan officer. Now he was the president of the Farmers Mercantile. Even though he was more than flush, the fear bred by the Depression was never far from him, and he held onto all that was dear to him—even his wife and daughter—as if they were his last two pennies. His concern that some harm might befall them became oppressive. Jean was always to call home at 8 and 10 p.m. when she was out with her friends. At college, she phoned each Sunday to let him know she'd made it safely through another week.

"Geez," Jean told Charlie once. "You'd think there was a killer around every corner."

Jean was thinking about all this as the principal, Mr. Pomeroy, stepped to the podium and cleared his throat. He was a short man who wore bowties and rimless eyeglasses that were too big for his face. He parted his hair in the middle and oiled it. Jean thought he looked like a man from another decade, like her father at the time the market sank. Mr. Pomeroy had that look of always being on guard, and Jean took strength from it, the thought that Mr. Pomeroy had a secret; no matter how many years he'd stood at that podium on the first day of school, a small part of him was afraid.

He turned to look at his faculty, sitting in a line on the stage. His gaze fell on Jean, and for just a brief moment she swore she saw a tremor of a smile at the corner of his mouth. She rose to that softening, as if it were all she'd ever wanted from her father. Her heart lifted and her smile grew larger. Then she thought, *I must look like the Cheshire cat, just grinning away like an idiot.*

Then Mr. Pomeroy was calling the students to order, and bit by bit the chatter ebbed and the laughter dwindled, until finally the auditorium was so quiet Jean could hear birds singing and the cars passing on the street outside the school. She barely took in what Mr. Pomeroy was saying. Something about the start of a new year and all the opportunities it brought.

Then he paused to look down at his notes, and a voice from the parking lot rang out. "Keep the change, bub. No need to wait. It's time for both of us to shake a leg."

She knew that the voice belonged to Charlie Camplain. Now Mr. Pomeroy was calling her to the podium, and Mary Ellen had to nudge her elbow and whisper, "Go on."

Jean sat there, frozen. She wanted the hands to fall from the clocks, the Earth to stop its rotation. She wanted time to stop, because she knew that once assembly was done, she would have to walk out into the hall, and there she would find Charlie waiting.

"You think it's over?" he'd said to her when she gave his ring back. "Listen to me and listen good: It's never going to be over between you and me. Never. Sweetheart, that's one thing you can take to the bank."

❧

The man in the gray flannel suit called out to her—"Miss. Oh, Miss"—just as Robbie was about to reach for the handle on the door that led to the auditorium. She was late for assembly. She'd been in the girls' room, locked in a stall, crying because everything she'd planned for the future was ruined, thanks to Tom Heath. She had his class ring clasped inside her closed palm, the chain digging into her skin. What a fool she'd been. She could hear her mother saying as much when she found out: *Oh, you little fool.*

And now here was this man, this strange man. He looked like he had expectations. Her father—he'd owned a real estate agency—would have called him a man with prospects. She took in his flannel suit, his snazzy necktie, his nicely cut hair, his grin, and she found herself aching for her father and the way he'd left the breakfast table each morning with a snap of his fingers, a tap of his palm against his fist—ba-da-bing!—and a "Gotta skedaddle, Robbie-Girl. There's money to be made."

Oh, how she missed him. She missed the smell of him those mornings when he kissed her on her forehead before leaving the table: shoe polish and leather, Aqua Velva and tobacco, Brylcreem and Dial soap. She missed the way he called her Robbie-Girl, and the times when they were alone in his car driving somewhere to look at a house he was putting on the market. She was always so excited watching him fit the key to the lock, swing open the door, and say, "This is it, Robbie-Girl. This is paradise." Sometimes he let her write the descriptions for the ads he placed in the *Daily Record*. He schooled her in the art of deceptive positivity. A rundown home became "A handyman's dream." Cramped spaces became "Cozy nests." There was always some way to make something ugly sound charming. "Look on the bright side, Robbie-Girl," he used to tell her. "Sell the people what they want."

If only he could have done the same for himself. If only he'd had the same light heart in their home as he'd had in the homes he arranged for so many others. There was something between him and her mother, some darkness that kept them from happiness. "Oh, we were in love once," she remembered her mother saying to her. "Everyone starts out in love. Everyone on this old Earth." Then what happens, Robbie wanted to know. "Time," her mother said with a sigh. "It just goes."

Robbie remembered the way her father seemed to go inside himself whenever he was with her mother. At home, he wasn't the man Robbie knew at all. He was someone strange and brooding, closed off to her. She couldn't come up with any kind of game to brighten him. Sometimes he lay on the floor watching television and pretended to be asleep if her mother came into the room. Other nights, he went out by himself, no invitation for Robbie to join him. She saw him once when she was walking to the library to study. He was sitting in his car—the Cadillac Eldorado convertible he'd been so proud of—and his head was down on the steering wheel and his shoulders were shaking, and Robbie knew he was crying. She didn't know how to touch his sadness—didn't even know what it was—so she walked on by, hurrying to the library where Tom was waiting for her.

That was the night her father died. That was the night his heart stopped. If only she'd gone to him, touched him, told him she loved him, maybe then everything would have been all right.

Now here was this man. He looked at her as if she were the very person he'd been looking for all his life, and he said, "I'm looking for Miss De Belle, Miss Jean De Belle. Could you please tell me where I might find her?"

From the auditorium, she heard Miss De Belle's voice. There was music in its bright tone.

Robbie opened the door a crack and saw her at the podium. The sun was shining on her and she was saying how glad she was to be there. "That's what I remember," Robbie would say later. "How happy she looked." Robbie let that feeling fill her up. She wanted the man to feel it too. She opened the door wider so he could see.

"That's her," she said. "That's Miss De Belle."

That's when the man came undone. He took a step forward, a single step toward that open door, and then, overcome by something Robbie couldn't name, he folded over, his hands on his knees.

"Are you all right?" Robbie asked.

The man straightened. He tugged at his cuffs and snapped them across his wrists. "I've come a long way," he said. "She'll see how far I've come. She'll see I'm a different sort of man. We'll be aces."

His voice was too loud, too jazzed up, too bright. It was the voice Robbie had heard from her father so many times, the voice of a man trying to sell. Kids in the auditorium were turning to look for the source of that voice. Robbie didn't know how she would explain what she had to do with the man who had asked this question of her, any more than she'd known what to do about her father the last night of his life when she saw him crying in his Eldorado.

"I have to go," she said, and she stepped into the auditorium, leaving the man outside.

The Golden One, Robbie's father told her El Dorado meant in Spanish. The mythical city of gold. Explorers had tried to find it but had never succeeded.

"Wouldn't it be something," he said to her once, "if it turned out to be true? We'd all be happy then."

The girl swung open the auditorium door, and Charlie saw Jean at the podium. He heard her sweet voice, and he nearly broke down, for he'd come to fear that he'd never hear it again, never see her, his Jean, who'd got all mixed up and run away from him.

He'd tried to tell her as much. "Jean, you don't know what you're doing," he said to her on the telephone—one of the last times she agreed to speak to him.

"I know exactly what I'm doing, Charlie Camplain," she said.

Then she went away. But now here she was, just a few feet away from him. She was smiling, and he imagined she was smiling because he'd come, and now they'd be able to put right everything that was wrong. He had the ring in his pocket, the one she'd worn when she'd promised to be his wife. He imagined her putting it on her finger again. He imagined everything being as it was once upon a time.

He'd quit drinking. All of his anger was gone. He'd soon have his driver's license back, and he'd be able to return to the road for the State Security Life Insurance Company. Everything would be on the square. He could be the man she deserved, the one she'd first fallen in love with that night she met him at the pond and told him everything she'd never been able to tell anyone else. He was a good listener. Despite his hearing aid, he knew how to pay attention. He'd tell her all of this. He'd say, *I love you, Jean De Belle, and I know you love me.* He'd just keep talking until she'd have no choice but to say, *Yes.*

The door was closing behind the girl, but that was all right with Charlie. He knew where Jean was. Finally, they were in the same place again. He had all the time in the world.

Jean saw him. For just an instant, she saw Charlie outside the auditorium doors. She stumbled over what she was saying. For a few moments, she couldn't make a sound. The time stretched on until she was finally aware that she wasn't speaking and the students were starting to notice, starting to elbow each other and whisper and smirk. Finally, she cleared her throat. She tried to resume what she'd been saying—something that now seemed uninspiring and vapid to her—about first days and new beginnings, but she stammered and had to stop and clear her throat again.

A boy somewhere in the auditorium called out, "Uh, uh, uh, uh," making fun of her stammer, and the entire assembly erupted in laughter.

Jean felt her face go hot. She heard a chair behind her scrape over the boards of the stage, and then Mary Ellen was at the podium, her face close to Jean's as she leaned toward the microphone.

"That will be enough," she said. "That will be quite enough." The laughter faded, and when all was quiet, she added, "You will give Miss De Belle the respect she deserves."

She put an arm around her shoulders and gave her a squeeze. For just a moment, Mary Ellen let her cheek rest against Jean's. Somewhere in the auditorium, girls began to giggle, and Jean thought back to earlier that summer, when Mary Ellen took her hand at the pool and those silly girls laughed. She pulled away from Mary Ellen now, and Mary Ellen nodded to her and then stepped away from the podium.

Jean was devastated. Mary Ellen had to come to her defense on the first day of school. How could the students ever respect her after that? She was ready to end it, to say how glad she was to be among them, but it hardly seemed appropriate after the titters and guffaws that had embarrassed her so. But what else was there to say? She'd failed miserably. She was about to simply turn and go back to her chair. Or maybe she'd just keep walking, disappearing into the wings of the stage and making her way out of the auditorium, out of the school, out of this new life she'd so desperately wanted for herself.

Then she saw Etta Lawless in the front row. Etta Lawless with her bobbed hair and her pale skin and those rimless glasses and her plain cotton dress. She was leaning forward, her thin lips parted, eager for Jean to overcome the difficulty of this moment, wanting so desperately to believe in her. Etta Lawless who loved books. Jean had promised they'd be friends.

So she said, "I'm looking forward to knowing you all better." Etta Lawless was smiling, and Jean went on. "I came here because I love books and I love teaching. I love this life I have, and you're all going to be a large part of it now, you and this school, which I've already begun to treasure. I truly believe we can have some wonderful days together this year, and in the years beyond. These are the good days. You might not think so now, but trust me, they really are."

And with that, she returned to her seat and sat with her hands folded in her lap and tried to smile so she could pretend that the laughter hadn't bothered her at all.

Then someone started to clap. It was Etta Lawless. The smile on her face was wider now, and she was leaning forward as if at any moment she would spring from her seat, run onto the stage, and give Jean a hug. She was clapping her small hands together, and slowly other students began to join in, until finally the auditorium swelled with applause.

Jean felt a warm glow rise up in her chest and spread to her throat. She'd done it. She'd almost lost them, but in the end she'd won them back.

"Thank you, Miss De Belle," Mr. Pomeroy said from the podium.

Another male voice rang out from the rear of the auditorium. "Ring-a-ding-ding," it said.

No laughter followed the remark. Only a single, low wolf whistle, which brought a rebuke from Mr. Pomeroy, who said he wouldn't tolerate such unseemly behavior.

Jean did her best not to let her face show how much it all pleased her, how much it meant to her to be liked, even if it was in what Mr. Pomeroy was now calling an "ungentlemanly" way.

For a while, she almost forgot that Charlie was waiting for her outside the auditorium. She knew why he was there. Surely, he meant to convince her to resume their engagement, to once again make plans for her to become Mrs. Charlie Camplain.

As if that would ever happen. Still, there was a part of her that felt sorry for him, sorry for herself, even, that things had come to such an abrupt end. One minute she'd been his fiancée, and the next minute she was gone.

She'd told him at the end of June, once she'd accepted the position at Lawrenceville High School. She'd managed the trip down for the interview by telling Charlie she was going to visit an aunt she'd invented. When she returned, Charlie took her to dinner at the Skyview Supper Club. He was wearing a white dinner jacket with a black bowtie. She was in a new emerald green taffeta party dress with a black velvet sash that tied at her hip. She picked at her Waldorf salad, barely touched her beef Wellington, declined Charlie's insistence that they have bananas Foster for dessert. He was on his third martini by this time and getting a little loose in the joints.

"Then let's dance," he said. The band was playing "You Belong to Me," and couples were doing the foxtrot. "It's our song. Come on and dance with me."

She said, "Not tonight, Charlie. I really don't feel like dancing."

"Sure you do, Tootsie." He took her hand. "Let's get cozy."

"Don't call me that." She pulled her hand away. "I'm not your Tootsie."

She saw the surprise and hurt on his face. He finished his martini and looked around for the waiter, holding up his empty glass to indicate he was ready for one more. At that moment, she knew she wouldn't get in the car with him. She'd call a cab, or if Charlie got hotheaded, she'd ask the maitre d' to call the police.

"You're drunk," she said.

He leaned back in his chair. "You're the one who needs to get a hold of yourself. I'm in perfect control."

That's when she slipped the engagement ring from her finger and laid it on the white tablecloth in front of his water glass. The grin on his face, fading now, had been so close to a smirk. He was so smug. He was sitting there like he had the world on a string, had *her* on a string, when the truth was she'd come to be afraid him—afraid of his drinking, afraid of his temper, afraid of the way she felt herself getting swallowed up in all of that. "Don't let a man take you away from who you are," her mother had told her, when Jean confided in her that she was thinking of breaking the engagement. "Don't ever let that happen, Jean. You'll regret it the rest of your days."

The truth was Jean had had quite enough. She was ready to call it quits with Charlie and walk away from him.

"Jean?" he said. "What gives?"

"I've taken a job."

"A job? Well, that's fine, Jean. We can use the extra dough."

"It's not like that," she said.

"No? Well, then suppose you tell me what it is like."

He had that angry edge to his voice, the one that tied her stomach up in knots. He'd punched a man once at a filling station because Charlie thought he was giving her the eye. "I won't have that, Jean," he said as they drove away. "I just won't." He'd never been violent with her, but his temper had long been a source of concern. She lived on tenterhooks when she was with him, never knowing what might set him off.

Now he was waiting. "If you've got something to say, then go on and say it." He glanced down at the ring. "Or maybe you want to reconsider?"

He was daring her. He didn't think she had enough backbone to say what he knew she wanted to say.

Maybe she didn't. Instead of getting right to it, she started to talk all around it. It was a job at a high school, she said. She'd be the school librarian and even teach an English class. The school was in Illinois, across the river from Vincennes. She'd be moving there. She'd be moving away.

He used his finger to push the ring back across the table to her. "You don't know what you're saying, Jean."

She looked at the ring a long time, so long that the band finished "You Belong to Me" and started playing "Don't Let the Stars Get in Your Eyes." Finally, she raised her head and met Charlie's gaze. She remembered when the two of them had been good together. Those days at Eastern Illinois, days when she sat beside him in English Literature class and the sun slanted across them, the night he came to her at the pond and all the nights when she told him what haunted her and he did the same. He told her all about the war and the hearing loss and the time he spent at Walter Reed. He told her what it was like to hear the boys in the rooming house call him "Dummy" when they didn't know he could hear them. At first, she tried to drink with him, but soon she saw that was a losing proposition. She couldn't keep up, and she grew tired of having to help him home and put him to bed and listen to his soft crying as he told her he was no good, told her she should get out while she could. "But I love you," she said, and she swore it was true.

It had taken her the rest of that school year and half of the summer to figure out that pity wasn't love, that a life with Charlie would be a life of caretaking, of always being on guard, of giving and giving and giving, and if it meant she was a bad person for not being able to do that—if she were selfish for believing that love meant something else—so be it. She'd made her decision, and even though there would always be a part of her that wondered whether she should have stayed—after all, he adored her, and he had a way of making her laugh, and she'd already promised him so much—she had to trust her instincts. A life with Charlie would be a hard life, a life that would take her away from herself.

"I know exactly what I'm saying." She pushed the ring back toward him, doing her best not to cry. She felt the familiar ache in her throat, and she swallowed it back down. "I can't go through with it, Charlie. I can't do this."

The waiter came with his martini glass balanced on a small silver tray. He was an older gentleman in a black tuxedo with a waist-length server's jacket and a wide black cummerbund. He'd been a waiter at the club ever since Jean was a little girl. She knew he lived in an apartment above the Walgreen's two blocks down and had no family. She knew this because her father had told her that during the Depression, he'd had a wife and a baby who left him because times were hard and he'd taken to drink. He got himself sober and wrote to his wife to tell her so, but by that time she'd fallen in love with a steel worker who lived in Hammond, and soon she sued her husband for divorce. He never remarried. Jean sometimes saw him coming out of the Ohio Theatre alone, taking the last bite from a giant Hershey's bar and then tossing the wrapper into the trash barrel on the sidewalk before stuffing his hands into the pockets of his jacket, bowing his head, and starting the walk back to his apartment. To see him now, having to serve drinks to the likes of Charlie Camplain, made Jean's heart break.

Charlie waved the drink away. "I didn't order that, Pops," he said. "You must have your tables mixed up."

The waiter had lifted the glass from the tray and was holding it in midair. "Sir?" he said.

"Take it away, Pops." Charlie raised his voice. "I said I didn't order it." He nodded toward the empty martini glass on the table. "What do you take me for? Some kind of lush?"

"No, sir. Of course not, sir. My mistake."

"Maybe you've had too many of those yourself. Maybe that's your problem."

"I'm not a drinking man," the waiter said.

"And I am?" Charlie pressed his knuckles into the table and started to lift himself from his chair. "What are you, some kind of wise guy?"

Then the maitre d', a thin man with a pencil moustache, was there. "Is there some sort of misunderstanding?" he asked.

"Pops here is trying to sell me drinks I didn't order," Charlie said. "He seems to have an opinion of me."

The maitre d' turned to the waiter. He pointed his chin at him, clearly expecting an explanation.

The waiter said, "A misunderstanding. I have no particular impression of the gentleman."

He bowed and backed away.

The maitre d' said, "My apologies, sir."

Charlie said, "I should think so."

He was so indignant, Jean couldn't keep quiet. "You know you ordered that drink, Charlie, and you know you've already had too many. The waiter may not have an opinion of you, but I do." She pushed her chair back from the table and stood up. She had her purse and the money inside it. "You really need to learn to take responsibility for yourself," she said, and with that she was gone.

She heard Charlie calling after her. "Jean," he said. "For Chrissakes, don't to this."

Heads were turning to see what the fuss was all about. Jean heard a crash of dishes, the maitre d' saying, "Sir, I must ask you to compose yourself." She glanced back once to see Charlie on the floor, his leg somehow tangled up in the tablecloth. He'd pulled the dishes down with him. He was trying to get up, but he kept slipping. The wire from his hearing aid had come out of his ear, and he was shouting, "Jean, Jean, Jean."

Her heart broke. He looked so pathetic. She almost went back. But something swelled up in her, some courage she'd almost forgotten, and she kept walking. She left the supper club and found an empty cab at the stand at the corner. She gave the driver her address, and she went home, thinking, *There, it's over, it's done.*

But it wasn't really. There were weeks of phone calls from Charlie and embarrassing moments in public when he would follow her and beg her to come back to him. He knocked on her door in the middle of the night, and her father, who now saw him for exactly what he was, told him to go away. Her mother hugged her and said, "Oh, Jean."

Then Charlie was arrested for drunk driving and lost his license. Her father read about it in the evening paper. "I guess we know him now, don't we?" he said.

Charlie frequented the bars downtown and got into fistfights. Jean saw him once, punching a man on the sidewalk in front of the Oasis downtown. She drove on by. *Good riddance to bad rubbish,* she told herself, and yet she was sad to know that Charlie had come to such destructive behavior. At heart, he was a good man. Of that, she had no doubt, but now he was out of control.

Then the night before she was to leave for Lawrenceville, he called. His voice was very calm. "Jean," he said, "it's Charlie."

She almost hung up, but there was something in his voice—some weariness, as if he'd resigned himself to what was going to happen— that kept her on the line.

"I want to wish you luck," he said.

"Thank you," she said, "that's good of you."

"Just remember." His voice was low now. "Nothing will ever be over between us. Nothing, Jean. We're meant to be together."

She hung up then. There'd been just enough menace in what he said to spook her.

The phone kept ringing throughout the night, and each time it did, Jean cringed. She let it ring. Finally, well past midnight, her father answered.

"Camplain," her father said, "if you don't stop calling here, I'll have the police around to get you. You understand? Leave my daughter alone."

And he had, until now—the first day of school. Jean sat on the stage, remembering all that had led to this moment. Soon the assembly would end, and she would have to go out into the hallway and meet what was surely waiting for her.

8

TOM HEATH GRABBED ROBBIE BY the arm as she left the auditorium. "Robbie, you've got to listen to me."

"Let go." She tried to pull away, but he held her fast. "I don't want to hear anything you've got to say. I don't ever want to talk to you again."

Students were pushing past them on their way to their classes. Someone bumped against Robbie, and she would have lost her balance if Tom hadn't been holding her arm. He dragged her to a corner near the staircase and pressed her back to the wall. The plaster was rough. She heard someone say, "You should let her go, bub," but she had no idea who had said it.

"It was just something that happened," Tom said. "It doesn't mean anything."

"Doesn't *mean* anything? It most certainly does. That poor girl."

"But you're the one I love."

"You don't know anything about what love is, Tom Heath."

"I know I want to spend the rest of my life with you."

"Then you need to act like it."

"So you're saying there's a chance?"

She'd meant no such thing, but in the clamor of the hallway—kids rushing past, locker doors slamming, Tom taking her by surprise— she'd had no time to think. Was there a chance? Was that what she wanted? She couldn't say. Everything was happening too quickly. Just a little over an hour ago, she'd been on top of the world, gliding along Tenth Street in Tom's Chevy Fleetline, certain of so many things. Now, here she was without a clue.

"I have to go," she said. "I'm going to be late for my English class."

Still Tom held her arm. "I'm not going to let you go," he said, "not unless you tell me we're through." He gave her arm a shake. "Can you say that, Robbie? Can you?"

That's when the man in the gray flannel suit stepped up and closed his hand around the back of Tom's neck. Robbie felt her arm come free. She saw Tom moving away from her. The man in the suit was walking him backward, turning him, pushing him up against the wall.

"Bub, that's no way to treat a lady."

Yes, she was sure, she would say later. He said *bub*. A man in a gray flannel suit. A maroon-colored tie. A crazy design of circles.

"You could get lost trying to follow those circles," she'd say. "Circles inside circles. You'd never know where you began."

◦⦿◦

Then Jean was there. One minute, Charlie was holding the boy by his arm and vowing to teach him a lesson about how to treat a lady, and then he didn't care a thing about that boy and that girl because here was Jean, the love of his life.

She had her head down, her hands stuffed into the pockets of her dress. Charlie noticed she had the Parker 51 fountain pen that he'd given her clipped to her breast pocket, and he took heart from that. She hadn't been able to throw it away. That meant something.

He called her name. "Jean," he said. "Jean, it's Charlie."

She kept walking. A mousy girl wearing wire-rim spectacles and holding a notebook to her chest was following her.

Charlie let the boy go.

"I don't know who you think you are, mister," the boy said.

Charlie stopped just long enough to let him know. "I'm Charlie Camplain," he said. "And don't you forget it."

He caught up with Jean at the bottom of the stairs. The students had thinned out, the last of them ducking into classrooms, but the mousy girl was still with Jean. She was chattering away.

"You were grand, Miss De Belle," she said. "I loved the way everything turned in your favor."

"Thank you, Etta."

Jean had noticed him. He saw her glance over the top of the girl's head to see him standing behind her. She pressed her lips into a tight line. Well that was all right, he thought. That was to be expected. He'd go slow. He'd let her get to know him again.

"That boy whistled," the girl said. "I guess you've got an admirer."

"She sure does," Charlie said, "and here I am." He stepped up beside Jean and put his arm around her waist. He hadn't meant to do that, but it had seemed so natural it was done before he knew it. "Hello, Jean."

She took a step toward the girl, and Charlie let his arm drop to his side.

"You should be in class now," she said to the girl, and the girl said, "Holy smokes. You're right. I'll come by the library and see you later, Miss De Belle. It doesn't matter to me."

"What doesn't?"

"I heard some girls talking about you and Mrs. McVeigh, you know, but it doesn't matter to me. It's okay if you're what they say you are."

"And exactly what would that be?" Jean asked.

But the girl was hurrying away, and Charlie and Jean were alone in the empty hallway.

"You have no right to be here." She was talking in a fierce whisper, her anger barely contained. "And to put your arm around me like that?" She snorted. "The idea, Charlie Camplain, and on this day of all days. The first day of school. You make me so mad."

"Calm down, Jean. I just wanted to let you know I'm here."

Much to his surprise, she took his hand and pulled him into an empty classroom. "I wasn't going to push anything," he said later. "Then she did what she did."

She closed the door, and there they were.

"I told you we were finished," she said to him. "I have this life." She opened her arms and spun around. "I have this wonderful new life. What makes you think you can take it away from me?"

"Jean, I want you to listen to me."

"What do you have to say, Charlie?" She crossed her arms over her chest. "What do you have to say that could possibly make a difference?"

She should have expected a stunt like this. Charlie had always been impulsive and bull-headed. What a fool she'd been to believe she'd left him behind.

"Jean, I've given up the booze," he said. "I haven't had a drink since you left. I go to meetings now. AA meetings, and I'm going to get my driver's license back, and then I'll start selling insurance again. It's just the start of things for me, Jean. I thought you'd like to know that."

She wondered if he were telling the truth. "So you're sober now?"

He reached into his trousers pocket and took out a bronze coin, which he placed in her hand. It had a triangle on it. One leg had the word "Unity" on it. Another leg said "Service," and the base said "Recovery." In the middle was a circle with the number 1 in it, and below that the word "Month." Curved around the top edge of the coin were the words, "To Thine Own Self Be True."

"That's my one-month sobriety coin. I want you to have it."

"No, I shouldn't take it." She tried to give the coin back to him. "It's yours."

"I want it to mean something to us. You're the reason I'm sober now."

"If I keep it, will you go?"

He was fumbling with something in the breast pocket of his suit coat. At first, Jean thought he was adjusting the volume on his hearing aid. Then she saw he had the ring, the engagement ring she'd returned to him that night at the Skyview Supper Club.

"I'll go if you'll agree to let me put this on your finger again."

"I have to be in the library now." She started to slip past him toward the door, but he grabbed her arm. "Let me go," she said.

"No, you're going to listen." He was pushing her back toward the chair behind the teacher's desk. He gave her a shove, and she had no choice but to fall back into the chair. He hovered over her, his hands on the arms of the chair.

"Don't you threaten me," she said.

"I'm not threatening you, Jean." His voice was calm. "I'm going to tell you what's what."

She wasn't afraid. She was more annoyed than anything.

"Charlie," she said as kindly as she could.

But before she could go on, he stopped her.

"Weren't we good together?" he said.

She told the truth. "Sometimes we were. At first."

"We could be good again."

"It's too late for that."

"No, Jean, it's not too late. We can go back and make things better. I know I wasn't always the sort of man you deserved, but I'm going to be that man. You'll see. We'll make everything new again. We'll make this nightmare go away. We'll be happy."

There'd been a time when she'd loved him—or at least thought she did—but she wasn't that same girl now. She was Miss De Belle of Lawrenceville, Illinois. She wasn't some moony lovestruck girl. She was a woman with a career, a librarian and a teacher, a woman who would have a proper position in the community She had a life that didn't include Charlie, and that was as it should be.

He had her left hand in his, and he was trying to slide the ring onto her finger. "You can stay here this year while we plan the wedding. Then, after we're married, you can come back to Madison, and we'll find the right house, and it'll be just fine, Jean. It'll be aces." He was looking down at her with that smile that had charmed her so. "Say you'll marry me, Jean."

She looked at the ring, and she remembered the night Charlie first put it on her finger. It was at the pond. Where else? It was the end of the school year. They'd gone for a walk in the twilight. The ornamental crabapple trees on campus were in bloom, pink and white. All around them was the scent of the green grass. They walked across campus to the athletic fields.

Jean heard the clacking of field hockey sticks, the pock-pock of tennis balls hitting rackets. She held Charlie's hand. He was quiet, which was unusual for him, but she didn't mind. The light was fading, the air was calm, and so was her heart.

They walked to the pond, the spot where she'd first begun to fall for him. Frogs peeped from the cattails. A mockingbird was singing somewhere. It was all so lovely, and then Charlie got down on his knee, and he said the words to her that he'd said again now. "Say you'll marry me, Jean." The ring was so modest—that diamond solitaire—that it made her feel tender toward him. She imagined him picking it out at Hanft's Jewelry Store downtown, choosing what he could afford, paying for it on time, looking at it time and time again when he was alone in his small room at the boarding house, imagining the day she would be his bride. "I will," she said. "Oh, yes, Charlie. I will."

Then had come the thrill of wearing that ring, of announcing to the world her engagement to Charlie Camplain. Those sweet days of love before the drinking became a problem, before he became so needy, so possessive. Those days before Jean realized she was disappearing.

Now she laid the sobriety coin on the desk. She took the ring from her finger and put it beside the coin.

"I'm sorry," she said.

Charlie was pacing back and forth in front of the desk now. He had one hand up to the back of his head. "Of course, if you want to work at another school closer to Madison after we're married, that would be fine with me. We'll get us a nice place. I'll be on the road some, but I'll be home every weekend, and boy oh boy won't we have us a time then. Dinner, dancing, whatever you want, Jean. Or if we have kids—we'll want kids, of course—why then we'll…"

"There you go." She interrupted him. "You haven't changed a bit."

He stopped pacing. He let his arm trail down to his side. "Jean?"

"You haven't been listening to me." She chuckled. "You're the same old Charlie. You only hear what you want to hear. Don't be such a dummy."

He narrowed his eyes. Through all the drunkenness and fights, she'd never seen such an ugly look on his face.

"Dummy?" He tapped the earpiece from his hearing aid. "What's that supposed to be? Some sort of crack?"

"No, Charlie. It's no crack. I didn't mean…"

"That what you think of me now? Are you like those boys in the rooming house? You want to make fun of me because I can't hear right? You want to call me a dummy?"

"Charlie, it's not like that."

"I know exactly what it is." He was fumbling with something in the inner breast pocket of his suit coat. Then he pulled out a gun. "I've heard it all," he said. "I've heard everything loud and clear."

9

GRINNY HEARD A COMMOTION AT the front of Mr. Heath's paint store, and he stepped out of the back room to see who was causing the fuss.

It was the two ladies at the counter. The one with the white gloves was flapping a paint sample strip in Mr. Heath's face. She was the more slender of the two ladies, and younger too. Her lipstick was bright red, and now she was so worked up, Grinny couldn't tell where the rouge on her cheeks stopped and the heat of her anger began.

"We have been waiting," she said. "We have been waiting patiently. Honestly, is this any way to treat your customers?"

The other lady—she had gray hair and a round face, and her eyeglasses sat on top of her full cheeks—said, "Indeed. Indeed."

Mr. Heath held his hands up in front of him as if he were getting ready to catch a ball or ward off a blow. The latter seemed the more probable to Grinny, who watched at first with a sense of amusement and then, as the tirade went on, a sinking realization that Mr. Heath would never make good on his promise to stand with him in the midst of this trouble with their children. When all was said and done, Grinny and his wife would be the ones to deal with Millie and what he knew now they would call her "little problem." Mr. Heath would find his way out of the situation, as he was doing now with his two angry customers.

"Ladies, how about I throw in a couple of gallons free? For the trouble I've caused."

"It's the least you could do," said the young woman with the white gloves. "It's a start."

The woman with the glasses said, "You know there's a paint store in Vincennes. I wouldn't want to take my business across the river, but really, Mr. Heath, you'd hardly be able to blame us if we did."

"And, of course, I'll let you have whatever else you need—rollers? trim brushes? painter's tape?—without charge." Mr. Heath let his hands drop. He turned them, palms up, as if he were about to hug the ladies in reconciliation. "Would that be some help?"

The ladies eyed each other. The one with the white gloves raised her eyebrows; the one with the glasses pursed her lips and gave her head an almost imperceptible shake.

"And free delivery, I assume?" the one with the gloves said.

"I'll have my son run everything over when he gets out of school today." Mr. Heath was smiling. "Now, shall I write up the order?"

The two ladies nodded at each other.

"Along with your apologies?" the woman with the glove said.

"A million times over," Mr. Heath said.

"Apology accepted," said the woman with the glasses.

Mr. Heath went behind the counter and started to write out the ladies' order.

The one with the gloves said, "It's your son's senior year, isn't it?"

"It sure is."

"Where will he go to college?" the other asked.

"I'm hoping the U of I in Champaign," Mr. Heath said. "That's where I went, you know."

"He's such a nice young man," said the one with the gloves.

"Always so well-mannered," said the one with the glasses. "You must be so proud of him."

Mr. Heath glanced up from his order book. Grinny glared at him.

"His mother and I are extremely proud of him," Mr. Heath finally said. "We think he has a bright future ahead of him."

Grinny saw it clearly now, the way everything would go on for the Heaths. Oh, sure, there would be a brief interruption, a period of

"How could you?" and "What were you thinking?" But in the long run, Mr. Heath's son would have his life back on track. And Millie? Well, she would have a longer, harder road. One thing Grinny knew for certain: there were people who had and people who didn't, and the ones who had always left those who didn't to shoulder most of life's burdens. The rich ones relied on their money, their reputations, their influence to help everyone forget whatever misstep or scandal threatened to unhinge them.

"Better ask your boy what he's been doing over at Westport." Grinny was moving now. What a fool he'd been. "Better ask him if he knows how to keep his pants zipped."

Grinny took delight in the shocked looks on the ladies' faces and the way Mr. Heath narrowed his eyes in fear.

The woman with the paint sample strip shook it in Grinny's direction. "Who are you to talk like that?"

He was so close to her, he reached out and snatched the sample strip from her hand. "I'm no one," he said. "No one who matters at all."

10

ROBBIE WAS WAITING FOR HER home economics class to begin when she heard a loud pop. She nearly jumped out of her seat.

"My goodness," she said. She put her hand to her throat and felt her heart beating.

Some of the other girls were giggling.

"What a fright," one said.

Someone else said the boys were working on an old jalopy downstairs in shop. That must have been what they'd heard. Just an old jalopy backfiring.

Then they heard five more pops in rapid succession. They sat there, no one laughing now, no one making a sound.

Their teacher, Mrs. McEllroy, a stern woman with her gray hair in a tight bun, opened the classroom door, and across the way, Robbie saw her mother coming out into the hall from her own class. Someone was shouting downstairs. Robbie couldn't tell what they were saying. There was more than one man's voice, but it was all just noise, frantic noise. Then Robbie's mother was running. She was running down the stairs. She was running the way she had the night Robbie's father's heart had stopped and she ran from room to room, crying, "Robbie, oh, Robbie," not knowing what in the world she should do.

Outside the school, Charlie opened the door of a car, a sharp-looking Chevy Fleetline, a gold Fleetline that looked like a million bucks. The boy behind the wheel was the boy from the hallway, the one who had treated that girl so badly.

The boy had been crying. He wiped at his eyes with the heel of his hand.

"Mister, I don't want any more trouble."

Charlie kept his voice even. "Son, what's your name?"

"Tom, sir. My name is Tom."

"Tom, do you know how to drive to Westport?"

"Yes, sir."

"You do that." Charlie nodded toward the windshield. "You do that right now, and we'll get along just fine."

❧

Jean was sitting in the chair behind the desk. At first Mary Ellen thought she must be ill, had fainted perhaps. Her head was tilted to the side, away from Mary Ellen, and she was slumped down in the chair, her left arm trailing over the side as if she'd been reaching for something that had fallen to the floor.

Mary Ellen called her name. "Jean?" she said. "Jean, are you all right?"

Then she saw that something was askew with her left ring finger. It was bent back and to the side at the first knuckle. It was in a position no one's finger should be in.

That was, Mary Ellen said later, her first indication that something was terribly wrong.

Then she noticed the diamond ring on the desk, and beside it a coin of some sort, and she wondered why they were there and what they had to do with Jean. But it was that finger that concerned her most, for now she saw the blood coming from it. It was dripping onto the floor.

Later, when she thought back to this moment, when she tried to describe it for Robbie, she said it was like she was nowhere and everywhere all at once. She knew she was in the high school, but she was also a million miles away, somewhere in space looking down on herself, that woman, that widow woman who was so intimate with grief, and the girl in the chair, the girl she'd thought would be her friend a long, long time, the girl she now knew was dead.

"And I thought of your father," Mary Ellen said to Robbie. "And of course, I thought of you and hoped that you were safe and that you wouldn't come to that room and see what I was seeing. I thought of people I hadn't thought of in years—my best friend when I was a girl, a woman I saw on a bus once and the scar on her face. It was like the world shook open and there we were, all of us, everyone all across time, and we all felt a chill go up the backs of our necks. Some of us were afraid, some of us felt like crying. Some of us ran home and hugged the people we loved. Some of us knew the most excellent ecstasy. For just an instant we were all alive to one another. Maybe that's what death brings us, Robbie. His name was Charlie Camplain. He was out there, and we didn't even know it until it was too late."

11

Lorene was sitting at the Gimbels lunch counter when Norville arrived. She hadn't bothered to take off the light blue smock she wore while she was sewing and doing alterations. She was sitting on a stool at the counter, flipping through the pages of a *Photoplay* magazine. She liked to keep up on all the movie stars and their latest fashions. She had her legs crossed, one foot in a simple black flat tapping a rhythm only she could hear, and she had a run in her stocking. For some reason, the sight of it made Norville feel tender toward her, and despite how she'd wounded him, he went to her and slipped his arm across her shoulders and said, "Look at this pretty girl."

This was the way he always greeted her, and her response today was the same as usual. "Maybe you need to have your eyes checked," she said.

Today, for some reason he couldn't name, he said something he'd often thought but had never had the courage to try to put into words. He said to her, "I'm not a particularly handsome man, and Lord knows I'm not rich, but I believe I'm a decent man. I really do, Lorene, and I believe you could do a lot worse than me." He took note of the surprised look on her face. Her lips parted as if she were about to speak, but he didn't let her. He pushed on. "This past year, when we've been spending time together, I've often wondered what it would be like if we'd make it a permanent arrangement. I'm not getting any younger, Lorene. I thought you liked spending time with me. I know

I like spending time with you. When we're apart, I feel so all alone, I don't hardly know what to do. This is the day, Lorene. This is the day I'm asking you to be my wife."

For a long moment, the only sounds were the grease spattering on the grill, the chatter from the other diners, the sound of silverware on plates, the cook calling out, "Order up!"

Norville knew right away that he'd made a mistake. He could tell from the momentary grimace on Lorene's face, the way she bit down on her lower lip and glanced away from him as she closed her *Photoplay* and ran her hand slowly over the cover. Ann Blyth was looking up at Norville. She had her arms crossed, her chin resting on her top hand. Her blue eyes were stunning with her dark hair. Her lipstick was a subdued red and her brown eyebrows were nicely arched. It looked to Norville as if she were in a pose of expectation, as if she were anticipating something she'd long looked forward to and knew was about to arrive.

Lorene turned to him. She said, "Norville, I know why you're doing this."

He was glad she knew, because he didn't. He'd come to Gimbels intent on getting her to admit she was sleeping with Raymond Hardy, but then he saw that run in her stocking, and he got all soft-hearted. He thought of her pressing a dab of fingernail polish to that runner to stop it from going farther. He thought of her pulling a stocking from a dresser drawer and running her hand up inside it. He saw the autumn light shining through a window and that window was in their bedroom—his and hers—and he was sitting on the bed waiting for her to finish dressing so they could go out and grab a bite to eat, maybe catch a movie, maybe *One Minute to Zero,* that new Ann Blyth and Robert Mitchum picture, and from there it just went on, his fantasy of a life spent together.

"I've always loved you, Lorene."

At that instant he forgave her for Raymond Hardy. They had no need to speak of it. All she had to do was to say yes and there they'd be, at the start of a glorious life together.

"It's Raymond Hardy, isn't it?" She was speaking softly, and it pained him to know that he'd forced her to speak of something that embarrassed her. "It's because you know what you know."

"I love you," he said, but even he could hear the confidence fading from his voice. "That's all that matters."

"I like you, Norville. I really do." She reached out, then, and touched his hand. "But we both know this isn't right. This isn't really what you want to do. Not now."

"Yes," he said. "I'm not sure. I think. Yes."

She was holding onto his hand, and her touch, despite all that lay between them, was the most wonderful thing.

He said to her then the thing he'd never been able to say to anyone. "Sometimes I just want someone to hug me, to hold my hand, just to remember what that's like."

She smiled at him. "We're doing that now, aren't we?"

He nodded.

"So why don't we have our lunch? Why don't we sit here and eat and talk about pleasant things. Wouldn't you like that?"

"Yes," he said, "I would."

"Good," she said. "For the time being, we don't have to know any more than this. I enjoy your company, and you enjoy mine."

Everything now seemed cut and dried to Norville. He'd go on living alone, go on being the night clerk at the Grand Hotel, go on being the man who wanted what he couldn't have because Lorene only liked him and didn't love him.

He cut into his hamburger steak. He listened to Lorene chatter. He accepted his fate. He was a nice man who would always be lonely.

Then, down the counter, he overheard a man talking. "I just came from the courthouse in Lawrenceville. I was there when the sheriff got a call about a murder."

12

A GOLD CHEVY FLEETLINE MADE a left turn onto State Street in Lawrenceville just as Grinny started to turn right. He had to slam on his brakes so fast, his left foot didn't find the clutch in time, and his cab bucked and stalled. An ambulance was coming up behind him, sirens blaring. The ambulance blasted its horn again and again and again, warning Grinny to clear the intersection.

It was all an embarrassment to him—first all he'd put up with from Charlie Camplain, then his encounter with Mr. Heath, and now this. Grinny was a good driver, and he took pride in that fact. He'd never had an accident in his cab, had won an award from the company, in fact, for his safe driving, so now to be stalled and in the way of an ambulance galled him.

"Goddamn," he said out loud. "Goddamn it all to hell."

His cursing was a further embarrassment because he was known as a man of faith who never used foul language. He was glad Millie and Peg weren't there to hear him.

Finally, he got the cab started, and he swung the wheel to the right and turned onto State Street in time for the ambulance to rush on through the intersection. He pressed down on the foot feed, speeding east, gaining on the Fleetline.

He'd glimpsed the driver and his passenger when the car cut him off at the intersection. It came to him with a sudden clarity. That gray flannel suit, that crazy tie. The man in the passenger seat of the Fleetline was Charlie Camplain.

What that meant, Grinny couldn't say, but he found himself giving the cab more gas, eager to stay close just in case.

❧

Charlie took the snub-nosed .38 from his suit coat pocket. He gave the chamber a spin and put the barrel to his temple.

"Keep your eye on the road." Charlie made sure to keep his voice low and even. "I want you to drive like your grandmother. You savvy?"

"Mister, don't do anything stupid."

"Too late," said Charlie.

The Fleetline moved slowly over the bridge across the Embarras River. The radio tower of WAKO was in sight. Soon the Fleetline would take the turn toward Westport and the Showboat, where Charlie had left his suitcase. He'd left it there in the event it turned out that he needed a change of clothes. He'd hoped such wouldn't be the case, but now it was.

"Tell me, Tom," he said. "What in the world could possibly be bothering you on such a beautiful day?"

"Sir?"

"You'd been crying when I got in your car. What's the story, sport? Girl troubles?"

Tom nodded. "I love a girl—the girl you saw me with at school—but I did something stupid with another girl and now she's pregnant."

"Oh, that blasted romance." Charlie chuckled. "What's a poor fella to do?"

"If I could just go back and change things," Tom said.

"Exactly, but you can't, can you? You can only live with what you've done. No way around that, bub. Believe me."

"Mister, I don't want you to hurt yourself. I don't want to have to see that."

"Tom, there are going to be people who'll ask you if I was crazy." Charlie grinned at him. "I want you to tell them about this."

He pulled the trigger, and the hammer snapped against an empty chamber.

"Good Lord, mister. Please don't."

Charlie spun the chamber again. "You just keep driving," he said.

Mary Ellen told the sheriff what she could. Yes, she rented out a room in her home to her new colleague, Jean De Belle, who'd moved in at the beginning of August. No, she hadn't known her to have any trouble. No, she hadn't had any callers. No one had come to visit her. No one had called for her on the telephone. She was friendly and excited about the first day of school.

"I liked her very much." Mary Ellen sat on a chair in Mr. Pomeroy's office, a handkerchief twisted in her hand. She had to stop from time to time to blot the tears from her eyes and to try to control her quavering voice. "I'm sorry," she said.

The sheriff was patient. She'd known him as a friend of her husband. His name was Gerald Malone—a stocky man with a red face, known for wearing a brown fedora hat. It rested now on Mr. Pomeroy's desk as he sat across from Mary Ellen. His hair was graying, oiled and combed back from his forehead. He'd been the sheriff for a long time. Mary Ellen knew he'd witnessed horrible automobile accidents, seen bodies burned in fires, stabbed to death, shot to death, but this—a teacher gunned down in broad daylight at the high school, and now the killer on the loose—rattled even him.

"You take your time, Mary Ellen," he said. "Just tell me what you know."

Mr. Pomeroy stood behind her, patting her back. "We'll help you get through this," he said. "You heard what you thought were shots, yes?"

"I heard the shots." Mary Ellen nodded. "And I ran downstairs. I don't know why, really. I'm usually no good in a crisis, but something told me to run. The door to the classroom was open, and I saw Jean slumped in the chair. At first I thought she'd taken sick. Then I saw her finger. It wasn't right. It was bent. It didn't look like a finger at all. That was the first thing that told me something was terribly wrong."

Mr. Malone asked if she knew of anyone who would want to hurt Miss De Belle.

Mary Ellen shook her head. "She seemed like a very happy girl. We were great friends."

Someone was tapping very lightly on Mr. Pomeroy's door. He opened it, and Mary Ellen saw the secretary, Lily Wagner, standing there, with her slender arm across Robbie's shoulders. Robbie had her arms across her chest, and she kept her head bowed.

"Mr. Pomeroy," Lily said, "I'm sorry to disturb you." She had on a white blouse that she'd buttoned to the top. She wore a gold pocket watch pinned to the blouse. "But Robbie has something to say, something I think you all should know."

Mary Ellen could hear the commotion outside in the hallway; she knew word was starting to spread. She got up from her chair. She went to her daughter. She took Robbie in her arms, and Robbie, who normally would have shrunk away from such a display of affection, clung to her as if she meant to never let go.

∽❦∾

Robbie sat beside her mother in Mr. Pomeroy's office, and she said what she knew about the man in the gray flannel suit.

"He asked me where to find Miss De Belle." Her mother had her arm around her shoulders, and Robbie snuggled in close to her, even laid her head on her chest. "I was late to assembly, and he stopped me outside the auditorium. I had the door open, and Miss De Belle was at the podium. 'That's her,' I told him, but I could tell he already knew who she was. He bent over and put his hands on his knees. I could tell he was overwhelmed."

"That's fine, Robbie." Gerald Malone leaned forward in his chair. He was scribbling something in a pocket-sized notebook that he held between his knees. "You're doing fine. What else can you tell us?"

"After the assembly, he got rough with Tom."

"Tom Heath?" Mr. Pomeroy said.

Robbie nodded. She could barely speak, her throat tight with the misery that Tom had brought her. "I'm sorry," she said in a hoarse voice "It's been quite a day."

Later, she would remember saying this—*It's been quite a day*—and she'd think it didn't sound like her at all. It was too mature a thing to say at this time when she felt like a little girl. She didn't know what to make of that. She only felt that something inside her was changing, but she had no idea what that something was.

"Honey, it's all right." Her mother patted her arm. "I'm right here with you, Robbie. Go on."

So she did. She explained how she and Tom had been having an argument and he'd grabbed her by her arm and wouldn't let her go. "That's when this man took him by the neck and backed him into the wall. 'Bub,' he said, 'that's no way to treat a lady.'"

"He said 'bub'?" Gerald Malone asked.

Robbie confirmed that he did. "He had Tom by the neck, but he let him go when Miss De Belle came out of the auditorium."

Gerald Malone snapped his notebook closed and said to Mr. Pomeroy, "I'll need to speak with Tom Heath."

"Of course," said Mr. Pomeroy. "I'll have Miss Wagner find him."

But it soon became apparent Tom was nowhere to be found, nor was his car in the parking lot.

"It's a Chevy, isn't it?" Mr. Pomeroy asked Robbie.

"A Fleetline," Robbie said. "A gold Fleetline." Later she would think she'd memorized everything about that car for exactly this moment. "A fastback with fat whitewalls and tons of chrome." Here she faltered, the memory of what else she had to offer nearly too much for her. "A piece of pink cashmere hanging from the rearview mirror."

Gerald Malone got up from his chair and grabbed his fedora from Mr. Pomeroy's desk. "I have a hunch if we find Tom Heath, we'll find the man we're looking for."

Robbie watched Gerald Malone rush out. Her heart was pounding.

She understood that Tom might be in danger, and then a flutter in her stomach told her she still cared about him, no matter what he'd done.

❦

Now the word was coming to the lunch counter at Gimbels. Another man slumped onto a stool and said he'd just heard that someone had shot the librarian at Lawrenceville High. Yes, shot her to death right there in the school. A man wearing some sort of crazy necktie.

"I know that man," Norville said to Lorene.

Lorene had been about to take a bite from her toasted cheese sandwich, but now she put it back on her plate. "Really now, Norville. How would you know someone like him?"

"He stayed at the Grand last night."

"You're sure?"

"A design on that necktie like nothing I've ever seen. You don't forget something like that."

"Goodness' sakes," Lorene said. "The police are going to want to talk to you."

He was already pushing himself up from his stool. He stood and took a five-dollar bill from his billfold. He folded it three times and held the rectangle out to Lorene. "This should pay for lunch. I'm sorry I have to go."

"Of course you have to go. Right now. This instant." She took bill in her palm, and at the same time she closed her fingers around Norville's hand. "You call me later," she said. "Promise me. I'll want to know that you're all right."

"I promise," he said.

She held to his hand just an instant longer. He looked into her eyes. She was looking at him with what he decided was concern and admiration. He might even call it love. At last, he thought. Here was something between them.

Outside Gimbels, he stepped inside a telephone booth on the corner of Second and Main and pulled the folding door closed behind him. He fumbled in his hip pocket for his billfold. He unsnapped his coin purse and fished out a nickel before remembering that in spring the cost of a call from a payphone had gone up to a dime.

He didn't have a dime. He had a nickel and two pennies. He thought about going back into Gimbels and asking Lorene for the loan of a dime, but he decided that would make him look weak, inept, and he couldn't stand the thought of that, not when she'd looked at him with such warmth. She'd even asked him to call her later to let her know he was all right. Just the way a wife would do, he couldn't help thinking. No, he couldn't go back in and ask for a dime like he was a little boy, or worse, an imbecile.

The street was full of people—women with boxes from Gimbels and men with garment bags from Albert's. He could tell any one of them that he needed to make an urgent phone call, or he could go into the Kresge store and break a bill. That's what he'd do. He'd buy something small—a pack of Wrigley's gum, maybe—and he'd make sure to have a dime.

He stepped out of the telephone booth at the exact moment that a police car pulled to the curb.

Norville surprised himself by opening the passenger-side door and calmly getting in.

The officer, a young man with a head of black, wavy hair and a dimple in his chin, laid his hand on his service weapon. The leather of the holster creaked as he shifted in his seat to take a look at Norville.

"Mister," he said.

Norville held up his hands. "Forgive the intrusion." He tried to smile, to make it clear that he was friendly. "I'm pretty sure that sooner or later, you're going to come looking for me."

13

GRINNY KEPT THE FLEETLINE IN sight. At the crest of the hill just east of WAKO, it turned south, and he followed suit. Soon the Fleetline and the Yellow Cab were winding back to the east and were on the flat plain of farmland. The soybean plants were browning and near to harvest; the cornstalks were also turning brown. The ears would harden in their dry husks and wait for the pickers. Grinny closed the distance.

He couldn't have said why it was so important to him to follow that Fleetline. Later, he would suspect it had something to do with Millie, and how badly things had gone with Mr. Heath, that made him want to be on the square with the straight and narrow. There was something about Charlie Camplain that seemed suspicious; he'd had a short fuse with Grinny in the cab ride earlier, and there was that matter of the suitcase left at the Showboat. If nothing else, Grinny wanted to see if the Fleetline might be going there.

Yes, he knew there was trouble somewhere in Lawrenceville, he'd say later, but he didn't know where or the nature of it. He had no idea whether the Fleetline and Charlie Camplain were involved, but he wasn't surprised when he found out.

"Something wasn't right about that fella," he'd say. "He was wound tight and just about to snap."

Now the Fleetline was drifting across the center line, then swerving sharply back into the proper lane. Grinny wondered what was happening in that car. Then he got close enough to see that Charlie Camplain had a gun, and he was holding it to his own head.

⌒◯⌒

The flat road T-ed into Illinois Route 33 just outside Westport. The boy sat at the stop sign, his fingers trembling on the steering wheel.

"Son, what's the holdup?" Charlie said.

"I'm scared." Charlie could see the boy was close to tears. "Stop doing that with your gun." Charlie had spun the chamber and fired the .38 into his temple again and again. "You *are* crazy. I'll tell them. Please, mister. No more."

Charlie lowered his arm and let the .38 lie in his lap. "Son, do you know where the Showboat is?"

"Oh, mister, please don't make me go there." The boy kept glancing in the rearview mirror, and Charlie imagined he knew what he was thinking—that once he'd had a life somewhere back there behind him, but now that life was about to disappear. "Please, mister," he said again. "That's where I met this other girl. That's where everything went wrong."

Just then, a car behind them honked its horn, startling Charlie. He hadn't known anyone was following them. He picked up the .38 and jerked around to see who it was. He saw the Yellow Cab and the toothless driver who'd taken him to Lawrenceville.

He raised the .38 and pointed it at the boy. "You've seen me snap down on all the chambers except this last one. Now, what does that tell you?"

The boy turned the Fleetline toward Westport.

"Smart boy," Charlie said.

The Showboat was just ahead, just a few seconds for him to figure out what to do about that cab driver, to hope that when the boy turned the Fleetline into the parking lot, the Yellow Cab would go on by.

If it didn't? Well, things might get a little messy.

"I don't want to die," the boy said.

"You're not going to die," Charlie said. "At least, not today. Just get me where I need to go."

The Fleetline slowed just before the rise to the Lincoln Memorial Bridge that carried traffic over the Wabash River in and out of Vincennes. Grinny tapped the brakes on the Yellow Cab and followed the Fleetline into the gravel lot of the Showboat. The Fleetline edged into a parking spot near the front door. The sun glinting off the chrome bumper nearly blinded Grinny as he cruised past and parked at the far end of the lot, where he could keep an eye on Charlie Camplain.

It wasn't long before Camplain got out of the Fleetline. The boy who was driving got out on the driver's side. He was a boy with ears that stuck out too far from his head and black-rimmed eyeglasses, a boy who wore a pair of blue jeans with the legs rolled above his black tennis shoes and a red and black plaid shirt. He bent over at his waist and put his hands on his knees. Grinny could only see his flat back and a bit of the Indian beaded belt he wore with his blue jeans.

He opened his door and got out. He stood there, undecided about what to do. Then he saw Camplain march briskly around the front of the Fleetline and yank the boy up straight. He had the boy by the belt, and he nudged him with the gun. He marched him up to the front door of the Showboat and then inside.

Grinny knew Peg would call him a fool, but he felt sorry for that boy. He didn't know who he was or what a man like him could do, but he couldn't let him go into the Showboat alone with Charlie Camplain. If some other man saw Millie in trouble, he'd want him to try to help. That was the bottom line. That was how he found himself moving across the parking lot, to the front door, to whatever might be waiting for him inside.

When Robbie and Mary Ellen finally left Mr. Pomeroy's office, they saw Lily Wagner trying to comfort a young girl, who was sitting on a wooden chair sobbing. A freshman, if Mary Ellen was any judge. The mousy girl, Robbie remembered. The one who had made such a fuss over Miss De Belle outside the auditorium. Etta, Miss De Belle had called her.

"Poor thing." Lily was kneeling beside her. She had her arms around her, rocking side to side. "She's beside herself."

Mary Ellen felt her heart come up into her throat. Watching that young girl cry, a girl obviously from somewhere out in the country, broke her to pieces.

School was dismissing, Lily told them. She'd called in the bus drivers to run their routes. Word had reached parents in town, and a number of them were coming to pick up their children. Through the windows, Robbie could see other students running across the front lawn. Many were shouting with glee, running wild with the thrill of escape—no school, almost another full day of summer. Some of the younger boys were pretending to fire guns, and others were pretending to fall over dead.

Idiots, Robbie decided. Every one of them.

Robbie and her mother stepped out into the empty hallway.

Her mother said, "Goodness, I can hardly think of what to do."

"I want to know that Tom's all right," Robbie said.

The words were out of Mary Ellen's mouth before she could stop them. "Tom Heath, Tom Heath, Tom Heath," she said. "You think the whole world revolves around that boy." She put her hand to her mouth. "That was a horrible thing to say. Robbie, I'm so sorry."

Robbie could hardly believe it. Inside Mr. Pomeroy's office, she'd felt close to her mother. Watching Etta sob, Robbie had imagined her own mother holding her close. Then she said those words and Robbie felt the old bitterness returning. She wanted her best friend—she wanted Tom—but she didn't know where to find him, or whether she'd ever be able to count on him again.

"He doesn't love me," she said to her mother. Her voice was cool, matter of fact. "He's got another girl now. There, does that make you happy?"

⌒◈⌒

"Spell it," the police officer with the black wavy hair said.

Norville obliged. "C-A-M-P-L-A-I-N."

"Armed, you say?"

"A snub-nosed .38. Said he had a girl in Lawrenceville. I saw her picture. He had an engagement ring for her. Said she didn't know it yet, but he was going to change her life."

⌒◈⌒

"He wasn't in a hurry," Grinny would tell Peg later. "He took his time. Like he didn't have a care in the world."

Charlie Camplain was standing at the end of the bar, just to the left of and a little behind the boy, who was sitting on a stool.

"A Coca-Cola for my friend here," Camplain said to Dick Dollahan. Dick was unwrapping a fresh King Edward cigar. "And a Schlitz for yours truly."

Grinny walked straight toward them. He kept his eyes on Camplain's right hand, which was still in his suit coat pocket. Grinny saw him turn his head. He saw his eyes narrow when he spotted Grinny.

Then, in a flash, he was smiling. "Well, looky here," Camplain said. "My friend from this morning. My grinning friend, the cab driver. Pull up a stool. What are you drinking?"

"I'm not drinking anything," Grinny said. "I'm working. I'm driving my cab."

Dick Dollahan set the Coke and the Schlitz on the bar.

"Here's to the working man." Camplain wrapped his hand around the Schitz bottle, lifted it to his mouth, and took a good, long drink. "I believe I may be done working for a while. If you ask me, I've earned this. Wouldn't you say so, son?"

The boy hadn't touched his Coke. He sat with his shoulders hunched, his head bowed, his hands braced against the bar. Grinny got the impression that he might spring up at any moment.

"Yes, sir," he said.

"It's been quite a morning." Camplain glanced at his wristwatch. "My friend and I can only stay long enough for this one drink." Then he said to Dick Dollahan, "I'll ask for that suitcase I left with you, and then we'll be out of your hair."

"Where are you going?" Grinny asked.

"Places to be, bub." Camplain took another long pull on his Schlitz. "Things to do. People to see."

"Doesn't look like he's in any rush." Grinny nodded toward the boy. "Hasn't even taken a sip of that Coke."

"Drink up, son," said Camplain. "Don't be shy."

The boy looked at Grinny, his eyes wide with fear.

"If you need me to carry you somewhere," Grinny said to Camplain, "I can."

Camplain shook his head. "I've got my personal driver here. Thanks all the same.."

Grinny stepped up close to Camplain, close enough to bump him. The wire running up to his ear waggled.

Camplain raised his left hand to his ear to make sure his hearing aid stayed in place. "Watch it there, bub," Camplain said.

Grinny kept his voice low. There were a number of diners at their tables, and he didn't want to alarm them. "I don't know what went on back there in Lawrenceville, but I know something did."

"Not your business."

"I was following you. I saw what you were up to."

"Like I said, not your business. Let it go."

Grinny leaned in closer and whispered into Camplain's left ear, "I won't let you hurt this boy."

The hearing aid squealed.

Camplain jerked his head to the side from the pain of it.

Grinny yanked on the wire and pulled the hearing aid free.

The boy sprang from the bar and ran for the door.

Camplain turned, the gun now in his hand. He pointed it at Grinny, and Grinny closed his eyes, bracing himself for the shot that never came. When he finally opened his eyes, he saw that Camplain had lowered the gun. He flicked open the chamber and spun it.

"No bullets." Camplain giggled. "How about that? Guess I used them all up. Looks like this is your lucky day."

Robbie didn't wait for her mother to respond. She turned and started walking toward the front doors of the school.

Her mother called after her. "Robbie, wait. Robbie, I feel just awful. Robbie, where are you going?"

She didn't know where she was going; she only knew she was getting away from her mother, and from the school where Tom had told her about this other girl, this Millie, and where a crazy man had killed Miss De Belle.

She trudged up Tenth Street, and was waiting to cross State when a black Buick Super stopped beside her. Robbie took in the sight of the three VentiPorts along the front fender, the ones that Tom had explained to her ventilated the engine compartment. She knew it was Mr. Heath behind the steering wheel even before he called to her.

"Oh, Robbie," he said, "it's just horrible, isn't it?"

His bowtie was crooked. That's what Robbie noticed first, that cockeyed bowtie. She would remember the colors of it and its awkward angle below Mr. Heath's Adam's apple the rest of her life. Sometimes it would come to her uninvited. That bowtie. That horrible day.

"Mr. Heath," she said.

"Are you all right?"

"They let school out."

Mr. Heath revved the engine. "I have to go. They've found Tom's car in Westport."

Westport. She never wanted to hear that word again. But they'd found Tom's Fleetline. She started to ask Mr. Heath if they'd found Tom. She wanted to know if he was safe.

But the Buick was already pulling away from the curb. She listened to it run through its gears as it headed out State Street just as fast as Mr. Heath could safely go.

❧

Dick Dollahan was not a man who took kindly to a patron brandishing a gun in his establishment. He kept a baseball bat and a sawed-off shotgun behind the bar to discourage such behavior.

When Charlie Camplain laid his .38 on the bar, Dick drew out the sawed-off shotgun and pointed it at Camplain's chest.

"Ruth," he said, "call the police."

The diners gradually started to notice that something was wrong. They saw Dick Dollahan and then they saw the shotgun. A woman screamed.

"It's all right," Dick said. "Nothing to worry about, folks. I've got this all under control."

The call to the police proved unnecessary, because at that moment the door opened and in walked Sheriff Gerald Malone.

He went directly to the end of the bar. "Something tells me you must be the man I'm looking for," he said. "Were you in Lawrenceville this morning?"

"I carried him there in my cab," Grinny said. "To the high school."

Malone nodded. "Did you go there to shoot Jean De Belle?"

Camplain chuckled. "Of course not, bub. I went there to ask her to marry me."

"You've got a strange way of proposing." Malone used his finger to nudge the .38 farther down the bar. "Bub."

Camplain hung his head. When he lifted it, he had a smile on his face. "She said no." He held up his empty palms and shrugged. "What else was I to do?"

"The sweetest smile," Grinny would tell Peg later. "You could almost believe he was really in love."

14

So AUTUMN DEEPENED INTO THE short days, and all through the Wabash Valley—in Vincennes and across the river into Westport and out along the prairie to Lawrenceville—the talk was about Jean De Belle and Charlie Camplain and the folks who had crossed paths with them on September 3: the desk clerk at the Grand Hotel in Vincennes, where Camplain had stayed; the cab driver who carried him to Lawrenceville; the English teacher who rented a room to Miss De Belle; the daughter who dated the boy who drove the getaway car after the deed was done. And there were others, unknown to most, whose lives were about to change because they knew, in one way or another, the people who had to testify about what they saw, what they heard, on that day in early September.

Millie Haines carried Tom Heath's baby. Tom's mother, grateful for his safety, told his father to go easy on him. Robbie McVeigh woke each morning, her heart aching, and she grew more distant from her mother, who wanted to know what had happened with Tom Heath: why had the two of them gone their separate ways?

"Maybe I set my sights too low," Robbie said. "Like you always told me, I've got my whole life."

Mary Ellen didn't believe it for an instant. Robbie was a girl who wanted what she wanted—when had she ever taken no for an answer?—but really, what was the point in pressing on a sore spot. Boys and girls came apart every day, sometimes with barely a thought, sometimes with a violent turn, as had been the case for Jean. Mary Ellen hardly slept at night, haunted by the image of her slumped in that chair.

The harvest moon hung full and bright outside the house on Dubois Street, and Mary Ellen sat near the window in the long hours of the night and watched that moon and told herself the next day would be a better one. She would be a better mother, a better teacher, a better friend. She let herself feel again the closeness she had felt with Jean. She remembered sitting with her on the porch swing those evenings after supper and how once she reached out and held Jean's hand, just like two girlfriends who had known each other all their lives. That and the evenings they went to dinner at the Candle Lite downtown on the square, or the times they played records on the stereo and even danced a little. So many memories from the short time Jean had been with her, but enough to remind her what might have been for them, if not for Charlie Camplain.

One morning at school, she walked into her empty classroom and saw what someone had written on the chalkboard: *Mrs. McVeigh + Miss De Belle, True Love?*

She erased it straightaway, and then was immediately disgusted with herself because she'd acted as if she were guilty. If Jean were alive, Mary Ellen felt certain, they'd share a chuckle over the idiocy of those gossipy students.

"Can you imagine?" Mary Ellen might say.

And Jean would answer, "They think they know so much when really they don't know a thing. If you ask me, they're just jealous. How rare it is to find someone with whom you can be so close."

Peg Haines clung to her husband in bed each night as if she were afraid to let him go.

"He had a gun," she said to Grinny that first night, the night of September 3, "and you walked right up to him."

"I didn't think about it," he whispered to her in the dark. "I couldn't let him hurt that boy."

Lorene Deveraux couldn't get over how Norville Rich had become all alive to her. He seemed like a different man. She didn't know what it was, but she knew it was there—that little flutter in her chest every time she saw him. Raymond Hardy said he was an imposter, a little man puffing himself up just because he happened to be working the front desk at the Grand the night that Charlie Camplain checked in.

"If you ask me," Lorene told Raymond, "you're being pretty small yourself right now. You have no idea what he's gone through. This has affected him deeply. It's *touched* him. I feel it, too. That's your problem, Raymond. You don't feel anything."

Out across the prairie that stretched from Westport to Lawrenceville, pumpkins lay fat and orange on the ground, ready to be snapped from the vines; cornstalks rubbed their dry leaves together in the autumn chill; combines worked the fields, cutting soybeans and clouding the air with dust. In the muted light, the tree lines couldn't hide the oranges and yellows and reds of their leaves: red oaks and sugar maples, hickories and sumacs, cottonwoods and sweet gums.

These were the dearest days of autumn—these last days before stark winter—and for some they were filled with mourning, or with the fear of what lay ahead, or with hope that fortune would turn in their favor, but always, not far from the thoughts of anyone who had brushed up against that moment in the classroom at Lawrenceville High School, was the terror and thrill of being in a place between a beginning and an end and not knowing which it would be.

Make a choice. Follow a direction. Robbie could have told them it was all circles. Left or right, something ended and something began.

Charlie Camplain had taught her that. Charlie Camplain and that crazy tie. Circles inside circles. Sometimes all you could do was surrender.

Take a step, Robbie thought. *Any step*. Like Jean De Belle, you had no way of knowing what might be out there waiting for you. But you had to find out. Otherwise, Robbie finally said to her mother, what was the use in living?

"I don't want to be afraid," she said. "I want my life. I want it, Mother. Whatever it turns out to be."

✦

All right, then, Mary Ellen thought. *All right*. She was tired of watching the moon at night and then feeling leaden all day. She was tired of walking the hallways at school and hearing students whispering. *She's the one who found her*. She was tired of the gossip about her and Jean, and the way it cheapened the memory of their friendship. But why hadn't she known Jean better? She'd never once asked her about her family or her home. Maybe if she had, she would have heard the story of Charlie Camplain, and maybe—just maybe—she could have done something. Jean would be up there in her room right now, grading her students' themes, or listening to the radio, or changing her clothes before coming down to supper.

"Oh, really, Mother," Robbie said to her. "What could you have done? What in the world could any of us have done?"

In the days immediately following the shooting, Mary Ellen sometimes found herself downstairs, shaken from a daydream by what she swore were footsteps above her, coming from Jean's room. But, of course, it was always her imagination. It was her hearing what she wanted to hear, wanting to believe that nothing had gone wrong that morning of September 3, that she and Jean had driven home together after school and Jean had been excited to tell her all about her day. Oh, how Mary Ellen had hoped that Jean's youthful exuberance would awaken the enthusiasm that she herself had once felt, not only for teaching, but for everything around her. Even before her husband's death, she felt as if a great weight were pressing down on her and she didn't know what to do to shake it off. She was forty-eight years old, and she knew her sadness was driving her husband away. Each day, she told herself she'd find something to be happy about. She went through the motions of preparing her lesson plans. She went through the motions of being a mother. She went through the motions of being a wife.

"I don't know where you've gone, Mary Ellen," her husband finally said to her. "I really don't."

She didn't either. She only knew it was somewhere dark and oppressive, and she couldn't get out.

Then he died. Her husband. Her Edward. His heart stopped, and he died, and her sadness reached a new depth that nearly drowned her.

But then the girl came. Jean De Belle. She was bright and new, and Mary Ellen loved her from the beginning.

Oh, what a glorious day it had been, that first day of school. Mary Ellen saw the sunshine that morning, felt the late summer breeze through her open window, and for the first time in years she felt excited about the new school year. She hoped she'd turned the corner and had started her way back to reclaiming the joy that had once been hers. She wanted her life, too, she'd tell Robbie, even now after Jean was dead. She'd always wanted her life, even when it seemed like she'd given up. She just hadn't known how to say that to anyone who might have helped, and she hadn't known how to help herself.

Jean's autopsy showed that Charlie Camplain had shot her six times, emptying all the chambers of his Colt Detective Special .38 . Two bullets to the heart, three others in the abdomen, and a single bullet to the head after it passed through her left forefinger.

Mary Ellen remembered Jean's bent finger. She knew now what it meant. The shot to the head had been first. Jean had known that Charlie was about to pull that trigger, and she put her hands up in front of her face. Mary Ellen couldn't let herself think about that, couldn't let herself imagine Jean covering her face and the long seconds before the gun fired.

Jean's parents came to town and made arrangements for her body to be brought home to Madison. Mary Ellen knew this because, one evening, there was a knock on the front door, and when she went to see who had come calling, she found a man standing on the porch. A man in a brown top coat because a storm had gone through and the temperature had dropped, and autumn was threatening to assert itself in earnest. He raised his head and blinked when she turned on the porch light, and it filled the lenses of his rimless eyeglasses. He was a well-dressed man, a tall man with slumped shoulders, and Mary Ellen knew, without having to ask, that he was Jean's father.

"I'm sorry to disturb you." He took off his brown fedora, and the sight of the few strands of hair combed over his balding head almost broke Mary Ellen. Without his hat on, he looked like who he was: a man beaten down with grief. "My wife and I." He waved an arm out behind him, where a black Chrysler sedan sat idling at the curb. A woman in a camel's hair car coat sat in the passenger seat, her head bowed. She had on a black pillbox church hat with black netting that came down over her eyes. "We're Mr. and Mrs. De Belle. We understand that this is where Jean stayed."

Mary Ellen nodded. She said, "I was the one who…"

"We know who you are," Mr. De Belle interrupted. His voice was shy. "You'll have to forgive my wife. She's had a difficult day."

"Of course." The wind was up. Mary Ellen had a light sweater over her shoulders and buttoned at her throat. She crossed her arms over her chest and shivered in the chill night air. "How may I help you, Mr. De Belle?"

He said his wife wanted him to see the room that had been Jean's. She wanted him to tell her what it was like, that room where their daughter had spent her last days. "She'd do it herself," he said, "but she just can't face it."

"The police have already been through it," Mary Ellen said.

They'd taken a few things: an address book, a letter she'd been writing her parents, a pocketbook. Everything else was still in the room, exactly how Jean had left it that morning when she and Mary

Ellen set out for school. Mary Ellen had closed the door to that room after the police had come and gone, and she hadn't opened it since.

Mr. De Belle made no response. Of course, Mary Ellen thought. One more thing he already knew. He leaned forward, coming up on his toes, and she opened the door wider and told him to please come in.

"Top of the stairs," she said, and he nodded. Then he grabbed onto the banister and bent his head.

Mary Ellen followed him up the staircase. Robbie was in her room listening to records. Mary Ellen heard the chorus of Doris Day's "A Guy Is a Guy." When Mr. De Belle reached the top of the stairs, he stood to the side and waited for Mary Ellen to open the door to what had been his daughter's room.

A gray wool skirt lay across the bed, discarded that summery morning of September 3 in favor of something more lightweight. A novel, Pearl S. Buck's *The Hidden Flower,* was on the night table. Mary Ellen knew the book was causing quite a stir in town for its portrait of an interracial love affair. A carousel music box sat on the dresser. Mr. De Belle went to it. He laid his fedora on the dresser, and then he turned the carousel top, winding the music box. When he was finished, he opened a small drawer at the base of the box, and the four horses went up and down their metal poles as the carousel turned. Mary Ellen had heard the song played countless times at merry-go-rounds at the county fair.

Suddenly, Mr. De Belle shut the drawer with a slam, and the music stopped. His shoulders were shaking. His right hand was curled into a fist.

"Mr. De Belle?" Mary Ellen said.

He turned to her, his face twisted with rage. "She tried to warn me about him." He could barely control himself. "Charlie Camplain." He turned back to the dresser and reached for his fedora. Mary Ellen knew he was fighting to control himself. But it was no use. He was sobbing now. "She tried to tell me he wasn't safe."

Mary Ellen went to him. She slipped her arm across his shoulders. She patted his arm. She steadied him while he cried, and when he was done, she said, "I didn't know your Jean long, but I could see she was a special girl."

"Thank you," he said. "Thank you for giving her a place."

"I loved every minute she was here. I think she felt at home."

"In a way, she never quite did in my house," Mr. De Belle said.

He drew back his shoulders. Mary Ellen felt the muscles in his forearm stiffen. She thought it wise to speak of something else.

"I can get boxes for Jean's things. I can help you carry them to the car."

He said, "That book, that skirt, all of these things. They're not the Jean we loved. They're someone we didn't know." He took a step into the middle of the room. He tipped back his head. "But do you smell that?"

Mary Ellen sniffed the air. "Sir?"

"Lilac."

It was there, just the slightest trace from Jean's perfume.

"That's our Jean," Mr. De Belle said.

Then he left. Mary Ellen watched him go down the stairs and out onto her porch. He left the front door open behind him. By the time she reached it, he was in the Chrysler. Mrs. De Belle turned toward the house, taking a last look as the car pulled away from the curb. She was still looking back when the Chrysler turned onto Tenth Street and disappeared.

Mary Ellen understood. She hadn't been able to see Mrs. De Belle's face behind the netting of her hat, but had she been able to, she knew she would have seen the look of a mother who had lost her little girl, a mother who was grieving now, and would be for some time.

She couldn't let that happen to her. No matter how sad she was over Jean's death, she couldn't let Robbie slip away from her.

❧

Robbie had just turned off her record player when her mother came into her room. Didn't even knock, no matter that Robbie had told her time and time again, for the love of Moses, to respect her privacy. Well, that was her mother. Since when had she ever cared a snap about someone else? Robbie supposed at some point her mother had loved her father, and surely there was even a time when she and Robbie were close, but now that was all just smog in the noggin. Just a wisp of a memory, here and gone.

"Oh, Robbie," her mother said. "It was the saddest thing just now."

She sat down next to Robbie on her bed, and Robbie felt the surrender in the way the weight of her body dropped. For an instant, she almost laid her hand on her mother's, because she knew that feeling of wanting to give herself over to someone, to have them rock her in their arms and tell her everything would be all right. She hadn't said a word to anyone about Tom, and, really, after the shock of Miss De Belle's death and the danger Tom had found himself in with Charlie Camplain, Robbie had found it easy to deflect her friends' questions with a sad shake of her head.

She was lost without Tom—and Miss De Belle? Robbie was ashamed of the way she'd treated her during the short time she'd lived in their house. Not only that, she felt guilty because she was the one who had let Charlie Camplain know that morning where Miss De Belle was. Sometimes Robbie thought she heard someone moving about in her room—just a few minutes before her mother came in, she'd thought she heard footsteps in there—and she feared she'd be forever haunted by the thought that if she hadn't opened the door to the auditorium that morning, hadn't pointed out Miss De Belle, then maybe she'd still be alive, and Robbie wouldn't feel guilty, and she could more easily play the role of the girl who got thrown over for someone else. A good girl, not someone fast and easy like this Millie Haines.

Robbie wanted to tell her mother all of this, but she'd spent so long closing off her heart, she didn't know how to open it again.

So she said, "You didn't knock. Mother, we've talked about this. You've no right to come in here without my permission."

Her mother's eyes filled with anger. She started to say something, but then she bit down hard on her bottom lip. She got up and went to Robbie's window—the window where Robbie had stood so many nights, waiting for the first glimpse of Tom's Fleetwood as he came to pick her up for a date.

"Jean's parents were just here. Her father wanted to come up and see her room." So Robbie had indeed heard footsteps coming from next door. "Her mother couldn't even get out of the car. That's how grief-stricken she is. But, Robbie, you should have seen the way she turned to look at our house when Mr. De Belle drove away. She looked until she couldn't see it anymore. That poor woman. I can't imagine." She turned from the window, then, and said to Robbie in a voice that was firm but not angry, "I have every right. I'm your mother."

Robbie had never heard what she heard in her mother's voice. She didn't even know how to describe it. A measure of control. A note of certainty. An undertone of caring and warmth. It was the voice Robbie had been needing to hear ever since that horrible morning. It was the voice of the woman her mother had once been, the teacher she'd once been, and suddenly Robbie wanted to tell her everything. But she couldn't bring herself to say the words.

Instead of doing what she wanted to do—to go to her mother and throw her arms around her—Robbie said, "What's there to see in that old room anyway?"

Much to her surprise, her mother didn't snap at her, or shake her head in disapproval, or click her tongue. She merely crooked her finger. She even grinned. She said, "Let's go find out."

Robbie dawdled. She watched her mother leave her bedroom, heard her footsteps in the room next door, but still she lingered, not wanting to admit that she was curious.

"Oh, my," she heard her mother say, her voice filled with wonder and just a hint of sadness. "Oh, my, my, my."

That was when Robbie's curiosity became too much for her, and she got up from her bed and went next door to see what her mother had found.

"Have you ever seen something so beautiful?" Her mother was standing in front of the closet, a dress held in front of her. An aquamarine chiffon party dress with a cinched waist and a flared skirt.

Mary Ellen smoothed the skirt across her own legs. "Oh, Robbie, I wonder if she ever had a chance to wear this. What a shame if she didn't. The thought just makes me sadder than sad."

"Don't think about that dress, Mother. Don't think about Miss De Belle."

"I can't help myself."

"Think about what's coming up."

"Homecoming," Mary Ellen said. "I bet Tom would love you in this dress."

"I told you, Mother. Tom and I are through."

"Oh, you've probably just had a spat. Nothing more than a lovers' quarrel. Things will get back to normal soon."

"I doubt that. I'm not going to the dance."

"Nonsense." Her mother brought the dress to her and held it across her front. "At least look in the mirror. I just know that Tom would love it."

Her mother let the dress go, and Robbie had to grab onto it to keep it from sliding to the floor. The chiffon felt so silky. She'd always wanted a dress like this, and, yes, Tom would love it, if they were still together, but they weren't, and the thought that they never would be again overwhelmed Robbie, and suddenly she was in her mother's arms, the dress crumpling between them, and Robbie was trying so hard not to cry.

Then she told her. She told her everything about Tom and that Millie.

"My poor girl." Her mother rocked her in her arms. "My poor baby girl."

"I wish Charlie Camplain had shot him," Robbie said.

Her mother said, "No, you don't wish that."

Her voice quavered, but her tone was resolute, and Robbie sensed she was speaking as one who knew. Had there actually been a moment when she had wished something similar on Robbie's father? Robbie didn't want to know the answer to that question. It was enough for her to know, in a way she never had, that there were people, and her mother was one of them, who knew more about loss and hurt than she did.

"Trust me," her mother said. "You don't wish that."

15

THE NEXT MORNING, A SATURDAY, Mary Ellen went to speak to Mrs. Heath. Mary Ellen had always thought her snooty, and in particular she harbored a grudge against her for something she'd said at Edward's visitation. She hadn't known that Mary Ellen had heard her, but she had. *Robbie told Tom things hadn't been happy between Mary Ellen and Ed for quite some time. It just goes to show you never know what's going on in some houses these days.* Still, Mary Ellen had come to let her know how bad she felt about what was now happening inside her own home.

"I'm sorry for dropping by without telephoning first." Mary Ellen could see that she'd caught Mrs. Heath unprepared for callers; she was wearing a pair of dungarees with the pant legs rolled to her knees, a kerchief tied over her head, and a man's shirt—maybe Tom's, maybe Mr. Heath's—with the tails hanging over her hips and the sleeves rolled to her elbows. She held a feather duster in her hand. "I've caught you cleaning house," Mary Ellen said. "My apologies."

Mrs. Heath was holding the storm door open with the toe of her canvas tennis shoe. "It's Saturday," she said, as if Mary Ellen didn't know that. "Saturday is the day I redd up the house."

"I beg your pardon?"

"It's an old Scottish saying." Mrs. Heath gave her feather duster a shake. "It means to make things tidy. On Saturdays, I redd up the house. When do you do yours?"

"I see." And indeed Mary Ellen understood that what Mrs. Heath was really saying was that she had everything in order while Mary Ellen was all at loose ends, running around town on a Saturday morning instead of seeing to her own housecleaning. "Later," Mary Ellen said. "Robbie and I will see to it later."

Mrs. Heath had a broad, flat face with a splotch of freckles across her nose and cheeks. A lock of auburn hair had escaped her kerchief to fall across her forehead, and she blew at it to keep it out of her eye. That puff of air sounded like a reprimand to Mary Ellen, as if Mrs. Heath were telling her to get to the point, for Pete's sake, so she could get back to her cleaning.

"It's about Tom," Mary Ellen said.

"Tom? What about Tom?"

"Well, really it's about Robbie and Tom. My Robbie. She's heartbroken by what's happened."

Mrs. Heath drew back her shoulders. She pressed her lips together in a tight line. Finally, she said, "And what is it that's happened?"

It was a cool, damp day. A misty rain had put a veil over everything: the cedar trees on the Heaths' long front lawn, the lighted red cross on the hospital's emergency entrance, the clock tower atop the courthouse downtown. Mary Ellen could hear the tires of cars hissing on the wet pavement as they drove past. Closer still, she could hear rain dripping from the eaves of the Heaths' front porch. The air smelled of wet cedar and the crushed rock from the circle driveway and the scents of ammonia and bleach that Mrs. Heath carried with her. A wind came up just then, and Mary Ellen felt a chill across her back.

"It's just that Robbie told me about Tom." Mary Ellen let her voice fall to a whisper. "Tom and that girl."

Mrs. Heath didn't say a word. She only glared at Mary Ellen, who went on to say, "It's so hard these days with teenagers. I want you to know that I understand. If there's anything I can do…well, I just want you to know that you have my sympathy."

"Your sympathy?" Mrs. Heath gave Mary Ellen a puzzled look. "I'm afraid I don't have any idea what you're referring to."

"Tom," Mary Ellen said. "My Robbie is heartbroken."

"Who's to say why young ones come apart. They fall in and out of love like changing shoes."

"That girl." Mary Ellen was suddenly quite aware of the real reason she'd come. Beneath her intention of offering condolence was the desire to make Mrs. Heath admit it all—to let her know that she knew the secret, that money or position or influence couldn't change facts. To let her know that her daughter's heart was breaking and it was her son's fault, and more than that, to let her know that she hadn't forgotten the pain she'd suffered at Ed's funeral. It gave Mary Ellen satisfaction to say now, "Millie. That girl from Vincennes. The one Tom…" How should she say it? "The one Tom stepped out with. The one he left with child. I imagine you've got quite the problem figuring out what to do about that."

Mrs. Heath narrowed her eyes. She studied Mary Ellen a good long while. Then she said, "I've heard that you and that teacher, Miss De Belle, were something more than friends." She gave Mary Ellen a smirk. "I've heard that you were lovers. You have my sympathies."

Mary Ellen felt the heat come into her cheeks. "Who told you that?" she said, but already Mrs. Heath had closed the door, and no matter how many times Mary Ellen rang the bell or knocked, she didn't return to answer the question.

All Mary Ellen could do was pound on the door, calling out again and again, "I know the truth, Mrs. Heath. Remember that. I know the truth."

∽✍↷

Day by day, autumn settled in. The Fall Festival took place in Lawrenceville on a glorious Indian summer weekend. A small carnival set up on the streets around the courthouse square—a carousel, a Tilt-a-Whirl, a small Ferris wheel—and food stands sold cotton candy, pronto pups, salt water taffy, lemon shakeups, snow cones. Politicians worked the crowds, handing out free yardsticks, free emery boards, free hand fans. The business club from the high school had an old

Ford with the windows broken out, and people were buying chances to take whacks at it with a sledge hammer. The Literary Society—Mary Ellen was the advisor—sold baked goods. The stores stayed open late and hosted sidewalk sales. Robbie and some of her girlfriends strolled around the square looking bored—looking, Mary Ellen thought, as if they'd seen it all and were so weary of this town. Tom Heath was there, taking photographs for the *Toma Talk*.

When his path intersected with Robbie's in front of George's Ice Cream, he said, "Hello there, Robbie."

Robbie and her friends just walked on by. Mary Ellen saw it all from the Literary Society's booth. Robbie gave no sign at all that she knew Tom Heath was alive.

∽◉∼

Oh, Robbie saw Tom Heath. Sure she did. Saw him there on the courthouse square, looking all down in the mouth when she walked by. He had his camera hanging around his neck. His hair was wet with Brylcreem, and she could see the tracks the teeth of his comb had left when he'd slicked it back from his forehead. The tips of his ears and his cheekbones were red from scrubbing. He had on a tweed sport coat with a plaid pattern of greens and browns. The polish on his wingtip shoes shined in the neon light from George's Ice Cream. His white dress shirt was buttoned to the throat. She imagined he was trying to look grown up, responsible. The sad look on his face told her he was sorry. In an instant, she took all of this in and kept walking with her girlfriends, leaving Tom on the sidewalk with his hand half raised in greeting.

"I wouldn't give him the time of day," she said to her friends after they were past, and she'd glanced back once to see Tom looking after her, the lights from the neon sign reflecting off the lenses of his glasses. Just a quick glance, which she disguised with a flip of her hair meant to indicate that she was poised and confident and a little bit haughty. "Who does he think he is, anyway?"

One of her friends was Lola Malone, a girl with thick legs and broad hips and a cute round face. She wore black-rimmed cat-eye glasses, and she was always freshening her lipstick. Her lips, she said, were her best feature, and she carried a tube of Max Factor Cheery Cherry with her, the lipstick that her favorite actress, Piper Laurie, used.

"I feel sorry for Tom," Lola said. "My father said he could have died." Lola was the sheriff's daughter. "He said Charlie Camplain could just as easily shot him dead."

"Oh, pooh," said Robbie's other friend, Dixie Dale. "That's just melodrama. Why would Charlie Camplain have done that? He'd already killed who he came to kill."

Dixie's father was the art teacher at the high school; she favored berets and Du Maurier cigarettes that she somehow got from Canada. How, she'd never say. "If I told you, I'd have to kill you." The Du Mauriers came in a flat red box, which Dixie would open rather dramatically before lighting up. She was smoking one now, unconcerned with who might see her because she was Dixie Dale and she fancied herself a rebel.

Lola lowered her voice to a whisper. "My father said he wet himself."

"Who?" said Dixie. "Charlie Camplain?"

"No. Tom. That's how scared he was."

Robbie let that sink in. She imagined what it must have felt like for Tom to have Charlie Camplain's gun stuck into his back. She wondered if he was scared now about that girl Millie and the baby. She wondered if he was scared about the rest of his life. She hoped he was. She hoped he was scared to death. But she also felt a pang of sympathy for him. He'd had everything mapped out, and now who knew what might happen? It was his own fault. Robbie was still angry about that, but still...

"I don't care about any of that," she said. "I'm not giving him the time of day."

"He doesn't deserve you," said Dixie.

Robbie hadn't been able to bring herself to tell her friends the truth, that Tom had made a baby with another girl. She'd only told them that he'd thrown her over for someone else, a Vincennes girl, someone he'd met in Westport.

"I thought he looked sorry." Robbie saw Lola turn her head to see if he was still watching them. "He looked really, really sorry, Robbie," she said. "Didn't you think?"

"I don't think about him anymore," Robbie said. "C'mon, let's ride the Ferris wheel."

She wouldn't admit this, but she hoped that when she was at the top of the wheel, she'd be able to look down on the crowd and pick out Tom. Maybe he'd be looking up at her. Maybe she'd wave and maybe he'd wave back.

But when she was on the Ferris wheel, and the car she was riding in with Lola stopped at the very top and swayed back and forth, she couldn't see him anywhere. She just saw the colors of people's coats and the neon lights.

"I would have been scared, too," she said to Lola. "If I'd been Tom, I'd have been scared to death."

Lola took her hand. "Me, too," she said.

From the car behind them, Robbie heard Dixie's complaint about being stopped so long. "Oh, for cripes' sake," she said. "Enough already. Move!"

"Hold on." Lola squeezed Robbie's hand. "Here we go."

The wheel began to turn again. They tumbled from the top, and the ground came rushing up to meet them, and then they were rising again and all the people below were shrinking. Robbie closed her eyes and hoped Lola wouldn't notice that she was crying.

❧

Millie Haines was scared. She kept going to her classes at St. Rose Academy for Girls, where she was a day student. She was one of the needy girls, at St. Rose by the good graces of the Sisters of Providence, who had determined that she was worthy of financial support. So early each morning, she put on her white blouse and her navy blue jumper and her bobby sox and saddle oxfords, and made the walk down second street to College to St. Rose, where she had a job in the cafeteria serving breakfast to the girls who lived in the dormitory on the grounds, and who all came from families with more money than hers. She hated the way they looked at her when she dished up bowls of oatmeal, or worse, the way they *didn't* look at her, the way they didn't notice her at all. She'd always felt she wasn't pretty enough, wasn't rich enough, didn't read the right books, didn't know the right people. Her father drove a cab, for Pete's sake. Her father had no teeth. Her father was too old to be a father.

And now she was pregnant, and her father was considering arranging for her to have an abortion. She knew this because one night, when they thought she was asleep, she heard her parents arguing.

"You can't possibly," her mother said. Her sweet mother who rarely raised her voice over anything. "Bert Haines, you know it's a mortal sin."

Her father said, "What will we do with the baby?"

"We'll raise it."

"We're old, Peg. We're too old."

"Then we'll put it up for adoption."

Her father was quiet for a good while, and as Millie waited to see what he'd say, she wondered what it was that she wanted. She rested her hand on her stomach. This was her baby, and it saddened her to admit to herself that she didn't really know what she wanted outside of turning back the hands of the clock and never drinking so much beer that night at the Showboat and never getting into the backseat of Tom Heath's flashy gold Chevy.

"Everyone will know." Her father's voice was fainter now, and she had to strain to hear it. She heard the fear in what he said, and she was overwhelmed with a feeling of guilt. "Peg, can you imagine the shame?"

Millie felt an ache in her throat, the feeling she always had when she was close to tears. Her father was a good man, a good Catholic. He'd never been anything but kind to her. *Millie-Dillie*, he called her. *Oh, my silly Millie-Dillie.* He'd come to be a father late in his life, but Millie knew how much it all delighted him, and now, *now* she'd done this horrible thing and left him in this crisis between his love for her and his love for his faith.

Her mother was crying. Her father was, too.

From her bed, Millie could look out the window and see the lights along the bridge over the river, and on the other side the lights at the Showboat, and she said a little prayer, which she knew she should have been doing all along.

"Ask God to help you," her father had always told her, "and He will."

She wondered where Tom Heath was now and what he was doing. He'd been such a nice boy. He'd been nervous and shy.

"I've never done this before," she told him.

"Me either," he said.

Then, in an instant, it was done. She could barely remember it now—just a brief moment—but she knew that soon she'd start to show, and she knew her parents were in anguish, and she knew it was her fault, and, the worst thing of all, she didn't know what to do.

16

MARY ELLEN AGREED TO CHAPERONE the homecoming dance. She found it to be a welcome distraction because by this time, early October, the gossip had spread. She'd started to notice a few lifted eyebrows and heard some whispered words when she walked into the shops downtown. Just that week—Homecoming Week—she'd taken Robbie into Delzell's for a corselette and a strapless brassier to wear beneath her dress, and Mary Ellen noticed two women at the hosiery counter. The older one she recognized as Mrs. Taylor, the dentist's wife. The younger was her daughter, Ramona Esther, who'd been one of Mary Ellen's pupils, a dour girl who'd always thought better of herself than she had any right to. Mary Ellen saw her lift her hand to her mouth and lean in to whisper something to her mother. Mrs. Taylor raised her head and caught Mary Ellen's eye, and then quickly looked away, pretending to be extremely interested in the stockings they'd been examining.

"We just got those in," the clerk, Midge, said to Mrs. Taylor and Ramona Esther. "The shade is called Crown Jewel. They're made by Roman Stripe."

Mary Ellen didn't let on to Robbie that the two women had been talking about her—gossiping, she felt sure, about the awful lie that she and Jean had been lovers. Mary Ellen was determined to not let that dampen her spirits, because she was thrilled Robbie had finally decided to go to the dance. Really she'd had no choice, not once she was chosen to be a queen candidate. Which then presented the problem of a suitable escort, a problem that Mary Ellen solved by "suggesting" to Clifford Gifford that he ask Robbie to be his date.

"Clifford Gifford?" Robbie had said. "Not in a million years."

Clifford was a chubby boy. "Not really chubby," Mary Ellen had pointed out to Robbie. "Stocky is more like it. Solid. Strong." And he was on the football team.

"Fourth string," Robbie said. "He never plays. He's only on the team because he's…so…stocky."

Oh, but he was a jolly sort. He was always laughing at something, always cracking a joke. Who wouldn't be able to have fun with a boy like him?

Finally, Robbie relented. She even agreed to wear the chiffon dress left hanging in Jean's closet, and that was what had necessitated this trip. Mary Ellen was carrying the dress in the Delzell's box that she'd found under Jean's bed.

"I'll be right with you." Midge waved a hand at Robbie and Mary Ellen. "You girls have a return?"

Mary Ellen laid the box on the counter right over the display of stockings that Mrs. Taylor and Ramona Esther were pretending to admire.

"Robbie would like to try on some things with her homecoming dress." Mary Ellen took the lid off the box and let Midge see the aquamarine chiffon. Of course, Mrs. Taylor and Ramona Esther saw it too.

"What a pretty dress," Ramona Esther said.

Midge put her hand to her mouth. She ran her hand over the silky chiffon. "I remember this dress," she said. "I sold it to…" For a moment, she couldn't go on. She bit her lip and shook her head. "To that new teacher, the one that man killed."

"You mean?" Mrs. Taylor was looking at Mary Ellen over the tops of her eyeglasses. "Surely, you're not letting Robbie wear that dead woman's dress."

"Jean," Mary Ellen said. "Her name was Jean, and yes, Robbie is going to look stunning."

"That would be highly inappropriate. Let that woman—whoever she was to you—rest in peace."

"I believe Jean would feel honored to know Robbie was wearing her dress. We were quite fond of Jean, and I happen to know that she felt the same way about us."

"Oh, I'm sure she did." Ramon Elizabeth glanced at her mother. "I'm sure you were *quite* fond of each other."

Robbie lifted the dress from its box and pressed the folds of the chiffon to her cheek. "It's so soft," she said, her voice the voice of a little girl full of love and awe. "Such a beautiful, beautiful dress."

Mary Ellen could see Mrs. Taylor and Ramona Esther were taken aback by the sight of Robbie fondling that dress. She knew it would be a story they would tell, but for the time, she didn't care. She could look at Robbie and feel how desperately she wanted to be loved. Jean had wanted that too, Mary Ellen felt sure, and she herself had wanted it for years and years. She could remember what it had been like when she and Edward first fell head over heels. She didn't know how it all changed. The years just went on, and there they were.

"It is," said Midge. "Just lovely."

Even Mrs. Taylor and Ramona Elizabeth had to admit it.

"Such an exquisite shade," Mrs. Taylor said.

Said Ramona Elizabeth, "It'll bring out the flecks of green in your eyes, sweetie."

And Mary Ellen, though she was seething over the two of them and their juvenile behavior, let it all wash away from her, not wanting to disturb this moment in which they all watched Robbie, and, perhaps, one by one—Mary Ellen decided it must be so—remembered what it was to be young, with all their lives ahead of them. Hushed, reverent, the women stood in the shop and looked at that beautiful dress.

Robbie waited until she and her mother were outside Delzell's. Then she said, "What was that all about? Those women."

It was late in the afternoon on a Wednesday, and they were alone on the sidewalk except for a few high school girls—Lola Malone was one of them—who'd just come out of George's Ice Cream. Lola waved at Robbie, and Robbie waved back. The stores around the square all had homecoming decorations in their windows: red and white crepe paper, plastic tomahawks, final score predictions (Lawrenceville 98, Bridgeport 0), an Indian brave with a bulldog, the Bridgeport mascot, on a leash, subdued. The sun was going down behind the courthouse clock tower. It was nearly five, and in the shade in front of Delzell's, it was just cool enough for Robbie to slip her arms into the cardigan sweater she'd draped over her shoulders.

"Oh, you know Mrs. Taylor and her daughter." Mary Ellen was holding the bag from Delzell's to her chest. Inside were the underthings—the foundation garments, Midge had called them—that they'd bought for Robbie. With her free arm, Mary Ellen gave a backhanded wave in front of her face as if she were fanning away a disagreeable odor. "They always need to look down on someone."

"What was that about you and Miss De Belle?"

"It was nothing."

"Mother?"

Robbie could always tell when her mother wasn't telling the whole truth. Mary Ellen twisted her hands together, and her eyes moved back and forth, looking for anything that would provide a distraction. She was doing both of these things now.

"Oh, look," she said. "Isn't that Lola with that group of girls?"

"Mother, is there something you're not telling me?"

Mary Ellen said, "You haven't heard anything, have you?"

"Anything about what? You and Miss De Belle?"

"It's all nonsense, of course." Mary Ellen handed the Delzell's bag to Robbie and took a handkerchief from her pocketbook. She dabbed at her eyes. "Rumors, just rumors. Sometimes people can be so cruel. You can't believe half of what you hear, Robbie."

"Are they saying that you and Miss De Belle were in love?" Robbie lowered her voice. "Is that what they meant?"

"So you *have* heard the gossip."

Robbie nodded. "I've heard a few things."

"Well, we don't need to talk anymore about the ugly business. What say we slip into the Candle Lite for supper?" Mary Ellen dropped the handkerchief back into her pocketbook and closed it with a snap. She smiled, but it was a shaky smile that wouldn't hold, and Robbie could tell she was doing her best to put on a brave face. "Their special is veal parmigiana tonight. You've always loved that."

"Isn't it a little early for supper?"

"Oh, come on, Robbie. I don't feel like cooking."

Robbie could see how much it mattered to her mother that they go to the Candle Lite, that they act like nothing was out of the ordinary even though so much had happened to put them in the public eye. Miss De Belle's murder, Tom's little secret (though Robbie hadn't yet heard word of that swirling around), and now this gossip about her mother.

"Please, Robbie?" Mary Ellen said. "Let's walk in there as big as day."

So they did. They walked into the Candle Lite, and they took a table by the window where anyone strolling by would be able to see them. Mary Ellen even ordered a glass of wine.

"Teachers should be permitted," she said. "All within moderation, of course."

Dusk came on, and the waiter lit the candle on their table. The cloth was red and white checked; the napkins were linen. Robbie spread hers on her lap and felt that this was all very nice, just the two of them, she and her mother having an early supper just because they could. It had been a long time since Robbie had felt this close to her. It was good to pretend, for at least a while, that everything was as it should be.

Then the door to the restaurant opened, and Mr. and Mrs. Heath stepped inside. He had on a jacket and tie, but he carried with him the distinct odor of turpentine. She had a fox stole around her shoulders and white gloves on her hands. They paused a moment, seemingly surprised to have found Mary Ellen and Robbie there, and something about the way Mrs. Heath looked at them—with scorn—told Robbie that whatever gossip was going around about Miss De Belle and her mother had started with her.

Much to her surprise, her mother stood up and went to the Heaths just as they were about to turn around and leave the restaurant. She grabbed Mrs. Heath by her arm and spun her back. Her fox stole slid off onto the floor.

"Just you remember." Her mother was whispering, but Robbie could hear every word. "I don't just think I know something. I *know* something, and if I start talking, it won't be gossip. It'll be the truth."

Then she did something Robbie would never forget. She stooped and picked up the fox stole and put it around Mrs. Heath's shoulders. She smoothed her hand over the fur. She looked her straight in the eye.

"Glass houses, Mrs. Heath," she said in her teacher's voice, the one Robbie had heard her use when she wanted to strike fear in a student's heart. "Glass houses."

On the Friday night of the homecoming football game, Mary Ellen sat in the bleachers and watched Clifford Gifford escort Robbie to the fifty-yard line at halftime. There, they joined the other four girls and their escorts, all of whom were football players. The white pants of their uniforms were grass-stained; their red jerseys were dark with sweat and the white numbers had flecks of blood on them. It had been a hard-fought first half, and the score was 0-0. Only Clifford's uniform was clean, because he hadn't played, and Mary Ellen knew that would embarrass Robbie.

Still she was trying to put her best foot forward. She was smiling and waving at the crowd. Clifford looked deliriously happy. He was beaming as he stood beside Robbie, her hand nestled in the crook of his elbow. His black hair was freshly cut and neatly combed. He was wearing his horn-rimmed eyeglasses, and the lights sparkled in the lenses. Mary Ellen could see he was having the time of his life.

Tom Heath, on the other hand, looked miserable, and Mary Ellen was ashamed to admit that she was glad. He stood at the edge of the field, about to take a microphone and, as president of the senior class, announce the name of this year's homecoming queen, a job he'd probably planned on handing off to the vice president when he thought maybe he'd be on the field with Robbie. But he wasn't. He was hunched in a dark suit, looking for all the world like an undertaker.

Mary Ellen sat next to Mr. Pomeroy and his wife, Betty. She was a trim woman with silver hair and excellent posture who taught Home Economics. She had a red and white pompom that she'd been shaking throughout the first half. Now it lay in her lap, the streamers trailing across the gray tweed of her skirt.

"Tom Heath looks about as low as low can be," she said. "Without Robbie, he's a sad sack."

Mr. Pomeroy wasn't concerned with the gossip of high school romance. His mind, Mary Ellen could tell, was working on something else.

"Mary Ellen," he said, "could you please stop by my office first thing Monday morning? There's something I'd like to discuss with you."

"Oh, Hugh." Betty picked up her pompom and shook it at him. It was strange for Mary Ellen to hear him called by his first name. "Can't you leave business alone? They're about to crown the queen."

Tom Heath was speaking into the microphone now, but his voice had no pep. He was trying, Mary Ellen could tell, but he wasn't having much luck.

"And the 1952 homecoming queen is," he said, and then paused.

All the girls except Robbie glanced at one another and giggled. They were so excited, they could hardly stand it. Robbie still had a smile on her face, but it hadn't changed a bit from when she'd first walked onto the field. She was staring straight ahead as if she were a mannequin on display in Delzell's window.

Then Tom Heath said her name. He said, "Robbie McVeigh," and his shoulders slumped, and Mary Ellen could see all the air go out of him.

That should have been enough to stop her. His misery should have been enough to keep her from saying what she was about to say. That, and the fact that her daughter had just been named homecoming queen. That should have been enough.

But it wasn't, because Mary Ellen was convinced that what Mr. Pomeroy meant to talk about with her come Monday was the rumor that she had engaged in an improper relationship with Jean De Belle.

Robbie was wearing a tiara now and cradling red roses in her arms. Clifford had his arms raised above his head, his hands clasped, shaking them in triumph. A picture every mother would want for her daughter, but for Mary Ellen, it barely registered. She was so afraid.

She said to Mr. Pomeroy, "I can tell you exactly what came between Robbie and Tom."

❧

The next evening—the night of the homecoming dance—Clifford arrived promptly at 5:45 so there would be plenty of time for Mary Ellen to take pictures. He was wearing a white dinner jacket with a black bowtie; she'd picked out a white carnation with tinges of green at the edges of its petals for Robbie to pin to his lapel. He had a gardenia wrist corsage for Robbie. When he took it from its box, the air was suddenly full of a sweetness that reminded Mary Ellen of humid summer nights and the taste of honey and heavy cream.

"Isn't that delightful," she said. "Robbie, doesn't that smell divine?"

"I guess," Robbie said. She'd pushed down the top of one white glove and was scratching her wrist.

"Robbie." Mary Ellen scolded her. "Clifford picked this out especially for you."

"The woman at the flower shop said it would be just the thing," Clifford said. "I hope you like it, Robbie."

"I do," Robbie said, remembering her manners. She slipped the corsage onto her wrist and raised it to her nose to take an appreciative sniff. "It's very sweet."

She didn't know that Mary Ellen had told the Pomeroys the story of Tom Heath and that girl from Vincennes. As soon as she'd revealed Tom's indiscretion, she wished she hadn't. Betty Pomeroy looked down at the pompom in her lap and smoothed its streamers with her hand.

Mr. Pomeroy gave her a stern look over the tops of his eyeglasses. "Be that as it may," he said, and Mary Ellen knew she'd done nothing to help her reputation. She'd revealed herself to be a gossip. "First thing Monday morning," Mr. Pomeroy said. "Don't forget."

Now she was ashamed and didn't want Robbie to know how low she'd stooped. Especially on this night when she was homecoming queen, even if it was an honor she didn't want. "It's embarrassing," she'd told her while waiting for Clifford to arrive. "It just proves to everyone that Tom and I are through, and I'm a loser who has to have Clifford Gifford as an escort."

"It's a night of your life," Mary Ellen told her. "A night you won't ever have again. Time never comes back."

Standing now in her entryway, Mary Ellen thought of Jean and how excited she'd been about this part of her life, how nervous she'd been on the stage of the auditorium when she stepped to the microphone, not knowing that time was about to run out for her. All that autumn, she should have been there. Mary Ellen should have heard faint music coming from her radio, should have shared so many meals, so many rides to school. Together, they would have gone to the fall festival, picked apples at the orchard, mulled cider on the stove, spent so many days and nights as friends, maybe even have chaperoned the dance together. She should be there now to see Robbie and Clifford off. Maybe she would have done better with Robbie than Mary Ellen had. Maybe eventually Robbie would have accepted her, grown close to her. Mary Ellen liked to think that Jean would have become the big sister Robbie had never had. She liked to think that in time they would have become a family.

But now it was just the two of them, just Mary Ellen and Robbie muddling through the best they could, trying to find their way back to each other.

"Say cheese." Mary Ellen was using the Argus camera that had been Ed's. "We want some good shots of you two on this big night."

She posed them at the foot of the staircase, on the loveseat in the living room, in front of the fireplace. Ed had always been the picture-taker, and it was the first time she'd ever used the Argus.

"Oh, these will be lovely," she said. "Now go on, go on. Shoo! I'll see you at the dance."

❧

It was Mary Ellen's job, of course, to make sure there was no untoward behavior. The boys sometimes liked to sneak in a pint of whisky; some of the fast girls liked to retreat to the dark heights of the bleachers with their dates and neck.

"Robbie makes a lovely queen." Mr. Pomeroy's secretary, Lily Wagner, pinned a corsage to Mary Ellen's dress. "You must be so proud."

Without warning, tears came to Mary Ellen's eyes, not because she was proud of Robbie—though of course she was—but because she didn't feel she had a right to this night. She'd let the scandal of Tom Heath make her smug, as if no sadness could ever touch her again. She knew now it was a foolish thing to believe. She knew they were all imperfect people and sad days waited for them all. Only Jean De Belle would stay pure, the young librarian with the cheerful smile and all her life ahead of her. They even had an enlarged "In Memoriam" photograph of her on an easel near the entry, a photograph Tom Heath had taken for the *Toma Talk* one day before the school year began. Jean stood in the library with a large book open and resting in her right palm. She was smiling at the camera. It broke Mary Ellen's heart to see that picture and to compare it with what she saw when she walked into that downstairs classroom and found Jean dead.

Lily was patting her arm. "Don't cry, Mary Ellen. Don't let those gossips ruin this night for you."

"Gossips." Mary Ellen drew back from Lily. "What have you heard?"

Lily hesitated. Then she said in a whisper, "I thought you knew."

"That's enough." Mary Ellen held up her hand, and it struck her with a swift sadness that this was what Jean had done when Charlie Camplain had first pointed his gun at her. "That's quite enough."

Lily's jaw went slack, and her mouth opened, and her chin began to wobble. Mary Ellen knew she should apologize, should make clear that it wasn't Lily who'd upset her but rather the ones spreading that wicked gossip, but just then she saw another set of chaperones walk in—Mr. and Mrs. Heath—and she forgot all about Lily. She left her in her misery and made a straight line toward the Heaths.

"Why do you want to cause trouble for me?" she said to Mrs. Heath. "Don't you have enough of your own?"

Mr. Heath was helping her off with her wrap—not the fox stole this time, but a white sateen cape.

"Why, Mrs. McVeigh," she said. "I've just now arrived. My word."

"Is there a problem?" Mr. Heath said, lifting the cape from his wife's bare shoulders.

"There most certainly is," said Mary Ellen. "Your wife is spreading an ugly rumor about me."

"I can assure you I wasn't the first one to sound that alarm," said Mrs. Heath.

Mary Ellen wouldn't let her pass. "Lies don't become you," she said.

"I assure you this is no lie. Talk to your daughter, Mrs. McVeigh. Ask her what she told me about you and Miss De Belle."

With that, Mrs. Heath brushed by Mary Ellen, and her husband followed, hurrying to catch up with his wife.

Mary Ellen stood there, stunned. Could it be that Robbie herself had cast suspicion on her? Surely Robbie wouldn't have. And how would Mary Ellen ever ask her? She certainly couldn't tonight. There she was, her daughter, dancing with Clifford Gifford. She'd allowed herself to lay her head on his chest. Her eyes were closed, and what she was dreaming Mary Ellen didn't know. She only knew she wasn't the only one watching. Across the gymnasium, Tom Heath stood with his camera. He had on a dark suit, the jacket buttoned, a red bowtie, but no flower pinned to his lapel. He'd come to the dance alone, and Mary Ellen knew she should feel sorry for him, but she couldn't manage it. He'd made his bed, now let him lie in it.

Just then, she felt someone take her hand. She turned with alarm and saw a girl in a dress that was obviously home-sewn, a girl with a blond bob done in pin curls, a girl with rimless eyeglasses that had slipped down her nose. Mary Ellen recognized her as the girl who'd been sobbing outside Mr. Pomeroy's office the morning of the murder.

"I'm Etta," the girl said. "Etta Lawless. I live out in the country, up near Pinkstaff. I don't have a boyfriend, but my mother said I should come to the dance because she never got to go to anything when she was in school, and she wants me to have an interesting life. She made me this dress. You're Mrs. McVeigh, aren't you?"

"Yes, that's right."

"Miss De Belle lived with you."

Ordinarily, Mary Ellen would have taken exception to this, would have thought it a prelude to more of what she'd gotten from Lily Wagner, but something told her this girl wasn't interested in the gossip. She was smiling so sweetly. Mary Ellen could tell she was a shy girl and she'd had to work up her courage to say anything. It had mattered that much to her. She was trying to do what her mother wanted. She was trying to have a more interesting life.

"She rented a room in my house," Mary Ellen said.

"She was sweet, wasn't she?"

"Yes, she was very pleasant."

"I talked to her that day. I talked to her in the library. She said she thought she and I were going to be great friends."

"I thought the same," Mary Ellen said.

The girl squeezed her hand more tightly. "I miss her."

Mary Ellen let her other hand rest on Etta's shoulder. She was such a slight thing, not much more than skin and bone. "So do I, Etta."

They stood there like that a moment more. The orchestra was playing a dreamy love song, "You Belong to Me." The gym was decorated to represent a Southern plantation. Mary Ellen and Etta stood under white garden arches, and across the stage was the façade of a stately mansion with tall white pillars. There were picket fences and trellises laden with flowers. A crystal ball hung from the ceiling to give the illusion of twinkling stars.

"I just wanted to know you," Etta said, and then she let go of Mary Ellen's hand. "I wanted you to know I saw the two of you that morning in the library." Then the girl disappeared into the shadows.

What a strange girl, Mary Ellen thought. What an odd thing for her to say, and just when Mary Ellen had decided that she'd been a gift. A chill went up the back of her neck. It was as if the girl had carried Jean to her. Mary Ellen was overwhelmed with the sense of her presence. She would never tell anyone this, but she swore she heard her voice. She heard her say, *You belong to me, Mary Ellen. Do I belong to you?*

Mary Ellen remembered the bright sound of Jean's voice, the way they'd lain in the sun at the city pool, each with a hand dangling from her deck chair, their fingers so close to touching. She remembered the poem she'd given Jean that first day of the school year, along with a chaste kiss on the cheek for luck. Oh, how she missed her. How she would always miss her company. Her lovely Jean. Of course, she belonged to her. "Yes," Mary Ellen whispered. "Yes, you do. Always."

❧

A time came when Robbie found herself alone. Clifford Gifford had gone to get them some punch, and she'd stepped outside to visit the little girls' room and found herself face to face with Tom.

"Robbie," he said, "you look…" He took a step back and looked at her with admiration. "You look swell, Robbie. Really swell. Congratulations on being queen."

Other kids were passing by, giving them the once-over, and Robbie didn't want to cause a scene. She thanked Tom for the compliment and tried to walk away, but he grabbed her hand and spun her around to face him.

"I've been miserable without you, Robbie."

She wanted to say that she'd been miserable since that first morning of school when he told her about Millie Haines, but she wouldn't give him that satisfaction. She also wanted to tell him to let go of her hand, but, truth be told, she liked the feel of him. Her hand in his was something familiar, something from not so long ago. For an instant, she let herself imagine that they could pretend this business with Millie Haines had never happened. They could go back to where they'd been before he told her the news; they could step through a door, and find themselves in a wonderful life. The soft strains of "The Tennessee Waltz" came from the gymnasium. Robbie closed her eyes and listened to the band's girl singer. Listening to that song, she wanted to believe she could forgive Tom and everything could be just fine, but she knew that girl was still out there, and she was pregnant with his baby, and how in the world would that ever be fine.

Robbie snapped her eyes open and said, "I thought you'd have a date."

Tom shook his head. "No date."

"What about that girl? What are you going to do about her?"

"I guess that's up to my mom and dad."

"Have you seen her?"

"No."

"You should." Robbie could imagine what she must be going through. She didn't mean to, but she couldn't help but feel sorry for her. "You should see her. You should make things right."

"My folks."

Robbie pulled her hand away from his. "They want to hush this all up, don't they? Your mother is spreading rumors about my mother just to keep people from finding out about you and Millie Haines."

There, she'd said it—the thing she'd been thinking ever since she knew Mrs. Heath had been the one to start the gossip about her mother and Miss De Belle. It was all a smokescreen, a lie meant to protect their reputation. Get enough people talking about Mary Ellen McVeigh, and no one would have an itch to poke around in the Heaths' business. "How dare she use Miss De Belle's death like that?" Robbie said. "How dare she spread those ugly lies?"

"Are they lies, Robbie? Your mom and Miss De Belle, they were… well, they were everywhere together. You told my mom about them sitting on the porch swing in the evenings. I even saw them once, and they were holding hands."

"There's nothing odd about that."

"You said they were lovey-dovey. That's the word you used. You said it like you were disgusted."

It was true that Robbie had resented the way her mother had taken to Miss De Belle. They'd gone to movies at the Avalon, eaten suppers at the Candle Lite, gone for ice cream at George's. They'd listened to records together, and once Tom had brought Robbie home and she'd found them dancing together in the front room—dancing with their arms around each other, she'd pointed out when she told the story to Mrs. Heath. She'd never meant to suggest anything untoward. She'd only been hurt because she'd felt so left out of her mother's affections.

"I never said anything to make someone believe…"

Tom interrupted her. "Why did Miss De Belle break off her engagement?"

"People fall out of love every day."

"Still, when you look at all the facts, it makes you wonder."

"They aren't facts, not the way you want them to be."

"Facts are facts, Robbie. You can't change them."

"I guess you'd know about that."

"Ouch." He put his hand over his heart. "That hurt."

"Lies are lies, Tom Heath."

"And everything tells a story, Robbie McVeigh. And this is the story you told."

"I only meant my mother was treating her like a…"

Robbie ran up against the word and couldn't bring herself to say it.

"Like a what, Robbie? Like a lover?"

"No." She was angry now. "Like a daughter," she said. Then she burst into tears.

The gym doors opened behind her, and she heard the music swell, and her mother's voice. "Robbie, hurry. It's time for the queen's dance."

But she couldn't face her mother just then, and she couldn't face the ever-cheerful Clifford Gifford. All she could do was push her way past Tom and hide in the ladies' and have herself a good cry, no matter how humiliating it all was.

❦

"Robbie, dear, you missed your own queen's dance." By Monday morning, Mary Ellen still felt sad for her. "A queen's dance with no queen. Oh, Robbie. Clifford looked so forlorn that Lily Wagner danced with him."

They were driving to school, and Mary Ellen couldn't stop thinking about the way she'd had to fib and say that Robbie had suddenly taken ill, but word had spread quickly from those who'd stood witness outside the gymnasium that something had happened between Robbie and Tom. "Everyone knew I was lying." Mary Ellen stepped on the brakes too hard at State Street and snapped back her and Robbie's heads. "Everyone. Honestly, Robbie Sue."

She'd managed to leave the subject alone after the dance and all of Sunday, letting Robbie sulk, but now, after Robbie had dragged her feet and made them late leaving the house, and on *this* day—a dreary, rainy day at that, when Mary Ellen was supposed to talk to Mr. Pomeroy—she couldn't stop herself.

"You'd think we could be decent people," she said. "You'd think we could live decent lives."

Robbie had her face turned away, and she wasn't saying a word. Mary Ellen felt so sad for her. Suddenly she remembered how at the dance Mrs. Heath insinuated that it was Robbie herself who had started the talk about her and Jean. "Robbie, what did you tell Mrs. Heath about Miss De Belle and me?"

Her Ford shot across State Street. Robbie didn't answer, nor did she when Mary Ellen asked her question again. "Robbie," she said, "I won't be mad." By this time, she'd yanked the Ford into a parking space. She let the clutch out too fast, and the Ford bucked one time before stalling. "Robbie," she said again.

But Robbie was trying to get out of the car. Mary Ellen grabbed her arm, and briefly Robbie spun around to face her. Her mouth was open, and Mary Ellen thought she'd finally say something, but then she pulled her arm free. Without a word of goodbye, she got out of the car and ran across the lawn to the school, her books hugged to her chest.

Mary Ellen glanced at her wristwatch. She wished she could run after Robbie. She wished she had the magic words to make everything all right, but time was short. Robbie would have to wait. Mary Ellen had an appointment to talk to Mr. Pomeroy.

He was standing by the tall windows behind his desk, the ones that looked out over the front of the school, when Lily Wagner showed her in. She knew then that he'd seen that little exchange between her and Robbie—seen her herky-jerky arrival and the way she'd grabbed Robbie's arm, and that moment when Robbie pulled away from her and ran. It would have been apparent to anyone watching, even if they didn't know a thing about the two of them, that here were a mother and daughter in the midst of something more than the ordinary teenage drama.

Robbie's snit at the homecoming dance had been more than a broken heart over a boy. Mary Ellen knew that. It had everything to do with how safe she felt in the world. Here she was, about to move into her adult life, and Mary Ellen knew she hadn't done much to give Robbie reason to believe in love's magic. Mary Ellen had lost touch with Ed long before he died, and after he was gone, she'd closed herself off from Robbie. Then Jean arrived, and it was like a gift had come to her, a reminder of what it was to love the world, to love her life. Then she was gone—murdered on that lovely autumn day that still had the feel of summer, killed in a place where the town's children were supposed to feel safe. Children like Robbie and Tom and even that odd girl, Etta Lawless. Now look at the ugliness that had come.

All the while, Charlie Camplain sat in prison and spouted off that the shooting had been all about love. Mary Ellen had read the newspaper articles and cringed every time. She'd tried to keep them from Robbie, but one night she found her with the *Daily Record* in her lap and tears streaming down her cheeks. "He says he loved her," Robbie said. The news article reported that at the time of his arrest, officers found a slip of paper in his billfold upon which he'd written a quotation from Oscar Wilde. Robbie read it out loud: "Each man kills the thing he loves. Do you think that's true, Mother?"

Mary Ellen snatched the newspaper away. "I most certainly do not."

Robbie sat there a good while. Then she finally said, "I think maybe it is. Love just goes away. At least that's how it seems to me."

It broke Mary Ellen's heart to hear her say that, but maybe there was some truth in it. Maybe everyone found ways to kill what they most loved. Maybe it was human nature.

That's what Robbie's snit at the dance had been about. Mary Ellen was sure of it now. Robbie had come up against a moment like the one Charlie Camplain had experienced, a moment when she knew that the love she'd once held so dear could never be that for her again—not with Tom Heath, not after what he'd done.

"Sit down, Mary Ellen." Mr. Pomeroy nodded toward a chair in front of his desk. "I'll get right to the point. You and Miss De Belle."

"I told you who started those rumors, and I think you know why." She couldn't believe Mr. Pomeroy would give them credence. "I've taught here nearly twenty-five years. You hired me, for Heaven's sake. Have you ever had reason to regret that decision?" She noticed framed photographs of Mrs. Pomeroy and their son and daughter on a bookshelf behind his desk. The boy and girl were away at college now, but Mary Ellen could still recall when they'd been her students. "I taught your children," she said.

Mr. Pomeroy nodded. "You've always been a fine teacher."

The office was too stuffy. Mary Ellen realized she was still in her coat, the red swing coat she'd taken from Jean's closet. She unbuttoned it. The steam radiator was forcing hot air into the room, and Mary Ellen felt faint.

"I've never given anyone cause to doubt my character," she said.

"No one is questioning that." Mr. Pomeroy came around to the side of his desk. He tugged at the bottom of his vest. Then his hand went to the knot of his bowtie. He cleared his throat. "I'm just going to ask you directly," he finally said. "Is there any truth to these rumors? Was there anything inappropriate between you and Miss De Belle?"

Mary Ellen stood up. She wouldn't sit there and be treated like a student accused of wrongdoing. "I can't believe you'd ask me that question." She drew back her shoulders with indignation. "I won't even honor it with an answer."

She turned to go.

Then Mr. Pomeroy said, "I think you should see this." Mary Ellen heard the sound of a drawer opening, and when she turned back to Mr. Pomeroy, she saw him take a sheet of notepaper from his desk. He held it out to her, a pained look on his face. "I don't know what to do with this, Mary Ellen. Can you help me?"

She recognized her handwriting immediately. She knew that Mr. Pomeroy had recognized it, too. She took the paper from him, but she didn't need to; she knew what she'd written on it. The poem. She'd jotted it down and slipped the paper into Jean's pocketbook that first day of school for her to find later. A keepsake from her first day as a teacher, something to remind her over the years what it had all meant to her, so she wouldn't forget that feeling of love shaking her heart.

"It's from the poet, Sappho," Mary Ellen said, and then handed the paper back to Mr. Pomeroy. "It was a gift from me to Miss De Belle."

"I know the poet," Mr. Pomeroy said in a stern voice. "Mrs. McElroy identified it for me."

In addition to English, Maude McElroy taught Latin. She was a stick of a woman with white hair that she kept in a wave and fingernails clipped straight across like a man's. A woman who'd never married. A teacher so severe she sometimes had her students in tears. She always called Mary Ellen "Mrs. McVeigh," and she was haughty about it, so much so that Mary Ellen sometimes felt like she, too, was one of the woman's pupils.

"Sappho was a Greek poet," Mary Ellen said. "Not Latin."

Mr. Pomeroy frowned. "I assure you, Miss McElroy is extremely well read."

"Then she surely knows that Sappho was a lesbian poet."

"Yes, she informed me of that as well. You know the police found this in Miss De Belle's pocketbook."

"Of course, I do. I just told you. I'm the one who put it there."

"May I ask why?"

"Am I now, or was I ever, a lesbian?" Mary Ellen couldn't help but parrot the question Senator McCarthy had put to so many people during his Communist witch hunt. "Is that what you really want to ask me?"

"It's just that some of the parents have been getting anxious."

"Parents like the Heaths, who have secrets of their own to deal with."

"The business with Tom Heath is a family matter."

"And what is this, Mr. Pomeroy? What is this business now between you and me?"

He laid the notepaper on his desk and ran his finger over the words. "This is a question of your suitability to teach our young people. Just give me the answer I'm looking for, and we'll consider this matter closed."

"And if I refuse to give you that answer?"

"I'll have no choice but to discuss this with the school board. You have a morals clause in your contract, Mary Ellen. Please just tell me this is what I want to believe it is."

She knew she should say it. She should tell Mr. Pomeroy the truth. She wasn't a lesbian, and what would it matter if she were? Did he think she would be the first lesbian to teach at Lawrenceville High School? What would it have to do with her ability to teach? She fumed over the insinuation—that a person's preferences when it came to matters of love might mean that she was immoral, that she might corrupt her students. Such thoughts were preposterous. Morals clause in her contract be damned. She shouldn't be standing there, having to defend herself.

"Mary Ellen?" Mr. Pomeroy said.

She could have told him that she left those lines for Jean as a kindness. She could have asked him what had happened to kindness these days, but her anger had the best of her, and she felt it was none of his business what she had felt for Jean. Still, she couldn't help but say something that was true.

"I cared for Miss De Belle," she said.

Then she walked out of Mr. Pomeroy's office. First bell was ringing, and she had a class to teach.

17

THE DOCTOR SAID MILLIE WAS nearly three months along. Dr. Claridge on Busseron Street, not Dr. Burns, the family doctor that Grinny and Peg and Millie always went to. They were trying to keep Millie's condition a secret.

"Just until we figure out the best thing," Grinny said that morning at the breakfast table.

"The best thing?" said Millie. "What does that mean?"

Peg glanced up from her oatmeal, and Grinny knew she was waiting for him to say something. He kept stirring sugar into his coffee. It had been nearly six weeks since Charlie Camplain killed Jean De Belle, but Grinny was still dumbstruck with the proof of how violent people could be, even people who loved each other, or had once upon a time.

And now here was Millie, his little girl, who'd consented to lie with a boy—what would Father Dufresne think of them all, of Peg and Millie and him? Grinny couldn't bear the thought of it. He looked up from his coffee. Millie had pushed her bowl of oats away and was leaning forward, waiting for Grinny to answer.

"You need to eat," he said. "The baby needs you to eat."

It was just after sunrise. Out the kitchen window, Grinny could see the golden cross atop the spire of the Old Cathedral. He'd seen that cross every morning for years, and it had always been a sight that lifted his spirits, but this morning he felt it was pressing down upon him, telling him to do the right thing. What that right thing was, he wasn't sure, but he knew Millie had to see a doctor—it wasn't like they could pretend that she wasn't with child—and he'd gotten permission to come into a work a couple of hours late this morning so he could be there with Peg and Millie when they went to see Dr. Claridge.

"Why aren't we going to see Dr. Burns?" Millie said.

"Dr. Claridge is a fine doctor," Grinny told her.

"I know it's because you're ashamed of me."

He knew he could tell Millie that he loved her, that no matter what, he would be her father and she would be his daughter, and she would always be able to count on him. He knew he had that chance. He could say it didn't matter what she'd done. Nothing mattered but her health and the health of the baby, and the love that held them all together, held them safe in God's grace, safe against harm.

Yes, he could have said exactly what he felt, but if he started, he'd have to say it all. He'd have to say that a sin was a sin, and even though confession could wipe it away, it would be a long time before he'd be able to move through this town, drive his cab, help out with the Knights of Columbus winter coat drive for needy children, go inside the Old Cathedral for Sunday Mass without feeling that people were sitting in judgment of his family. Yes, there was that shame, and Grinny didn't want Millie to know it.

"Everything will be fine," he said. "You'll see."

Immediately, he felt the emptiness of those words.

Millie got up from the table. "Let's just get this over with," she said.

Now she was leaving Dr. Claridge's examination room, where her mother was still talking to the doctor. Grinny was sitting in the waiting room, his porkpie hat on his knee. Millie told him the doctor said he should go on back.

"Is everything all right?" he asked her, and she said, "I guess."

She flopped down in a chair and started leafing through a copy of *Look*. Marilyn Monroe was on the cover, pretending to be a college coed because this was the college football forecast issue. She was wearing a white letter sweater with a golden "T" on it. She had a gold pennant on a stick balanced on her left shoulder, and with her blond hair and her big smile, she looked wholesome. Grinny knew it was a trick. He'd seen some of her pictures, and he knew what she was all about. Still, to see her on that magazine, obviously so full of pep and with white letters in script that said "YEA GEORGIA TECH!"—MARILYN MONROE, made it painfully clear to Grinny that he feared the sort of life Millie might be making for herself, and he wondered where his own blame lay. What had he done, or not done, that had led them all to this?

In the exam room, Dr. Claridge told Grinny and Peg that there was no reason Millie couldn't have a healthy baby; everything was as it should be, and even though a first birth could sometimes be taxing, Millie was a strong young girl, and she'd come through it just fine.

"She's not but sixteen." Peg held her pocketbook upright on her lap. A big black pocketbook. She'd put on just a touch of lipstick, but she looked tired; her brown hair was streaked with gray. "That's so young," she said. "That's too young."

Dr. Claridge was a bald man with heavy jowls. He wore a head mirror on a strap around his forehead. He took a Roi-Tan cigar from the pocket of his white coat and began unwrapping the cellophane from around it. *Man to man, smoke a Roi-Tan!* Grinny knew the slogan from the commercials on that *Leave It to Joan* radio program.

"You drive that cab, don't you?" Dr. Claridge stuck the cigar in the corner of his mouth. "I've seen you around town driving that cab."

"Yellow Cab," Grinny said.

Dr. Claridge had found a kitchen match in his pocket. He struck it on the sole of his shoe and held the flame to the end of his Roi-Tan. He squinted at Grinny through the wisps of smoke.

"You're him," he finally said. "You're the one who drove that killer to Lawrenceville. I read about you in the *Sun-Commercial.*"

Grinny was uncomfortable with the notoriety that Charlie Camplain had brought him. He hadn't liked telling his story to the sheriff. He hadn't liked seeing his name in the newspaper or all the attention he got from the other cab drivers. He didn't like knowing that he'd eventually have to tell his story to Charlie Camplain's lawyer and to the state's attorney. He'd even have to testify at the trial. He felt like he'd never escape that story; he'd always be the man who drove a murderer to a fateful meeting with the woman who'd refused to marry him. That day, once Grinny knew that the boy Charlie Camplain had taken hostage was all right, all he wanted to do was disappear. And what he'd felt once he knew that boy was Tom Heath? He'd have to confess to Father Dufresne that he'd had a wicked thought in exchange for the way that boy had hurt Millie, hurt all of them, really.

"You're a hero, brother." Dr. Claridge was smiling now. "I'd like to shake your hand."

His hands were broad, his fingers thick. He swallowed up Grinny's hand and squeezed so hard that Grinny winced.

"You're famous now," Dr. Claridge said. "Yes, sir. Everyone knows who you are."

That was what did it, that feeling of being trapped in the public eye, that made Grinny say, "Peg, go on out there with Millie. I want to talk to the doctor."

"Bert," Peg said, using his given name, which she only did at moments of great importance. "We said we'd talk."

"Go on," he said. "I won't be long."

She frowned at him. "I know what he's going to ask you," she said to Dr. Claridge. "He's going to ask you if you can get rid of it. The baby. He's a good Catholic, and he's going to ask you that." She took her pocketbook by the strap, stood up, and started for the door. She turned back and narrowed her eyes at Grinny. "Maybe that's what comes of keeping time with a murderer."

Dear God, Grinny thought. To hear Peg say that, to know what she must think of him. It was a good while after she'd gone, slamming the door behind her, before he could lift his head and look Dr. Claridge in the eye.

"I know a man named Raymond Hardy," Grinny said.

He started to go on, but there was no need. "I can do it," Dr. Claridge said, "but it's pricey. I'm taking a chance, you see. I could lose my license, go to prison. I have to make it worth the risk."

"How much?"

"Five hundred dollars. The earlier we do this, the safer it will be. We really can't wait too much longer."

"There's a danger?"

"There's always a risk. The later in the pregnancy, the greater the chance."

Grinny nodded. He said he'd have to give it some thought. Then he thanked the doctor and went out to face Millie and Peg.

18

Norville Rich couldn't shake the memory of September 3. That evening, he'd reported for work at the Grand as usual. He hadn't slept at all. He'd been too jazzed up. When he was sitting in the police car on Main Street telling the officer with the curly hair about Charlie Camplain, a call had come in over the officer's two-way radio telling him to make tracks—that's how Norville chose to characterize what he'd heard the dispatcher say, when he told the story, again and again, to anyone who was interested in hearing it—to make tracks pronto to the Showboat, where a murder suspect had last been seen.

"It was the perp," Norville told people. "Camplain. We had to get there a-sap before he took it on the lam."

The officer told Norville to get out of the car, but somehow the heel had broken off one of Norville's loafers, and as he fumbled to pick it up, the officer said, "Oh, Jeezy Pete. I don't have the time to spare. Whatever you do, you stay in this car. I can't have a civilian getting shot."

And then they were off. The officer hit the siren, and they raced across the bridge to Westport.

When they got to the Showboat, the Lawrence County sheriff was already outside with Charlie Camplain. He had him in handcuffs.

"Bracelets," Norville told his listeners. "He was wearing the jewelry."

What happened next was fairly dull. The officer got out of the car to see if he could be of any help, and the sheriff said no, he had everything in order. He'd gotten the stories of all the witnesses. Norville saw the cab driver, Grinny Haines, come out of the Showboat, along with a boy wearing glasses, a boy who looked like he might faint. Dick Dollahan was standing in the doorway with a sawed-off shotgun still in his hand.

As for Charlie Camplain, he had this little smirk on his face. His white shirt was still crisp. His necktie was still knotted and clasped with that tiger's eye clip. He looked much like the man who'd checked out of the Grand that morning, and not like man who'd just shot a woman to death at Lawrenceville High School.

"I've got someone over there you'll probably want to talk to," the officer said to the sheriff.

The officer pointed back to his car. Norville saw both the sheriff and Camplain look in his direction.

Camplain even lifted his cuffed hands in greeting. "Well, hello there, bub," he called out, and Norville gave a shy wave.

When he told his story, he left out the part about the wave, because he felt embarrassed that he'd acknowledged Camplain at all. What he told people instead was that he got out of the police car and walked over to where the officer and the sheriff and Camplain were standing, and he said, "I'm Norville Rich. I'm the night clerk at the Grand Hotel. This is the man who checked in late last night. He left early this morning, and I helped get him a cab to carry him to Lawrenceville. He said he had a girl there he was going to ask to marry him. I even saw her picture. Yes, that's the one. And he had a gun, a snub-nosed .38. Right again. Yes, that looks like the one I saw in his pocket. Said he was a traveling man. Said he couldn't be too careful."

And indeed that was what happened eventually, when a deputy from the sheriff's office came to interview him. What was the harm of telling a few of the details in the wrong order? He wasn't claiming he'd said anything he hadn't.

Except for one thing. He told people that Camplain said to him, *You're a dirty stoolie, mister. Lucky thing I'm in these bracelets, or I'd make you sorry you ever laid eyes on me.*

"And you know what I said back to him?" Norville asked his listeners. "I said, 'But you are in those bracelets, aren't you, bub?' Then I said to the sheriff, 'Take him away. You've got your man.'"

Norville felt bad about that one little lie, but not bad enough to stop telling it. He told it to the old German with the bushy eyebrows and the leather apron who cobbled shoes at Grundman's on Seventh Street, where Norville had gone to have the heel of his loafer repaired. He told it to the people in the Dinky Diner on Busseron, where he went to have a sandwich that evening. He even stopped in Alice and Woody's, a place he'd never been, and told the story to a group of men while sipping a Sterling beer—LIFE AT ITS MELLOW BEST, the neon sign behind the bar said, and indeed Norville took great satisfaction from the fact that Raymond Hardy was sitting by himself at the far end of the bar, the only one in Alice and Woody's who seemed to not be interested in what Norville had to say, but Norville knew he was listening because when he got to the line, *But you are in those bracelets, aren't you, bub,* Raymond snorted. He ground out his Pall Mall in a glass ashtray and made his way out of the bar.

His exit pleased Norville, and he grew even bolder in his telling. "Then I said to him, 'You're the lucky one, Camplain. I don't like what you did, and if we were alone, I'd hurt you the way you hurt that poor woman. I'd make sure you never hurt anyone ever again. It's scum like you, Camplain, that turns my stomach. You're nothing but trash.'"

"You didn't say that," a skinny man with an engineer's cap pulled down to his eyes said.

"Oh, yes, I did," Norville said with so much gusto that even he almost believed it had happened.

He told the story to Zelma Partridge, who'd worked a double shift at the Grand but still seemed chipper. She leaned her elbows on the counter and put her chin in her hands and gazed adoringly at Norville, who was suddenly aware, as he beheld the way she looked at him, that he was now someone different—someone larger, more important. Someone with options.

"Imagine," Zelma said. "A killer. And you stood right up to him."

Norville opened the guest register and pointed to where Charlie Camplain had signed. "Guess we're notorious now, Zelma. How about that?"

"Guess we are." She let her hand fall lightly onto Norville's, and he let it linger there. "I'm all right with that," she said.

He noticed that she'd rouged her cheeks, that she'd used mascara, that her lips were redder than lips should ever be. At one time, he might have laughed at how hard she was trying to be pretty, but not tonight. Tonight, he was a different man, and she was a different woman. A woman a little on the fleshy side, a little past her best years, with skin a little too loose on her throat and the backs of her hands, but truth be told, he'd never been much to look at either. But on this night, because of Charlie Camplain, none of that mattered a bit. Her hand was warm on his, and he felt a stirring inside, something rising up that had nothing to do with their shortcomings and everything to do with the people they could be.

"I guess I am, too," he said.

At that moment, Lorene walked into the lobby. Norville, spotting her, felt like time stopped for a long, long moment; he knew she was taking in the sight of Zelma's hand on his, and there was nothing he could do about that, even as it was coming to him that he'd promised to call Lorene to let her know he was all right, and he'd gotten so caught up in telling his story that he'd forgotten. All of this in an instant before Zelma moved her hand and said, "Good evening, Lorene." All of this in a fraction of time, but it was enough to make all the difference.

"You said you'd call." Lorene ignored Zelma. "You *promised* you'd call." She had her arms crossed over her chest. "I came down here to make sure you were all right." She glanced at Zelma, who'd retrieved her pocketbook from under the counter. Lorene's face went hard as she looked back at Norville. "But I see you're doing just fine."

"I'm sorry, Lorene," he said, but she'd already turned on her heel and was pushing her way through the door.

One night, Norville stepped outside to help a guest into a cab. The guest was an elderly lady in a plain cotton housedress and a thin coat, unbuttoned, and stockings rolled down to her ankles. She had a small gray overnight case with a white handle that Norville gave to the cab driver, who by chance was once again Grinny Haines.

The woman had been in town from Loogootee for the funeral of an old friend. She'd spent a good deal of time while she waited for the cab telling Norville the story of her friend, another spinster woman, who had died in her chair, a copy of Daphne du Maurier's *Rebecca* open on her lap.

"We were girls together," the guest had told Norville. "It seems not so long ago. She was so dear to me."

The guest had gone on to say that she and her friends had been schoolteachers, but that time was long behind them now.

"I still get so sad this time of year, when the children go back to school," she told Norville as he helped her into the cab. "I keep thinking there's somewhere I need to be."

Just then, Ruth, the waitress from the Showboat, came around the corner from Second Street. She had a bag of popcorn in her hand and a tiny plastic umbrella—the sort that would come in some exotic drink—in her hair.

"It's you," she said. She dropped the bag of popcorn on the sidewalk and came running to Norville. She threw her arms around his neck and kissed him on the cheek. He smelled the alcohol on her breath, and he was ashamed of this display in front of the elderly guest. "You're the one," Ruth said. "You're a hero."

Grinny had just lifted the trunk lid on the yellow cab and was peering over it at Norville. If anyone was a hero, it was him, Norville knew. He felt like an impostor.

He disentangled himself from Ruth's embrace. "I didn't do anything," he said.

Ruth shook her finger at him. "Don't be so modest. You're the talk of the town."

Grinny closed the trunk lid and got into his cab. "Where to?" he asked Norville.

"The bus station," Norville said.

"And you're the cab driver," said Ruth. "You're the one who followed Charlie Camplain that morning."

"My word," the guest said. "I must be in the company of famous men."

Neither Grinny nor Norville said a word. Norville gently closed the cab door, and Grinny pulled away from the curb.

"Tell me all about Charlie Camplain," Ruth said.

"I don't feel like talking about that," Norville said, and he went back into the Grand, leaving Ruth with popcorn scattered at her feet and a dismayed look on her face, as if she'd walked into a party just as it was ending.

Norville thought of the guest and her friend who'd died, and of all the people who lay down each night alone—even if someone lay next to them—and waited for morning to come.

Norville wanted to explain it all to Lorene—how stupid he'd been, how puffed up and full of himself, how he loved her and only her, how he'd always hoped they'd marry and be companions the rest of their days. The truth was, he'd had nothing to do with the capture of Charlie Camplain. The Lawrence County sheriff already had him in cuffs by the time the Vincennes police officer arrived with Norville in tow. Really, all Norville could claim was that he'd been working the front desk at the Grand when Camplain checked out that morning. He'd helped him get a cab. He'd sent him on his way. And, oh yes, he'd seen that snub-nosed .38, but that was it; that was the extent of his story. The further truth was that he wasn't interested in Zelma Partridge at all, and what Lorene had seen—Zelma's hand on his at the Grand—hadn't meant a thing.

One evening in October, just as dusk was coming on, he thought he'd take a chance and drop by Lorene's house. He'd tried once before, the day after she'd seen him and Zelma at the Grand, but she'd turned him away. "Maybe it's just best," she'd said, "if we didn't see each other anymore." He'd tried calling after that, but each time she heard his voice on the other end of the line, she hung up. He'd tried waiting for her outside Gimbels when he knew she'd be getting off work, but she was unwilling to entertain his apologies. Sometimes she was with one of the other ladies who did alterations, and then he didn't even try to approach her, out of the humiliation he knew he'd feel if she were to turn a deaf ear in the presence of someone else.

Then one evening, she came out of Gimbels on the arm of Raymond Hardy. Norville was standing on the sidewalk, a copy of the *Sun-Commercial* under his arm. He'd just been reading about Dr. C. Walton Lillehei, who'd performed a successful open-heart operation on a patient at the University of Minnesota. Imagine that, Norville had been thinking, holding someone's heart in your hands. Then he saw Lorene holding onto Raymond Hardy, her head tossed back as she laughed at something he'd just whispered in her ear, and Norville felt like someone had squeezed the life out of his own ticker.

"Lorene." He spoke before he could think. He only knew he couldn't stand there like a dummy while Raymond Hardy and Lorene walked on by. "Lorene, it's me."

He noted the look she gave Raymond just before patting his arm and moving away from him. He went on down the sidewalk, and Norville watched him open the door of that sky-blue Caddy, the one with the fat white walls, and slip inside to wait for Lorene. The look she'd given him was one that said, *I'm sorry, but I don't know what else to do but to talk to this love-struck sucker, and then you and I can be on our way.*

"Norville," she said to him, "do you really want to keep on with this?"

It was a Friday evening, and the sidewalk was full of shoppers. The neon lights in the store windows were just beginning to get their luster: FRESH BAKED GOODS, 19¢ HAMBURGERS, BUSTER BROWN SHOES. Teenagers were cruising down Main Street in their cars, pennants waving from radio antennas—green V's with the word ALICES, the mascot for Vincennes Lincoln High School. White shoe polish on the car windows, CAGE THE LIONS—the Loogootee Lions, that night's gridiron foe.

Down the street, a car horn tooted out "shave and a haircut." Norville knew it was Raymond. Lorene lifted her hand and waved.

Norville couldn't think of a word to say.

"I'm trying to be kind, Norville," Lorene finally said. "But I think the smart thing is for you to let me be, at least for now."

Then she hurried down the sidewalk.

At least for now, she'd said. Meaning, Norville figured, maybe sometime. He took heart, and then one October evening, he thought he'd chance a visit. The leaves were in full color, and in the muted light of dusk, the yellows and oranges and reds gave him a cozy feeling.

He opened Lorene's gate and saw her in the lighted window. She was sitting in a chair by a table where a lamp was on. She'd put on a pair of pedal pushers after work, and she had her legs tucked under her as she worked on her nails with a file. A bottle of Schlitz sat on the table, and from time to time, she'd put down the file and take a sip. She was wearing a white blouse with its pointed collar turned up about her neck. From this vantage point, she reminded Norville a bit of the actress Lucille Ball—that same red hair, dyed to be sure, a strand of beads close to her throat. Sure, she was older than Lucy, but she had that same spark, that same sense of adventure about her. A life with her would never be a dull life, to be sure, but Norville told himself to remember it was that lust for adventure that had probably led her into Raymond Hardy's arms. Still, standing there on the front walk, looking at her through the window, Norville got the notion that she might look his way at any moment and give him a wave and a smile the way she had when they were still spending time with each other, those days before this business with Charlie Camplain that had turned Norville into an idiot.

"I'm just an idiot," he said to Lorene when she answered his knock on her door. "That's it, plain and simple. I'm the stupidest man alive."

He stood there on her porch and let her look him up and down. She still had the nail file in her hand, and finally she reached out and tapped its point against his chest.

"I believe you might be right about that." She turned and walked back into the living room, her hips swaying inside those pedal pushers, and she left the door open. Norville hesitated. Finally, she said, "You going to stand there all night, or are you going to come in?"

She turned on the television set and went back to her chair. "It's time for *The Lone Ranger*. You still like RC Cola?"

"Yes, please."

And like that, they started up again. They didn't talk about anything important that night. They mostly didn't say anything at all. They watched *The Lone Ranger* and then *The George Burns and Gracie Allen Show*, and once she asked him if he'd like some Ritz crackers, and he said that would be fine.

"With salami?" she asked.

"I'm surprised you remember," he said.

"Ah." She threw her hands up in surrender. "What's a dame to do?"

When George and Gracie said goodnight, Norville put his empty RC bottle on the table, brushed some Ritz crumbs from his tie, and said, "Time to make a dollar."

She walked him to the door. "Say goodnight, Gracie," she said

"Goodnight, Gracie," said Norville, and then he stepped out into the night. The breeze was out of the south, and he took that as a sign that Indian summer was about to set in.

19

It was a season of sunshine and warm breezes, a reminder of summer before the final turn toward winter. Peg opened the small window above the sink and listened to birdsong as she washed the dishes. Millie came home from school, the sweater she'd left home with tied around her waist. Grinny drove his cab with the windows down, and it was neither too hot nor too cold. Men were in their shirtsleeves. Downtown, women's high heels clicked smartly along the sidewalks. It was a merry sound, one Grinny liked to hear—that and the slap of a shoeshine rag outside the Pantheon Barber Shop, the sizzle of the hot grill at the Dinky Diner, the sound of combines working out on the prairie, the creak of swings at Gregg Park, the pock-pock of tennis balls going back and forth over the nets.

And in the evening, there was the soft light that fell over the Wabash River and the Old Cathedral, and Grinny made his way home, still undecided what to do about Millie and the baby.

"I don't have the money," he said to Peg one night. "Five hundred dollars?" He shook his head. "I'm not a rich man."

They were sitting on the steps after supper, taking in the night air. Peg's stockings were rolled down to her ankles, and she'd untied her apron and left it on a nail in the kitchen pantry. In the glow from the porch light, Grinny took in the worry lines on her forehead, the gray at her temples, the curve of her back, and he thought she looked like a million tons were pressing down upon her.

"We've raised a baby before," she said. "We know how to do it."

A couple came down the sidewalk. They were shadows at first as they passed under the canopy of a large oak tree. Then they came out to where the streetlamps reached them, and Grinny saw it was Norville and the woman he used to go walking with quite often. Grinny hadn't seen the two of them together for some time. In fact, he was under the impression that she was keeping time with Raymond Hardy now. She gave a cheery wave as she and Norville strolled past, and Peg said, "Good evening."

"Such a fine evening it is," said the woman.

Norville kept his eyes straight ahead. Grinny didn't say a word. He knew how Norville had been talking big about Charlie Camplain. "You're the talk of the town," that woman who worked at the Showboat had said to Norville in front of the Grand, and Norville had just soaked it in. Right there in front of Grinny, who'd been the one to take the real chance. That was just like some folks, he thought. Always landing on their feet, always smelling like roses.

"You look so tired, Peg," he said, after Norville and the woman had gone on. "I know it's my fault."

"She's our little girl." Peg reached over and took his hand. "Doesn't that mean something?"

"Of course it does," he said.

"Do you want to put her in danger?"

"Dr. Claridge said it would have to be done soon."

Peg let go of his hand. "I can't believe you, Bert Haines. Honestly, I don't know who you are anymore."

"I'm the same man you married. I'm your husband."

Peg stood up. She looked down on him from the porch. "And you're Millie's father," she said. "You're supposed to take care of her. You're supposed to love her, no matter what."

"I do love her," he said.

Peg was halfway to the front door when she stopped and turned back to him. She said, "But it looks like you love yourself more."

Grinny was glad Millie couldn't hear that. He was glad she was in the house, upstairs in her room, doing her homework.

Only she wasn't doing her homework. She was busy making plans. She opened the drawer in her desk and took out the King Edward cigar box where she kept the money she'd saved from babysitting and the summer job she'd had at Wally's Root Beer Barrel in Westport. She started to count, hoping that she'd have enough to do what she'd decided to do.

20

One evening, Norville heard a tap on his front door. He thought it must be Lorene, but they'd already said goodnight, and why she'd be stopping by so late was a mystery to him. He was getting ready for another night shift at the Grand. She'd be asleep by now. When he opened the door, he was surprised to find Grinny standing there, his porkpie hat in his hands.

"I saw your light," he said.

A wind had come up since Norville had left Lorene's, and the leaves were rattling on the maple trees along the sidewalk. A taste of winter was in that wind. Norville hated the thought of another winter—those bleak days of little light, the snow coating the streets. He had a car—an old Nash that had been his mother's—but generally he kept it in the garage off the alley and walked most everywhere he needed to go. He lived in an old shotgun house on Busseron not far from the Grand, and a hop, skip, and a jump from Main, where he had everything he needed. To get to Lorene's, he walked down Second past the Old Cathedral, a short enough walk, or else she'd pick him up in her Packard, and they'd go out driving somewhere—maybe over the bridge to Westport, maybe through Gregg Park, sometimes over to Lawrenceville where they'd sit a while in the high school parking lot and talk about Charlie Camplain and that poor woman, Jean De Belle. "It gives me the shivers," Lorene said once. "That blasted romance." Like most people, she'd read in the newspaper how Camplain described what led to the shooting. All in the name of love, Norville thought. Love was a complicated matter. Look at what had gone on with him and Lorene and Raymond Hardy. Thank goodness that was over. Norville didn't want to know anything more than what he did about their time together. He never asked, and she never volunteered to talk about it. He gave thanks, instead, for the fact that he and Lorene had found each other again. Even though winter was coming with all its gloom, he felt hopeful that his life was about to change for once and for always.

"Well, sure love's complicated," Lorene said. "Otherwise, it wouldn't be love, would it?" Norville couldn't argue with that. Those nights when they sat in the high school parking lot and thought of the terrible thing that had happened there, they invariably ended up holding hands. "Just think," Lorene said. "You sent him on his way that morning."

And now the man who had driven Camplain to that place with murder in his mind was standing on Norville's step.

"Is there something you're wanting?" he asked Grinny.

"I thought you might know of a way for a man to lay hands to some extra cash."

Grinny kept his eyes down. From his position at the top of the steps, Norville could look down on his bald head. He could see his cheeks suck in, no teeth to give them shape when he spoke. The words came out all mushed together, and Norville found he had to listen carefully. He remembered the conversation he'd had with Grinny before they even knew Charlie Camplain existed—a night when he'd confessed to Grinny that he was afraid someone might try to rob him of the cash in the safe at the Grand. Grinny had admitted that he was often afraid of the same thing, not knowing who might step into his cab and knock him in the head, or worse, for the money he had on him.

"What makes you think I'd know something like that?" Norville said.

"You know," Grinny said.

Norville was stunned at what Grinny was about to ask of him, and he could tell that Grinny was equally shaken. He raised his head and looked up at Norville, and something in his eyes—some trouble deeper than any Norville had ever known—rattled him. Here was a desperate man, Norville could tell, caught between the devil and the deep blue sea.

He knew that there were always people who just wanted someone to ask what was troubling them. Maybe if he'd said the right words to Charlie Camplain that morning in September, Jean De Belle would still be alive. So he said to Grinny, "What's the story?"

"I've got this girl," Grinny said. "My daughter. She's sixteen, and she's in trouble." He paused to let those words sink in. He glanced down and then back up again, and Norville nodded to let him know he understood what sort of trouble. Then Grinny said, "I need five hundred dollars to be able to make that trouble go away. I think you know what I mean."

Norville nodded again. He'd heard the rumors about Dr. Claridge and what he could do for the right price, but he'd never quite believed them.

"You think I'd give you $500 that doesn't belong to me?"

"I thought you and me. I thought we had something between us. All those nights we talked. That Charlie Camplain." Grinny was talking fast now. "You and me were the ones with him right before he shot that lady. I was coming apart that morning. Nothing's been right for me ever since."

Norville said, "A thing like that happens, and you think it's got nothing to do with you. Then you find out you were wrong. I was a fool for a while, all puffed up and running my mouth. Now I just want a regular life."

"Do you have a church?"

Norville shook his head.

"I go to Mass," Grinny said. "I'm a Catholic. We believe you can get forgiveness for your sins if you confess them."

Norville knew, and had for some time, exactly where this conversation was going. The safe at the Grand. "It'd be my job," he said. "We'd both end up in prison."

Grinny put his porkpie hat back on his head. He stuffed his hands into his jacket pockets. "Just forget I came over here," he said. "I don't even know who I am anymore. I just thought you and me…"

"You think we've been marked somehow by Charlie Camplain?"

"He'll be the shadow over us the rest of our lives. We'll always be the ones who helped him get to that lady so he could kill her."

"It could have been anyone here in town."

"Yeah, but it wasn't anyone. It was us."

"We were just doing our jobs."

Grinny came up the steps until he was standing eye to eye with Norville. He lowered his voice to a whisper. "We could have stopped him. You know that."

"Stopped him? How?"

"You saw he had that .38 that morning. I thought something was fishy when he dropped his grip at the Showboat. He had a short fuse. I could tell something was about to pop inside him."

"That's not the way it works. You don't think about these things until later."

"Well, maybe it ought to work that way. Maybe people ought to pay more attention. Maybe they ought to know when someone's in trouble."

The wind was stronger now. It was out of the north, and it was blowing into Norville's face. He stood there, aware that Grinny was giving him one more chance to say he'd help him.

"Maybe just a little at a time," Grinny said. "Maybe a couple hundred skimmed off the top one week, and another couple hundred the next. Maybe like that."

"I'm sorry things are such that you feel you have to ask me this," Norville said.

"Sorry?" Grinny chuckled. "Well, mister, that's a thing we all know something about. Just don't go thinking you're better than me, because you're not."

"I didn't say I was."

"All right then." Grinny backed away from Norville until he was standing on the walkway. Before he turned and retreated into the darkness, he said, "You forget all about this, you understand? You forget I was ever here."

But Norville couldn't forget. It haunted him all that night, a night when he stood behind the counter at the Grand and watched the rain. It slanted down through the streetlamps and the headlights of the occasional car going past. The awning shook in the wind. A man hurried by with a black umbrella, and the wind caught the umbrella and turned it inside out. Not a fit night, Norville kept thinking. He was all on edge. He kept glancing at the small safe beneath the counter. He wished Grinny Haines had never paid him a visit, had never asked him what he had. It gave him the same sick feeling in his gut that had come over him once he knew Charlie Camplain was the man who'd killed Jean De Belle.

A slow night at the Grand. Most of the night, Norville tried to keep his mind off Grinny Haines. He watched the rain. He tried to get interested in a story he was reading in the *Saturday Evening Post*. But always his mind kept coming back to Grinny and what he'd said about his daughter.

Once the rain had stopped and it was finally daylight, he picked up the phone and called Lorene. He knew she'd be up, having her coffee, picking out her clothes for work, and putting on her face.

She answered on the first ring. "I've had quite a night," Norville said.

"I barely slept a wink," she said, "what with the wind and the rain."

Then he told her about Grinny's visit and what he'd suggested when it came to his daughter and the money he needed.

"*That* kind of trouble," Norville said.

Lorene sounded tired, all washed out. "That sort of thing happens sometimes," she said.

"But to ask me to steal money from the Grand? What does he think I can do?"

"Sometimes people are desperate. You can't blame him for that."

"But to expect me…I feel like there ought to be something I can do. I'm really shaken by this, Lorene."

"It's not your problem. It's his."

Norville knew that was true, and yet he remembered what Grinny had said about people needing to pay more attention, needing to help one another.

"I feel bad for him," Norville said.

"Don't."

"Easy for you to say. You didn't see him. I could tell it hurt him to tell me about his daughter."

"Girls," Lorene said. "They can be little fools."

"We don't know her story."

"It's an old story. Been going on since the dark ages, and women just go on being fools."

"Have you ever heard that Dr. Claridge can help a girl like that? Make her trouble go away?"

At first, Norville thought that Lorene must not have heard him. She made no answer. Then, enough time passed—enough silence—to make him feel uncomfortable, as if he were crossing over a border he didn't know into territory he didn't want to visit.

"People talk, Norville." Now her voice had an edge to it. "You can't believe everything you hear. Now I have to go. I have to get ready for work."

Just like that, she hung up, and Norville felt his heart beating fast. He didn't know why, but as the day went on, it would finally come to him. He had the distinct feeling that what Lorene hadn't been able to tell him was that at some point in the past she'd known the same trouble as Grinny's daughter, and she'd gone to Dr. Claridge for relief.

❦

When Zelma Partridge arrived for her day shift, Norville already had on his coat and hat. "You look like a man in a hurry," she said. She'd been good-natured about him picking things back up with

Lorene. "You look as stormy as the weather was last night," she said. "Don't worry. You know where she lives and where she works. You've got plenty of time."

But it didn't feel like that to him. He had to know what was what, and he had to know it now.

He caught Lorene just as she was stepping out her door. She had the house key in her hand; her pocketbook dangled by its strap from the crook of her elbow. She fit the key to the door lock and turned it. Then he called her name, and she glanced back over her shoulder, and for just a brief instant, Norville registered a look of annoyance on her face, and from that he knew that she'd been expecting this moment to come, had been dreading it, and now here it was.

"You didn't answer me," he said, "when I asked whether you'd heard what Dr. Claridge might do for a girl."

"I answered," she said. "People talk. That's what I said."

"I can see it in your face. You've been to him, haven't you?"

She opened her pocketbook and dropped her key inside. Then she closed it with a snap, squared her shoulders, and said to him in a very firm voice, "If we're to continue. If you and I are to have a life together, you'll stop this right now. Do you understand me, Norville?"

The problem was he understood too much. "When?" he said.

"I warned you, Norville. You need to listen to me."

"Was it Raymond Hardy's?"

Without warning, she was hitting him, striking him on his chest and arms with her fists. Her pocketbook was banging into his ribs. She was hitting him, and she was crying, and he took her around her wrists and squeezed until finally she could hit him no more. She looked up at him, and he thought her face beautiful with misery. He let go of her wrists, but instead of letting her arms drop to her sides, as he'd imagined, she put them around his neck, and he had no choice but to wrap his arms around her waist.

In time, she would tell him the story—the one about her and Raymond Hardy and the baby she decided to let go and the anguish it brought her, but look at her: she was a woman nearing middle age, a woman without a husband; what kind of life would she have been able to give a child? "We could have raised it together," Norville would say. "You and me. We could have had a family." And she would say, "You would have done that?" And he would answer, "Nothing gets in the way of love, Lorene. It abides."

But that morning, they didn't know any words to say. So they stood there, holding each other, holding on.

21

ONE NIGHT, IN THE BACK room of Alice and Woody's Cocktail Bar, Grinny stayed until the poker game had broken up and the losers had gone home to piss and moan. He waited to have a word with Raymond Hardy.

He needed help, he said. He needed, to be exact, five hundred dollars.

Raymond was sitting at the table, counting out a stack of bills. He licked his thumb before peeling back each one. A lit Chesterfield balanced on the lip of a glass ashtray. He stopped counting his money and picked up the Chesterfield, pinching it between his thumb and his first two fingers. He took a drag and let the smoke come out his nose. He squinted at Grinny. Then he lay the Chesterfield back on the ashtray and said, "That's a tidy sum. What might you be wanting it for?"

Grinny had always stood in judgment of Raymond, but now circumstances had taught him a lesson about pride. Standing there at the table, his hands in his pocket, his head bowed, he was shy and ashamed of having to answer the question.

"My girl," he said.

Truth be told, he was full of disgust. He could barely stand to be inside his own skin. All he wanted was peace. He wanted this nightmare to be behind him. He wanted to go back to the man he'd once been—just a working Joe with a gift of making people laugh, a happy-go-lucky cab driver who liked to lean out his window, flash a fare a toothless grin, and say, "So where ya goin'?" And more than that, he wanted to be the man who could step inside the Old Cathedral for Mass and feel God's peace. But how would he ever be able to do that if he couldn't bring himself to confess his sin and ask for absolution? That would be a hard thing, to kneel inside the confessional—*Bless me, Father, for I have sinned*—and to tell Father Dufresne exactly what he'd done.

He heard Raymond's throaty chuckle, and he lifted his head. Raymond was leering at him, the way he might have had Millie been standing there. The smirk on his face, that wicked chuckle, turned Grinny's stomach.

"Has your girl been naughty?" Raymond winked at him. "She need to see Doc Claridge?"

Grinny knew he was at a point where he could call Raymond Hardy a lousy bastard for talking that way about Millie. He could walk away and do the courageous thing: he could face the truth of his life. This was his last chance for that money. He had no other way to get it, outside of the crazy thought he'd had of stealing it from the safe at the Grand Hotel, but he knew he'd never get away with it. Raymond Hardy was the only one he knew who might help him, and that meant having to take whatever he wanted to dish out.

"My girl," Grinny said again. "Yes."

He knew he was agreeing. He knew he was leaving the best part of himself behind.

"You know I'll expect interest," Raymond said. "Twenty percent."

Grinny nodded, and Raymond began to count out the bills.

"No one gets off easy," he said. "Ask old Charlie Camplain."

❧

Robbie couldn't help herself; she had to see Millie Haines. She'd spent night after night wondering about her—wondering, to be more specific, what Tom saw in her outside of the fact that she'd opened her legs to him. Robbie hated to be ugly about it, but there it was, the truth: Millie Haines had been willing to give Tom what Robbie had refused him. That was all she really needed to know about Millie, her friends told her. She was fast; she'd brought this trouble on herself. But there was something else nagging at Robbie. What was it about Millie Haines that had first caught Tom's eye? Robbie lay awake at night wondering. At odd times during the day, the question kept coming to her. Why hadn't she been enough for Tom? What had made him turn to Millie Haines?

Dixie Dale was exasperated with her. "He's a boy. That's all you need to know."

But one evening, Robbie asked her mother if she could borrow her car to drive to Dixie's house. They had a project due in their US History class the next day and they still had work to do, and it was raining, one of those dreary autumn rains that plastered the fallen leaves to the sidewalks, streaked the windows, and left Robbie feeling melancholy. She didn't want to walk all the way to Dixie's in this dreadful weather, and couldn't she please borrow the Ford?

Mary Ellen handed her the key. "Take it," she said. "Just leave me in peace."

Robbie knew her mother was being called up in front of the school board over these nasty rumors about her and Miss De Belle. "I could lose my job," her mother told her, and then she started to sob. Robbie's heart went out to her. She took the key to the Ford and threw her arms around her mother's neck.

"I won't be too late," she said, and then she was free from the chronic sadness that now filled their house. She was in her mother's Ford, and she was on her way to Vincennes.

She drove out of town, past WAKO, and took the right-hand turn toward Westport. Suddenly, she found herself overwhelmed with a sympathy for Tom. This was the route he'd driven that first day of school with Charlie Camplain in the front seat, a gun in his hand. How terrified he must have been. Lola Malone's father said he'd wet his pants. That scared. Robbie felt a shiver go up the back of her neck.

She was hunched over the steering wheel, her hands at the proper positions of ten and two o'clock, holding a safe speed as she drove on through the darkness, past fields of corn stubble, past pumpkin patches where the vines were starting to wither. Out there, alone in the wet, dark night, she wondered what Tom was doing at that exact moment. She had the urge to turn the Ford around and drive back into town to find him, to put her arms around him and hold him and tell him she forgave him everything: his insinuations about her mother and Miss De Belle, even his night with Millie Haines. They'd go back, she'd tell him. They'd go back to who they'd been before Millie, before Charlie Camplain and Miss De Belle. They'd be Robbie and Tom again. They'd look forward to the rest of their lives.

But she knew it could never be like that, no matter how truly she forgave him. There would always be Millie Haines and the child that Tom had given her. So she kept driving, and soon the lights of the clubs and bars of Westport were in view, and then she was driving over the Wabash River, and she saw the cross atop the Old Cathedral, and she said a silent prayer. God help me, she said. God help us all.

She found a telephone booth on the corner of Second and Main outside Gimbels. She parked and made a dash for it. Inside the booth, she looked through the directory until she found a listing for Bert Haines. She remembered the name of Millie's father from the newspaper accounts of the shooting. Bert Haines had been the cab driver who'd taken Charlie Camplain to Lawrenceville that morning. *203 South Fourth Street.* That was it.

She wanted to drive there right away, wanted to see Millie Haines with her own eyes, but how would she explain her visit to Millie's parents? Without thinking, she put a dime in the telephone and dialed the number.

The woman who answered sounded worn to pieces. When Robbie asked to speak to Millie, the woman said, "Millie's not here. She's at the cathedral. Who is this anyway?"

Robbie said, "A friend."

The woman's voice brightened. "Oh, how nice," she said. "I'll be sure to tell Millie you called. What's your name, dear?"

"I'm just a girl," Robbie said, and then she hung up, her heart pounding.

❧

A few minutes later, she opened the door to the Old Cathedral and stepped inside. She'd never been in a Catholic church. She took note of the font of holy water, the confessionals, the stained-glass windows, the candles burning at the altar. An old woman with a humped back lit a candle and then made the sign of the cross. A few others sat on the wooden pews, all separate from one another. A man in a wool topcoat held rosary beads in his hand. A mother with a baby in her arms wore the most serene look on her face. A very tall woman with a goiter stepped out into the aisle, where she bent one knee to the ground before turning to leave. As she passed Robbie, she said, "Peace be with you."

That's when Robbie heard the muffled sound of someone softly weeping. About midway up the aisle, a young girl sat with her head bowed, rocking gently. She knew it must be Millie Haines.

One by one, the others left the cathedral, and still Millie wept, and Robbie stood there listening to the sound of her crying, until finally she couldn't stand it any longer. She walked up the aisle to the pew where Millie was sitting, and she went in and sat beside her and put her arm around her shoulders and rocked her back and forth.

Millie Haines was a tiny girl with dark hair and the palest skin. She was wearing a navy-blue jumper with a white blouse. The toes of her saddle shoes were dirty and scuffed. Her bobby sox were stretched out and sagged about her ankles. She'd gotten wet outside, and the little bit of eye makeup she had on had smeared and run.

Even though Robbie had spent days despising her—this plain, small girl who wasn't remarkable in any way—she now felt a tremendous sadness for how alone she seemed to be.

"Here," Robbie said. "You can use my hanky."

Millie took the handkerchief from Robbie and blotted her eyes. "Do I know you?" she said.

"You just looked like you could use a friend," Robbie said.

"I'm Millie."

The wind was blowing now, the rain pelting the stained glass windows. "It's a miserable night," Robbie said. "I have my mother's car. Would you like me to take you home?"

"I'm going to the bus station," Millie said.

She started crying again, harder this time, and Robbie patted her arm and let her cry.

"On a night like this?" Robbie said.

"You don't know," said Millie. "You just don't."

"If I take you to the bus station, will you tell me?"

Millie nodded.

"Do you have a suitcase?" Robbie asked.

"I couldn't risk it. I couldn't let my parents know."

"Are you running away?"

"I have a place to go."

"It's a miserable night out there."

"Every night's a miserable night," Millie said.

❦

The bus station was only a few blocks away at Fifth and Main, catty-corner from the Pantheon Theater. It was almost time for the seven o'clock show—Gregory Peck and Ann Blyth in *The World in His Arms*—and a few folks were still in line at the ticket booth, rain beating down on their black umbrellas.

Robbie found a parking place down the street from the station, and she and Millie sat there, both of them looking at the Arrow Coach, its motor running. Its wipers swept back and forth over the windshield. Above it, in white letters, was the destination: EVANSVILLE.

"I'm going down there to a home," Millie said. Her voice was soft, and she wouldn't look at Robbie. "A home for unwed mothers."

Robbie pretended to be surprised. "Oh," she said. "I never would have guessed…"

"Why would you? I'm not even showing."

"Are you sure you want to go now, without any of your things? I mean, if you're not showing, couldn't you wait a little longer?"

Why Robbie was trying to talk Millie out of going, she couldn't say. It was something about how small the girl was, how frightened, that made it hard for Robbie to think of her disappearing into a night like this.

"I don't have that much time," Millie said. She reached into the pocket of her coat and drew out a fistful of bills. "I've got money for the ticket."

"Your parents don't know you're going, do they?"

For a good while, Millie didn't say a word. Robbie watched a colored man loading suitcases in the baggage hold beneath the bus. Passengers were starting to come out of the station into the rain to board.

"My father," Millie finally said. "He's going to make me have an abortion."

Now Robbie was the one who was quiet. Of course she knew about such things—knew that certain doctors sometimes performed them illegally—but she'd never run with the sort of girls for whom this was information they would ever need. Millie was a different kind of girl. No matter what she did about the baby, she'd never be the girl she'd been. That part of her was gone, and Robbie felt the sadness of that loss.

"I don't know what to say," she finally said.

"You don't have to say anything." Millie grasped the door handle. "You did me a favor. You gave me a ride. I thank you for that, but you don't have any responsibility to me now. You can go back to your life."

Robbie nodded. But still Millie sat there, staring at the bus, not moving.

"You don't want to do this, do you?" Robbie said to her.

"I don't know what I want." Millie's voice was trembling. "I just wish this had never happened. I wish I'd never met that boy. He said he had a bottle in his car. He said, 'You like whisky, don't you?' I'd never had it before, but I didn't want him to know that. He seemed like a nice boy, so I went with him."

Robbie didn't want to hear anymore. "Sometimes," she said, "when you don't know what to do, it's better to do nothing."

"But if I don't do something soon, my father will make me go to that doctor." She had her hand flat on her stomach. "He'll take the baby. He'll just make it go away. At least at the home in Evansville, the baby will have a chance. I'll hope some couple will give it a beautiful life." She bit her lip. "I just feel so alone right now."

Robbie remembered how the woman on the phone—Millie's mother, Robbie assumed—said, "Oh, how nice" when Robbie said she was a friend. She realized now that the woman said it because Millie didn't have any friends. Here she was on this rainy night, about to get on a bus and run away, and Robbie knew she couldn't let her do that. Dixie Dale would never understand—*Good riddance to bad rubbish*, Robbie could hear her saying. *She made her bed, now let her lie in it.* But it wasn't like that, not here in this moment when Millie was about to open the car door and step out into the rain, step out into the rest of her life. Robbie did feel responsible. She felt very much responsible. As much time as she'd put into hating her, she felt her heart go out to this slight girl who was in so much trouble.

"I'm here with you," Robbie said.

Millie glanced back at her. She had the door open and one foot out on the pavement. She reached out her hand, and Robbie took it. Millie squeezed it hard.

"Don't go," Robbie said. "Don't do something you'll later regret."

Millie took a breath and let it out. "What else am I to do?"

"Come with me." Robbie dropped the gear shift lever into low. "Close the door and come with me."

"Are you an angel?" Millie asked.

"No, I'm no angel. Not by a long shot."

Millie closed the door. "Who are you, then?"

"You might not want to know." Robbie pulled away from the curb. "For now, let's just say I'm someone who wants to help. Okay?"

"Okay," said Millie, and then the two girls were quiet. There was only the slap of the windshield wipers and the hiss of the tires over the wet pavement. Soon Robbie was driving the Ford over the bridge into Westport and then the dark prairie beyond, thinking she was probably crazy, but maybe that's what this night required—something so crazy it might just work.

"Where are we going?" Millie asked.

"We're not going to Evansville," Robbie said, "and we're not going to an abortion doctor. Is that all right with you?"

"It is," said Millie, and Robbie drove on through the rainy night.

⟋⟋⟍

Mary Ellen was coming down the stairs when the front door opened and Robbie walked in holding the hand of a girl her mother didn't know. Such a tiny thing, with dark hair all stringy and wet. At first Mary Ellen thought she was a child, a little girl who was lost, someone Robbie had found wandering about in the rain. Then the girl lifted her face, and Mary Ellen could see she was a girl near Robbie's age, but she was no friend of Robbie's that Mary Ellen knew.

"Oh, Robbie," Mary Ellen said. "Look at the two of you. You're dripping on my floor."

"It's pouring rain outside," Robbie said. "God, Mother."

Mary Ellen hadn't meant to be sharp in front of company.

"You've brought home a friend," she said in her kindly teacher's voice. "How delightful." She came on down the stairs. "I'm Robbie's mother. I don't believe I know your name."

"This is Millie," Robbie said. "Millie Haines from Vincennes."

Mary Ellen stopped on the bottom stair. She clutched the banister. Of course she knew who Millie Haines was. The girl who was carrying Tom Heath's baby.

"I'm afraid I don't understand," she said. "I thought you were with Dixie."

Millie had let go of Robbie's hand. She had her arms crossed over her chest, shivering.

"I went to find Millie. I had to see her. I wanted to know."

Millie spread her arms, presenting herself to Mary Ellen. "Not much to look at, but a whole lot to know."

"Robbie," Mary Ellen said. "What in the world?"

"She knows who I am," Robbie said. "Mother, I didn't know where else to turn. I need your help."

Mary Ellen heard the anguish in Robbie's voice. Her heart went out to her—her mother's heart—and even though she had no idea what help she might be able to provide, she knew she wanted to do whatever she could to take the misery away from Robbie, and from Millie, too, for whom she suddenly felt responsible.

"Mrs. McVeigh, I'm sorry about your floor," Millie said, her voice filled with regret.

Mary Ellen went to her and put her arm around her shoulders. "Not to worry," Mary Ellen said. "Let me get you a towel. Then, after everyone is dry and warm, you'll tell me everything I need to know."

‿୧⁊◠

So they sat around the kitchen table, the girls and Mary Ellen, and Robbie told her the story. Mary Ellen had made hot cocoa, and the steam was rising from the mugs. Millie had dried and combed her hair and pulled it back into a ponytail. Robbie sat with her legs tucked beneath her.

"It's a horrible thing," she said.

"My father's not a bad man," Millie said.

"Of course he's not," said Mary Ellen. She remembered the accounts of how Bert Haines had stepped into the Showboat that morning in September and marched right up to Charlie Camplain because he knew that Tom was in harm's way. "He's just put upon right now."

Millie ducked her head. "I guess that's my fault."

"What good does it do to think about blame?" Mary Ellen said. "It's better to come up with a solution."

"That's why I brought her here," said Robbie. "I knew you'd be able to help."

It moved Mary Ellen that Robbie trusted her. This is what it was to have a child, to be there for them when they needed you, no matter what. Mary Ellen reached across the table and took her hand. Then she reached out her other hand to Millie, and Millie took it.

"I don't know what I'm going to do," Millie said.

Mary Ellen knew she'd have to ask a hard question. "Have the Heaths been in touch with you? Have there been conversations with your family?"

"My father tried talking to Mr. Heath once, back in September, on that day when…"

Millie's voice trailed away, and for a long moment they all sat there, not speaking, recalling the day that Charlie Camplain had come.

"That's not right," Mary Ellen said. "That boy is responsible."

∼⊚∽

While the girls finished their hot cocoa, Mary Ellen excused herself and went upstairs to her bedroom to use the telephone. Her first call was to Millie's parents.

"Are you Millie's mother?" she asked the woman who answered.

"Yes, this is Peg," the woman said.

"I hope you'll excuse me for being forward," said Mary Ellen. "You don't know me, but I have news about your daughter."

"Our Millie." The woman's voice rose with excitement. "Oh, my word. We've been worried sick."

Mary Ellen sat on the edge of her bed, the phone cord twisted around her finger, and she did her best to assure Peg Haines that there was nothing to worry about. "Millie is here with me. I'm a teacher in Lawrenceville. Everything is fine."

"A teacher," Peg said slowly. "In Lawrenceville."

Mary Ellen knew she was thinking about Jean, and her husband's part in the events of that day. Peg didn't say anything, and in the silence Mary Ellen heard the burden of her life.

"My daughter," Mary Ellen finally said. "My daughter brought Millie here."

"I didn't know Millie knew anyone in Lawrenceville…well, except for one person."

"We need to talk, Mrs. Haines."

Again there was a long silence, and then Peg said, "If you'll be so kind to give me your address, I'll send my husband to fetch Millie."

"I think it would be better, Mrs. Haines, if I brought her to you."

But first Mary Ellen decided to stop at the Heaths'.

"Mother, no," Robbie said. Mary Ellen was slowing to make the turn into the driveway. "Mother, you can't be serious."

"Trust me, Robbie," Mary Ellen said. "You girls wait in the car."

Millie leaned forward from the backseat, and Mary Ellen smelled her still-damp hair. "Where are we going?"

Mary Ellen said, "There's someone I need to talk to before I take you home."

This time, it was Mr. Heath who answered the door. Mary Ellen stood in the flow from the porch light, and she said, "Mr. Pomeroy tells me you're calling me up before the board."

Mr. Heath had a highball in his hand. Loud dance music was playing somewhere in the house. Two other cars were parked in the driveway; one of them, Mary Ellen knew, belonged to Mr. Pomeroy. Mr. Heath took another step so he was on the porch, and he closed the door behind him.

"This could all be avoided, Mary Ellen," he said. "All you have to do is tell the truth. I'm not after your job. I just want you to come clean about your relationship with Miss De Belle. I just want everyone to know who they're dealing with. Do I think you're seducing our young girls? Not for a minute. I just think those girls have a right to know this about you."

"Then I think there's something you should know." Mary Ellen turned and looked back at her Ford, which was beside the gaslight in the front yard. In that glow, it was easy enough to see Robbie sitting in the front seat and Millie in the back. "That girl in the backseat? That's Millie Haines. I doubt you've ever seen her. I doubt you've given her much thought at all. Such a tiny thing, isn't she, but she's the mother of your son's baby, and her father is going to make her have an abortion. I thought you and your wife should know that, Mr. Heath. I thought you should have a chance to take responsibility for Tom's actions."

Mary Ellen started down the porch steps. Then she stopped and turned back to Mr. Heath.

"I suppose I'll see you at the board meeting."

"What am I supposed to do? Insist that Tom marry her? Throw money at her? Raise the child as our own?"

"I suppose, Mr. Heath, that's entirely up to you."

When Mary Ellen got back in the car, Millie said, "This is his house, isn't it? This is where Tom lives."

Robbie sat with her arms folded across her chest, staring straight ahead.

"Yes, it is," Mary Ellen said. "Now don't you worry, dear. Everything is going to work out just fine."

And Mary Ellen believed it would. She believed that the Heaths would do the right thing to prevent the death of that unborn child. She believed it all the way up to the moment when she knocked on the Haineses' front door, and Mr. Haines came to answer it.

"This isn't none of your doing," he said. Then he took Millie by the arm and yanked her inside and slammed the door before Mary Ellen could utter a single word of protest.

"We've made a mess of things," Robbie said. "Oh, Mother, we really have. That poor girl."

❧

Norville didn't know the woman and girl on the front steps of Grinny Haines's house. He paused at the end of the walk, not sure whether to approach them. The rain, which had been steady since early evening, had now stopped, and all around them was the sound of water dripping from the leaves, that and the smell of coal smoke from chimneys because it had gotten cool enough for folks to light a fire.

He'd heard what the girl had said—*Poor girl*—and he imagined she was talking about Grinny's daughter. That's why he'd decided to pay a visit; he didn't want Grinny to do anything stupid.

The woman was holding the girl's hand. Norville imagined they must be mother and daughter. What business they had at the Haineses' house, he didn't know, but he could tell from the way the girl held to the woman's hand that something had gone awry.

Norville discreetly retreated into the shadows so the two of them could pass by in private. A black Ford with Illinois plates waited for them at the curb.

But then he heard the girl say with disgust, "Oh, that Tom Heath. Damn him, and his parents, too. Hell's bells and buckets of blood."

The woman said, "You know I detest that expression, but in this case, I'll join you. Yes—hell's bells and buckets of blood."

Norville knew that name, Tom Heath. He knew he was the boy Charlie Camplain had held at gunpoint while he drove from Lawrenceville to Westport.

"Excuse me." He couldn't stop himself from stepping out of the shadows to speak to them. "I didn't mean to eavesdrop, but I heard you mention the name Tom Heath. You must be from Lawrenceville, then."

"That's right," said the woman. "I teach at the high school there."

"Such a sad story about your librarian."

The girl said, "She roomed at our house."

"You must be Mrs. McVeigh," Norville said.

The woman studied him, a frown on her face. "You seem to know an awful lot about us."

"I'm Norville Rich," he said. "I'm the night clerk at the Grand Hotel. I was the last person to talk to Charlie Camplain that morning. Well, except for Mr. Haines."

"Mr. Haines can kiss my foot," Mrs. McVeigh said. "If you're a friend of his, you should talk to him. You make him come to his senses. Aren't there any decent people left in this horrible world?"

Norville didn't know what to say. Mrs. McVeigh kept staring at him. She lifted her eyebrows as if she were trying to prod him to answer. She must have done this countless times with her students, and like a dunce, he stood there, mute, until Mrs. McVeigh and her daughter brushed past him, got in their Ford, and drove away, leaving the question resounding in his ears.

He carried it with him up the walk to the Haineses' front door. He wanted to share that question with Grinny. He wanted to say, *What's happened to us? Why can't we all have decent lives?* He wanted to tell Grinny how Lorene was haunted still by the decision she made to give up her baby. He wanted to say, *Aren't you a good Catholic man?*

Just as he stepped up to the door, he heard the voices inside. Loud, angry voices, and a woman, Grinny's wife, pleading, "Please, please. My god."

"You talked to that woman and her daughter about this?" Grinny was shouting. "You let them into our lives?"

"They wanted to help me. Daddy, please."

"Help you? How can they help you?"

"They took me to the Heaths. She said they should take responsibility for what Tom did."

"She had no right. No right."

"Bert, please," Mrs. Haines said again.

"I want to have this baby," Millie said. "I want to have this baby." She wouldn't stop. Her voice rose higher. "I want to have this baby."

"Jesus," Grinny said. "Jesus, oh, Jesus, oh Jesus."

The house was full of the sound of crying. Norville was frozen in place, ashamed to be listening to this conversation, but unable to walk away.

"Oh, my little girl," Mrs. Haines said. "My precious little girl."

"Mama," said Millie. "Oh, Mama."

Grinny stomped across the floor, and Norville felt the house shake.

"Bert, what are you doing? Bert, don't."

Mrs. Haines's voice faded, and Norville heard her own footsteps, and he knew she was following Grinny to the back of the house. Then there was the sound of the back door opening and slamming shut. It wasn't long before Norville heard a car motor turning over, and then that motor's roar and the spray of cinders along the alley behind the house. Norville listened to the car, and from the sound of it he knew it was headed west over the bridge and into Westport.

"There wasn't anything I could do," he'd say to Lorene later. "Not a thing but just let him go. Not a thing for his wife. Not a thing for his daughter. All this trouble, and not a thing I could do."

Said Lorene, "You know that's not true. When people are in trouble, there's always something. We just have to have the courage to do it."

❧

Grinny was driving fast, much too fast, he knew, for the wet road. He didn't care. He just wanted to move. He just wanted to be somewhere else, away from his house, which was a house of sadness now, and sadder still because it had once been a place of so much joy.

A memory came to him: a Sunday morning from last summer, when he came down the stairs and heard Peg's and Millie's voices coming from the kitchen. They'd just returned from early Mass on an August day that would get hotter and hotter as the sun moved across the sky, but for the time, it wasn't bad at all. There'd even been a bit of a breeze off the river as they left the Old Cathedral. Grinny stood still on the stairs and listened to the sound of his wife and daughter talking about Millie's job at Wally's Root Beer Barrel.

"I try really, really hard not to mess up," Millie said, "but sometimes I just get so nervous."

Peg reassured her. "We all make mistakes sometimes," she said, "but people are usually understanding."

Millie laughed. "I spilled a root beer float once. Dumped it right in a man's lap."

Peg laughed, too. "Oh, really, Millie. You didn't."

"I most certainly did. And you'll never guess who it was—Father Dufresne. I thought I'd die, but you know what he said? He said, 'Dear God in Heaven, that certainly cooled things off down there.'"

Then Peg and Millie were both laughing, and the sound of it was enough to fill Grinny with thanksgiving. All the early years with Peg, they'd both longed for a child, and now here she was on this glorious morning, and Grinny was about to step into the kitchen and say, "What's so funny?" And he would feel so incredibly happy when both Peg and Millie would try to get serious and say, "Nothing, nothing at all." Then they would burst out laughing again. His heart would be full of all of this. His heart would long for nothing more.

Then September had come, and with it Millie's news, news she'd now shared with strangers. Grinny couldn't bear the thought of that.

He was out past the Showboat now and Wally's and the Allison Drive-In. The lights faded behind him. He was still driving fast in the black night. The barren fields flashed by him on the long straightaway before the curve to Lawrenceville. He was coming up on a slow-moving car. His headlights filled it, and he made out what he imagined were the forms of the woman and the girl who'd brought Millie home.

He blasted his horn and pulled out to pass. As he pulled even with the car, he glanced over and saw it was indeed the woman and the girl.

Then he was into the curve and starting to slide, his tires refusing to grip the wet pavement, and he said out loud, "God, dear God. God, help me."

Robbie said, "He's not going to make the curve." Her mother slowed down. The other car, an older model with bulky fenders and fat whitewall tires, fishtailed on the wet road. Its rear end slid off onto the grassy shoulder, and for a moment it appeared the car would leave the pavement and spin off into the field. It looked like it was going sideways. The headlights from her mother's Ford shined directly onto the driver, who was working furiously with the steering wheel, and Robbie saw who it was. "Mother," she said, "it's Mr. Haines."

Somehow, he righted the car. The rear end slid back into place. The car came out of the curve and shot ahead.

Robbie's breath was coming fast. "Oh, my goodness." She placed her hand flat against her chest. "That scared me to death. He was lucky, wasn't he, Mother? He's a lucky man."

"He's a damned fool," said Mary Ellen, and Robbie saw her press her foot down on the gas pedal. "And I intend to tell him so."

⁂

She caught him east of Lawrenceville, near the radio station. By this time, he was well within the speed limit, so much so, in fact, that Mary Ellen had to tap her brakes to keep from following too closely.

"Maybe now he's come to his senses," she said. "Do you think that's possible?"

She followed the car into town, past WAKO and the King Pin Bowling Lanes and Bottoms Up Liquors. Then the long climb up the hill past the grand two-story brick homes to the courthouse square and through the first intersection by the Hotel Lawrence. The square was nearly deserted—just a few cars parked on the north side near Studley's Rexall and The Square Deal Grocery.

The Pontiac—Mary Ellen could now see the make of the car she was following—turned left at the next light and pulled into a parking place in front of Heath's Paints. The store windows were dark. Mary Ellen angled beside the Pontiac and told Robbie to roll down her window.

Mr. Haines was already out of his car.

"I'm shaking, I tell you." He put his hands on the door of Mary Ellen's Ford and bent over to talk through the open window. "Did you see that back there? I thought I was a goner."

"You should have been," Mary Ellen said. "I don't know what saved you."

"I do," said Mr. Haines in an earnest voice. "That was God calling me back to him." He bowed his head, and when he finally raised it, he was grinning. "Oh, mercy," he said. "That was God getting me back on the right track."

"I don't know about that," Mary Ellen said. She wasn't the sort to believe in miracles, but if he was, so be it. "But something sure saved you. It was like there was an angel on your shoulder."

"Exactly. Ma'am, that's exactly what it was like. I've got my angel with me now, and she wants to know could you show me the way to Mr. Heath's house. Him and me, we've got some talking to do."

"I can do that," Mary Ellen said.

Mr. Haines went back to his car. Robbie rolled up her window.

"I thought you were going to tell him what a fool he was," she said.

"Sometimes no one has to say it." Mary Ellen reached across the seat and found Robbie's hand. "Sometimes we just know."

Grinny followed the Ford along the main street through town, past the Christian Church, a funeral home, the hospital. There, the street came to a Y, one lane veering right out to U.S. Route 50, one lane continuing on out of town toward Bridgeport and Sumner. In the crotch of the Y, set back far from the street, was a grand home, a home of red brick with a sprawling wraparound porch and a peaked roof with two chimneys. Grinny drove slowly up the driveway toward the lights of the house. Clouds were moving past the moon now. Rain still dripped from the trees, but it would be a clear night after all. Grinny parked and sat a while looking at the lighted windows of the house, imagining the life of ease that must go on in such a place. He wanted that comfort, that peace. He wanted to be able to lie down each night secure in the love of his family. He'd come near to ruining everything—he could imagine now how a man like Charlie Camplain could let crazy thinking take him by the collar and make him cruel and stupid —but he was in his right head again. He wasn't so far from the person he was to find his way back to him.

Mr. Heath was laughing when he opened the door, but when he saw Grinny standing on his front porch, the laugher stopped, and he set his jaw and narrowed his eyes.

"It's you," he said, and Grinny could tell that he'd convinced himself that he'd never see him again, that he could just forget that day in the paint store, could forget what his son had done, could just go on with his easy life.

"Here's the thing," Grinny said. He said it in a quiet, measured voice, stating the fact, saying the thing he'd made up his mind to say. "That day in the Showboat in Westport. You know the day I'm talking about. I was the one who saved your son. If it hadn't been for me, who knows what might have happened. Who knows if he'd even be with you now. He might have ended up dead if not for me. Are you telling me that doesn't count for something?"

Grinny saw that he'd touched something inside Mr. Heath. He could tell by the way he winced, ever so slightly, at the thought of his son dead.

"You and me are both fathers," Grinny said.

Mr. Heath put his hand to his mouth as if he didn't want Grinny to see that his lips were quivering, that he was close to coming undone. He drew in a breath, and his shoulders went back. He moved his hand to the top of his head. He said, "What is it you want me to do?"

"Maybe you should invite me in," Grinny said. "Maybe Mrs. Heath should hear this. Maybe we should talk like the decent people I'm sure we all are."

Still Mr. Heath hesitated.

"Or I could go home," Grinny said, "and tomorrow I could come back, and I could make my way around the square. It's my day off tomorrow. I'll have plenty of time. I'll go into every store, every café, every bar. I'll go to the school, even. I'll tell everyone what your son did to my daughter. I'll spread the word, Mr. Heath, unless you're willing to listen to reason."

Mr. Heath took in a long breath, his shoulders drawing back. He was bracing himself, Grinny knew, as he tried to decide how much he could risk. Finally, he let out his breath. He pushed the door open and stepped aside.

"Come in, Mr. Haines," he said. "Welcome to my home."

22

ROBBIE WAS GETTING READY FOR bed when her mother knocked on her door and asked if she could come in.

"Just a sec," Robbie said.

She finished buttoning her pajama shirt. Then she opened her door and was taken aback by the look on her mother's face—her lips pressed together, her eyes narrowed so that the two worry lines at the bridge of her nose deepened. It was the severe look Robbie had seen her give her students countless times.

"I need to know what you told the Heaths about Miss De Belle and me," her mother finally said.

Robbie went to the window. She looked out on the wet street and saw her own image in the glass, her face ghostlike without her eye shadow and mascara and lipstick and rouge. The face of the little girl she felt herself to be as she turned back to her mother and said in a voice that was barely more than a whisper, "I never meant to do any harm. I was just talking."

"Robbie, what did you say?"

"I said you and Miss DeBelle sometimes sat in the porch swing and sometimes you held her hand."

"That's true," her mother said. "There's nothing odd about two women feeling affection for each other. I treated Miss DeBelle the way I'd treat my…" Her voice faded away, and Robbie knew what she'd been about to say. "What else did you tell them?" her mother asked.

But Robbie wouldn't let it go. "Your daughter," she said. "Is that what you were about to say? You treated her the way you'd treat your daughter?"

Her mother said, "It doesn't mean I don't love you. It doesn't mean that at all."

Robbie was shaking her head. "I always knew she was who you wished I could be."

"That's not true," her mother said. "Not for a minute."

She went to Robbie and tried to hug her, but Robbie turned away. Her mother wrapped her arms around her waist. She kissed her head.

"Don't touch me," Robbie said. "Don't touch me like that."

"Oh, Robbie. Why are things always so hard between us?"

"I mean it, Mother. Don't."

"You're my only child."

Robbie tried to squirm away from her mother's embrace, but her mother held her more tightly. Finally, Robbie said, "I told them you and Miss DeBelle were lovey-dovey. That's what I said."

She was able to break free then. She crossed the room to her dresser and stood with her back to her mother, her arms crossed over her chest, waiting to see what would happen now.

Finally, after a long silence, she heard her mother's high heels on the wood floor. Out of the corner of her eye, she saw her moving toward the door.

"You have no idea what you may have caused, Robbie. None at all."

"What do you mean?" Robbie said.

"I'm to appear before the school board Monday evening. They'll determine whether I'm fit to be a teacher. They'll use your words against me."

"I didn't mean it that way," Robbie said. "Not the way they're making it out to be." She turned to face her mother. "You know that, don't you?"

"What you say and do is who you are, Robbie. You need to remember that."

With that, Mary Ellen stepped out into the hall and very softly closed the door to Robbie's bedroom, the room where Robbie would lie awake most of the night, listening to her mother toss and turn in her own bed, each of them alone with her misery on this rainy night, each of them wishing that Jean De Belle had never come to live with them.

But it was Jean, Mary Ellen knew, who'd brought joy back to her. She listened to the rain dripping from the eaves, heard the courthouse clock strike one, and then two, and then three. She was still awake when the sky started to brighten in the east. She remembered the first morning of school back in September and how she'd heard Jean moving about in her room early, before anyone else was up and around. Mary Ellen had been thrilled for her. It was only the beginning, she told herself. They would have years and years. Neither of them knew that Charlie Camplain was about to check out of the Grand Hotel in Vincennes and engage Grinny Haines to drive him to Lawrenceville.

Mary Ellen lay in bed now, thinking about how people always left her. Edward died, and Robbie said it was because he was so desperate to get away from her. Surely, it wasn't true. Surely he'd loved her as she'd loved him. It was just that time got in the way—time and what it did to people.

She heard Robbie's footsteps in the hall, and she almost called out to her, but something held her back. It was as if there was always something between them, some barrier that they'd almost broken down in the aftermath of Jean's death, what with the story of Tom Heath and that girl, Millie Haines, but now there was what Robbie had said about Mary Ellen and Jean, and the meeting with the school board that evening, and it was too much, it was all too much, and as Mary Ellen listened to Robbie come back from the bathroom and shut her bedroom door behind her, she wondered how it was that love ever survived.

Had she loved Jean? She most certainly had. Had they been lovers? No. Had she wanted them to be? Mary Ellen imagined these sorts of questions and more from Mr. Heath at the school board meeting. No, she hadn't. She'd only wanted...what was it exactly that she'd found with Jean? Where were the words to make that plain? She didn't have them. She only knew how she'd felt when Jean was near. She'd felt happy. She'd felt truly, truly happy, and what's more, she'd felt as if she'd had a reason to get out of bed each morning. She had this lovely young girl. She had someone who needed her.

Now Mary Ellen feared what was to come—not so much what would happen with her job, although she would be sad to not be able to keep it, but more what damage might result with Robbie, who had started talking about going to college now that she no longer had dreams of marrying Tom Heath. Somewhere away from there, she said. Champaign, maybe, or Carbondale, Bloomington. Somewhere, Mary Ellen knew she meant, where she could hide, remake herself, forget all of this. Somewhere where she'd be like Jean, starting over, having a new life, and Mary Ellen wouldn't be there to share it with her. That was her biggest fear, being alone while her daughter became the woman she wanted to be.

The courthouse clock struck six. With a sigh, Mary Ellen lifted herself from the bed. Nothing to do but get ready to face the day, perhaps the last day she'd be able to call herself a teacher.

Not a sound from Robbie's room, and Mary Ellen assumed she'd finally fallen asleep. Soon she would have to call for her, but not now. For now, she'd let her sleep. Robbie was her daughter. It was still Mary Ellen's prerogative to make her a gift like this. Over the years, she'd paid her countless sacrifices and acts of kindness, many that Robbie had never even known. Here was one more: a few more minutes of escape into sleep before she would have to come back to her life.

❧

On the way to school, Robbie barely said a word. She sat in her mother's car, her schoolbooks cradled to her chest, and stared straight ahead down Tenth Street. It was a sunny day, but wet leaves were stuck to the sidewalks and street from the rain the evening before, and there was a cold wind blowing. A boy walking to school had his hand clasped on top of his head, holding down his red ball cap. He leaned into the wind.

Finally, Robbie said to her mother, "What time are you to be at the school board meeting?"

"Seven," her mother said.

"I want to go with you."

Her mother came to a stop at State Street and waited for traffic to clear. She frowned at Robbie. "Now why in the world would you want to do that, Robbie Sue?"

"I'll tell them the truth. Whatever they want to know about you and Miss De Belle, I'll tell them."

"Perhaps you've already said enough."

Her mother pressed down on the gas pedal, and the car shot across State Street and then dipped down the long hill to the high school with a force that made Robbie's stomach drop. She'd always liked it when her father had done that, and he'd said, "Don't lose your gizzard." This morning, though, she didn't like it a bit.

"Have you ever thought about that?" her mother said. "Maybe you should leave well enough alone."

But Robbie couldn't stop thinking about it, the fact that what she'd said might cost her mother her job. She'd said those things out of jealousy because her mother had been so close to Miss De Belle. Every time she saw them sitting together in the porch swing, every time her mother held her hand or called her *Jean, dear*, Robbie felt as if she were very, very far away, a stranger to her mother, who had found the daughter she'd always longed for in the company of Miss De Belle.

Through all of her classes, Robbie kept checking her wristwatch, watching the minutes move toward midmorning, and then noon.

And when noon finally came, she found herself walking to the cafeteria just like this was any ordinary day. As she got closer, she heard the rattle of dishes and silverware and the rising voices and laughter of those already inside. Then she heard a quiet voice behind her say, "Robbie. Robbie, please wait."

She knew it was Tom Heath, and when she turned around, sure enough, he was there.

"What do you want?" she said.

She kept her voice stern, but the truth was, inside, she felt her stomach flip—a flash of recognition, a spreading glow of happiness—just like she'd always felt seeing Tom when they were steadies. He'd just had a haircut, and she could see the white skin above his ears. He raised a hand and patted the side of his head, and she knew that he was self-conscious about the new haircut and how it made it seem that his ears were even bigger and stuck out even more. She knew so much about him. She knew he cried last summer when his collie dog, Scout, got sick and died. She knew he liked to do impressions of celebrities—John Wayne, Jimmy Stewart, Jimmy Durante—but he'd only do them for her. She knew that sometimes he liked to go to the Old Cathedral in Vincennes, even though he wasn't Catholic, just to sit and think.

These were their secrets. What was she to do with them—what was she to do with all these things she knew—now that they were no longer a couple?

"You look nice today," Tom said. "But, heck, you look nice every day."

He was blushing. Robbie felt a smile forming and she ducked her head so he wouldn't see how much he'd pleased her. She looked down at the skirt of her plaid jumper, at her bobby sox and saddle shoes. Nothing out of the ordinary. Nothing special.

"It's just me," she said with a shrug of her shoulders. She pressed her lips together in a tight line.

"Here's the thing." Tom swallowed hard, and she watched his Adam's apple slide up and down in his throat. "There's so much happening right now. I'm going to have to testify, Robbie. The state's attorney told my dad I'm going to be called as a witness for the prosecution."

"Charlie Camplain?" Robbie said.

Tom nodded. "I feel my whole life changing, and the only one I want to talk about any of it with is you, but I know I can't because I was stupid."

"Yes, you were," Robbie said.

"I don't want to be a witness." He lowered his voice to a whisper. "And I don't want to be a father."

His voice was shaking. Robbie could tell he was close to tears. She tried to harden herself to him, but it was all she could do to keep from reaching out and touching him on the arm.

"It's a little late to do anything about the second one," she said, and he gave her a sad smile.

"Her dad and my dad had a talk."

"I know. My mother showed Mr. Haines how to get to your house."

"They've agreed on some things." Robbie waited for him to go on. "Looks like my mom and dad are going to raise the baby."

Robbie felt her cheeks go hot. "*Your* baby," she said.

"Yes, *my* baby. But that doesn't mean that Millie and me are going to amount to anything."

"I guess you never know," Robbie said.

"No, trust me."

She laughed. "Trust you. Ha! That's the funniest thing I've heard all day."

And with that, she turned away from him.

"Maybe I could call you sometime?" he said. "Maybe that would be all right?"

She kept walking, her heart beating fast. The last thing she heard him say was, "You know if I have to testify, you can bet you will, too."

❧

And indeed that afternoon's mail brought subpoenas for both her and her mother.

"Now of all times," her mother said, and then she went upstairs and Robbie heard her close the door to her bedroom.

The phone rang, and Robbie picked it up.

It was Tom calling. She'd picked up that phone countless times and heard his voice on the other end. "Hidey-hidey-hi," he always said, and they gabbed for hours. Then he told her about Millie Haines, and just like that, she felt herself cut away from him. Now he was back.

"Hidey-hidey-hi," he said, in a timid voice.

For a good while, she didn't answer. She stood at the front window, looking out on the twilight. The streetlights were on. The tree limbs were stark against the dimming sky. Robbie pressed her palm to the glass and felt the cold outside. A shiver went down her neck.

"Robbie?" Tom said.

She knew she could hang up, *should* hang up, but she finally said, "I'm here."

"Would you maybe want to go for a drive tonight? You know, just to talk, just to be together."

"Not tonight. I can't tonight." She bit her lip when she realized what she'd said and what he'd heard: *Not tonight, but maybe some night. Maybe yes.* "I can't," she said. "I just can't." Then: "Don't you know what's happening tonight? Surely you must."

"That's why I thought you might like to go for a drive. You know, to get your mind off your mother and the school board."

"You don't know anything, Tom Heath." She heard the snap in her voice. "Your father's out to ruin my mother. You ought to know that."

Then she hung up. She heard her mother moving around upstairs. Robbie checked her wristwatch. It was nearly six thirty. Her mother had insisted again that Robbie not attend the school board meeting: "There's nothing you can possibly do to help."

Robbie grabbed her coat and purse from where she'd thrown them on the sofa. She opened the front door as quietly as she could and slipped out into the night.

❧

Mary Ellen took a deep breath and opened the heavy door to the auditorium. The school board members were gathering on the stage.

They were shaking hands and clasping elbows. Seven of them, some of them in suits of dark serge or gray flannel. A few of them in sport coats of tweed or corduroy, the collars of their shirts open.

From the back of the auditorium, Mary Ellen recognized them all—Mr. Cunningham, the attorney; Mr. Bennett, the insurance agent; Mr. Lankford, the doctor; Mr. Yosowitz, the tailor; Mr. Piper, the owner of the radio station; Mr. McGaughey, the pharmacist; and, of course, Mr. Heath. He was standing behind a folding chair at the head of a long table on the stage. He had a leather-bound portfolio open on the table and was reviewing his notes, a fountain pen in his right hand. Lily Wagner was already sitting on a folding chair to his right, her steno pad open, a pencil lying on top of it and another one behind her right ear, prepared, as she always was, Mary Ellen thought, for the unexpected glitch as she was taking the minutes. She raised her head and looked at Mary Ellen. She even ventured a shy wave and a grin. Lily had a paisley scarf of red and white candy cane stripes around her neck and knotted at her throat, and Mary Ellen thought, *How pretty.* It made her think of how soon the holidays would be upon them, first Thanksgiving and then Christmas, and who knew whether there'd be any joy for her then?

Mr. Heath put his hands on the back of his chair, leaned toward Lily and said something to her. She didn't appear to hear him. She was still looking to the back of the auditorium. Mr. Heath followed her gaze and saw Mary Ellen. He rocked back on his heels and let his fountain pen drop onto the open portfolio. He put his left hand into his trousers' pocket, very casual, as if this were just any old night—just another school board meeting, ho-hum—and not the night when they would all decide Mary Ellen's fate.

She knew these men, had known them for years. She'd shopped in their stores, utilized their services, asked their advice, taught their children. Now she was to sit before them, forced to defend herself when she was innocent, and even if she were who they said she was, where was the shame in that? Why would that be something that needed defending? Her only fault was she'd loved Jean De Belle too much, and she'd wanted Jean to love her in return. Given all the loneliness in the world, where was the crime in that?

"Don't be scared, Mary Ellen." Mr. Pomeroy was at her elbow. She could smell the cold air on him and the strong menthol of his Aqua Velva aftershave, the same lotion her Ed had always worn. "This isn't the Nuremberg Trials," Mr. Pomeroy said.

Mary Ellen narrowed her eyes and glared at him. "More like the Salem witch trials," she said, and then moved on down the aisle toward the stage.

She was never able to walk into the auditorium without thinking of the morning of September 3, the morning she had sat next to Jean on the stage and told her not to be nervous, everything would be just fine. Then Charlie Camplain had come, and Mary Ellen had heard the shots, and she ran down the stairs and found Jean in that empty classroom, slumped in the chair behind the desk, her finger bent in such an unnatural way. Little by little, Mary Ellen came to understand that she was dead, that someone had shot her, and that was the beginning of everything that led to the here and now.

Mr. Lankford snapped off the punch line to a joke. "One's a snack cracker, and the other's a crack snacker!"

Mr. McGaughey and Mr. Piper tossed their heads back and laughed. Then Mr. Yowowitz, who hadn't been amused, saw Mary Ellen, and he put his hand on Mr. Lankford's shoulder and leaned in close to say something to him. Then all of the men were looking at her, and Mary Ellen could tell from the way they acted like boys who'd been caught at something—ducking their heads, sticking their hands in their trouser pockets—that the joke, whatever it was, had been one they hated thinking that she might have heard.

"Gentlemen," Mr. Pomeroy said, all business. He picked up his fountain pen and uncapped it. "Mrs. McVeigh is here. We can begin."

She sat at a chair to Mr. Pomeroy's left, her back to the empty auditorium because this was a special closed session, not open to the public as the regular monthly meetings were. Lily Wagner sat across from her, and she was all business now, too, because this was a serious meeting, one intended to determine, Mr. Pomeroy said, whether the district should terminate Mary Ellen's contract.

The men had questions for her. Later, she would try to recall who had said what, but it would all be a blur of voices, a gathering of coughs and sighs and cleared throats, a flash of gold tie tacks and cuff links, a compilation of scents: tweed and hair oil and shoe polish and ink.

They wanted to know about the nature of her relationship with Miss De Belle. *She lived with you in your house, didn't she?*

"She rented a room from me."

And your feelings about her?

"We were friends...colleagues. I believed we might have become great friends, had we had the chance."

A brief silence fell over the meeting at that point, everyone acknowledging the tragedy of Jean's murder.

Then Mr. Heath—Mary Ellen would remember this part quite well— said, "We have information that leads us to believe that you and Miss De Belle might have…" Here, he seemed to lose his words. He reached for the pitcher of water on the table and poured some into a tumbler. "That you might have…" He started again, but Mary Ellen wouldn't let him finish.

She said, "That we might have been lovers? Is that the word you're having trouble finding, Mr. Heath?"

"There are rumors, Mrs. McVeigh," Mr. Yozowitz said. He was a kindly man, a survivor of the Dachau death camp in Germany. A polite, soft-spoken man with a slender frame and a bald head. Mary Ellen would later feel guilty for how she snapped at him.

"And are rumors the purview of this board?" she said.

Mr. Yozowitz cast his eyes to the table.

Mr. Piper took up the line of questioning. He was a beefy man with a red face. His forehead was sweating, and his large Masonic ring kept clinking against his water glass as he spoke. "Our job is to investigate, Mrs. McVeigh." He had that deep, sonorous radio man's voice. "Our job is to get to the bottom of things."

"I won't be on trial here," she said. "I've done nothing wrong. Nothing to be ashamed of. Nothing to feel guilty about."

"We have this note." Mr. Lankford slid it across the table so Mary Ellen could see it. He was the family doctor, the only one Mary Ellen and her family had ever seen. He had a pencil moustache and a scent of antiseptic about him. "Do you recognize it?"

Of course she did. She didn't even have to look. The paper on which she'd written those lines from Sappho, those lines about love shaking the heart, which she'd left for Jean to find. Those lines she'd imagined Jean saving, and then, when she was as old as Mary Ellen and the day in and day out had started to wear on her, she'd look at those lines and remember what it felt like the very first day she was a teacher. That would be enough to remind her of what she loved. That would be enough to save her.

"I've already discussed this with Mr. Pomeroy," Mary Ellen said. "It was a gift to Miss De Belle. Something to mark her first day as a teacher." Here, Mary Ellen's voice broke, and tears came to her eyes. Lily Wagner took a white hankie with an embroidered border of purple from the sleeve of her blouse and reached it across the table. Mary Ellen took it and dabbed at her eyes. "I thought Jean would appreciate it. It was a kindness, nothing more."

What about these other things? the men wanted to know. *What about the reports of holding hands, of being seen together at Delzell's, or the Candle Lite, even the Avalon Theater.*

"Can't two women be friends?" Mary Ellen said.

Mr. Heath cleared his throat. He lifted his chin and pointed it at her. "What about the fact that your own daughter described your relationship with Miss De Belle as…" He glanced down at his notes, then looked at Mary Ellen again. "Lovey-dovey," he said. "That's the words she used."

He made a check mark by that note with his fountain pen and waited, one eyebrow lifted, for Mary Ellen to answer.

But what came instead was a voice from the back of the auditorium, a voice Mary Ellen immediately recognized as Robbie's.

"I didn't mean it," she called out, and Mary Ellen turned and saw her there, looking so small at the end of the aisle. She was wearing the pale blue swagger jacket that she wore to church, the one with the black mohair collar, and the three-quarter length sleeves that flared at her elbows. She had on a white blouse and a black pencil skirt, and Mary Ellen's knew she was doing her best to look grown up and responsible. "I said a silly thing." Robbie was walking down the aisle toward the stage. "It wasn't true." The men on the stage sat there, looking down on her, their faces severe. Even though Mary Ellen had told her not to come, here she was, and Mary Ellen thought how brave she was to face these men who sat in judgment.

Mr. Heath was the first to speak to her. "Robbie, this is hardly the place for you tonight."

"It's exactly the place for me," Robbie said, and Mary Ellen was proud of the clarity of her voice. "This is my mother you're talking about. I won't let you make something of her that she's not. She's a good teacher is what she is." Robbie caught Mary Ellen's eye and held it for a moment. "She's a good mother, too," she said.

Mary Ellen wanted to go to her and wrap her up in her arms, but she knew this wasn't the time to show how much she admired her, how much she loved her, how sorry she was for the years of distance between them. This was a time for strength. Mary Ellen knew that, and she could tell that Robbie did, too.

Mr. Heath said, "Are you saying that you lied? Young lady, are you saying we can't trust anything that you say?"

Mary Ellen knew that Mr. Heath was trying to twist logic and catch Robbie in its snare.

"Mr. Heath," Mary Ellen said with indignation—but she soon saw she needn't worry about Robbie, for Robbie said, "Mr. Heath, if you want to talk about trust, perhaps we should begin with your son."

Mary Ellen saw Mr. Heath take in a breath. He seemed to hold it. Then he let it out with a sigh, and it was like the air was going out of him. His shoulders slumped. His chest deflated. He could no longer look at Robbie. He looked at Mr. Pomeroy instead, and Mr. Pomeroy said, "Thank you for coming, Robbie. I'm sure your love for your mother is very great. But we now have business to finish, and this *is* a closed session. I'm sure you understand."

"I do," said Robbie. "I've said what I came to say. There's not a word of truth to these rumors. I was a silly girl for a long time, but I'm not now. I'm telling you straight out. The students of this school need my mother. You'll be hurting them if you let her go."

With that, Robbie did an elegant turn, the skirted swagger coat swirling about her legs, and with her shoulders back and her spine straight, she left the auditorium.

"We have one more testimony to investigate," Mr. Heath said. "The testimony of…" Again, he glanced down at his notes. "Etta Lawless."

At first, Mary Ellen didn't know who he meant. Then it came to her. Etta, the girl who'd said that odd thing at the homecoming dance, that thing about seeing Mary Ellen and Jean that morning in the library.

"Now you're taking the word of odd ducks like her?" Mary Ellen said.

She knew right away she'd been wrong to say it. She seemed defensive and insensitive to students like Etta. She wanted to take it back, but it was too late.

Mr. Pomeroy gave her a stern look over the tops of his spectacles. "We have to remember," he said, "that not all of our students have had the same advantages. Surely, you'd agree with that, Mary Ellen."

Mary Ellen had no response. She folded her hands in her lap and sat there, chastised.

Mr. Heath went on, reading from his notes. "Miss Lawless reports that on the morning of September 3, the first day of classes, she saw you kiss Miss De Belle in the library."

"On the cheek," Mary Ellen said. "A friendly kiss on the cheek for good luck."

The men sat there for a good while, none of them saying a word. Lily Wagner kept looking down at her steno pad, a blush creeping up her neck to her cheeks.

Mary Ellen knew how it all looked, if that's what someone was indeed hoping to find. The note left in Jean's purse, the number of times the two of them had been seen together uptown or on the porch swing at the house, the kiss in the library. Mary Ellen had no idea that Etta Lawless had seen that kiss, and even though there was absolutely nothing for Mary Ellen to feel guilty about, she couldn't help but feel, here in the presence of these men, that the girl had seen something she shouldn't have. And why had she come forward? The kiss should have meant nothing to her at all, but obviously it was something that she kept worrying and worrying until she felt she had to tell someone.

Finally, Mr. Heath spoke. "Do you deny the kiss?"

It had happened. To say it hadn't would be to deny all that she'd felt for Jean—all that she felt still—and more than that, it would feel like a betrayal of this young woman who had come so briefly into her life at exactly the time she needed her youth, her enthusiasm, her blessing.

"No, I don't deny it," Mary Ellen said.

"I didn't think so," said Mr. Heath.

A few more uncomfortable moments of silence went by. Then Mr. Pomeroy said to Mr. Heath, "Do you have everything you need?"

Mr. Heath glanced around the table. "Gentlemen, are we all satisfied?"

One by one, the men nodded their heads.

And with that, Mary Ellen was free to go—free to wait, she knew, for Mr. Pomeroy to call and let her know what the board had decided.

"You're making a mistake," she said. Then she gathered up her coat and her purse and left the auditorium.

Robbie was standing outside the doors. "What now?" she said.

Mary Ellen gathered her into her arms. "Now, we go home," she said.

23

THAT RAINY NIGHT, THE VERY night that Grinny Haines came close to dying but didn't, Norville went to Lorene and said, "It doesn't matter what you did in the past. None of it matters to me. Lorene, I love you, and I'm ready for us to have the life we both deserve."

They were standing in her living room. He'd caught her about to go to bed. Her hair was in curlers. She was wearing a chenille bathrobe. Her glass held the last swallow of a Schlitz. She put it down on the coffee table.

"Are you asking me to marry you?" She reached up and took one curler from her hair. The lock it had been holding sprang out wildly over her forehead. She started to reach for another curler and stopped, her hand in the air. "Surely you're not," she said. "What would you want with someone like me?"

The living room was neat and cozy. Old quilts hung from the walls and on wooden racks. A Bible with a pair of wire-rimmed eyeglasses on top of it—her father's—lay on the fireplace mantle. Oil lamps with their tall glass chimneys sat at either end. A blue wicker sewing basket sat on the floor by Lorene's armchair. The basket's lid was open, and Norville could see a skein of red yarn and two knitting needles.

He wanted to lose no more time. He wanted to be able to switch off the tea lamp on the table by the window and take Lorene's hand and lead her off to bed. He wanted to sleep beside her all the night through, comforted by the steady rhythm of her breath, the warmth of her body. He wanted to have this life with her in this home where he felt at ease.

"That is what I'm asking." He got down on one knee—so many times he'd dreamed this moment—and he took her hand. He didn't have a ring to offer her, but he was determined to wait no longer. Something about his experience at Grinny's house, the ugliness of the loud voices inside, had left him impatient with loneliness. "It's exactly what I'm asking. Lorene Devereux, will you do me the honor of being my bride?"

She let her free arm drop to her side. Her voice was barely a whisper. "I never thought," she said, and then for a moment, she couldn't go on. Norville squeezed her hand. "I never thought anyone would want me," she said. "Not after what I did. I never believed I'd find love, and now here you are."

"Here I am, Lorene."

"Aren't we a pair?"

She got down on her knees in front of him. She took his face in her hands and brought her lips to his. He thought of the September morning when Charlie Camplain had checked out of the Grand and he'd dropped that picture of Jean De Belle. He said he had a ring for her. He said he was going to change her life. Norville hadn't known the long path he was about to go down because he'd bumped up against Charlie Camplain. He hadn't known where he was going, but he did now. No one was there to stand as witness, but here they were—he, a man of a certain age; she, a woman of like years—and though Norville knew it was insignificant really, in light of all the suffering that people endured, just a speck in the dust of the universe, he still felt himself tremble here on the verge of the rest of his life. He'd dreamed it so long—this moment, this surrender, this love.

"Are you saying yes, Lorene?"

Her arms were around his neck, and she was holding him as if she never wanted to let go. "Yes," she said. "Yes, I'm saying yes."

∽❧∽

Norville received the subpoena that Monday. It arrived by certified mail. An order to appear before the state's attorney in Lawrenceville in the matter of the murder of Jean De Belle.

"It's starting," he told Lorene that evening, when they were having supper at her house. She'd been talking to him about wedding plans. She'd been saying that she wanted to get married at the Old Cathedral, and, yes, she wanted a white wedding dress, because she'd never walked down the aisle before and she meant to do it up in style.

Then he said, "It's starting," and she said, "Well, forgive me for acting like a love-struck girl. I thought you'd be happy."

"I am happy," he said. "I'm ecstatic."

Then he showed her the subpoena.

"What's this mean?" She laid the subpoena on the table by her dinner plate and tapped it with a fingernail. "Norville?"

"I'll have to give a deposition." He sat with his fists on the table, his fork in his right hand, his knife in his left. "They'll want to know what I remember from that morning in September." He turned his head so he could see out the dining room window. The days were growing shorter. Already dusk was coming on. The temperature had only been fifty-three that afternoon, and now a cold front had moved through. He could see the wind moving through the holly bushes outside. On his walk from his house to Lorene's, he'd felt the cold, and now he swore he saw a few spits of snow in the air. "It's starting," he said again. "They're getting ready for Charlie Camplain's trial. I'll have to testify."

He laid down his knife and fork and got up from the table. He walked over to the window and stood there feeling the cold air that was leaking in around the frame. He'd have to remember to run a bead of caulk around it. It was time to get ready for winter.

Lorene came to him, and she put her arm across his back and rested her head on his shoulder.

"Is that a bad thing?" she said. "You seem so sad."

"That morning," he said. "I remember everything about it. I remember Camplain checking out and how he showed me the ring he had for her, for Miss De Belle, and how it gave me the nudge I needed to ask you to marry me."

"You never told me that."

"I got off work, and I walked straight over to Raymond Hardy's to tell him to leave you alone, to tell him you and I were going to be a permanent couple." Here, he stopped, and he moved away from Lorene so that she wasn't touching him anymore. "That's why I don't like remembering that morning. Not because of Camplain and what he did. Because that was the day I found out that all along you'd been with Raymond."

"It was a stupid thing." She sighed. "It was always you I loved, Norville. I swear."

"I'm just saying it still hurts to know what I know." He stuck his hands in his trousers pockets and rocked up on the balls of his feet. He shrugged his shoulders. "Sorry. Can't help it. That subpoena called it all up in me."

She was beside him again. She touched his face. "That's all behind us now," she said. "You know that, don't you. I'm going to marry you."

"Yes," he said, "I know."

"You'll do what you have to do at that trial, and our life together will go on. It'll be glorious, Norville. I've dreamed of it for so long."

"I just want you to know that sometimes it comes up on me unexpected, and I'm standing at Raymond's door again, and I'm hearing the shower running, and then you ask him to bring you a towel, and…well, it's all too much for me."

"Me, too," she said. "I wonder, though, if we have to remember those times to remind ourselves how lucky we are. We lived through all of that, and here we are, still in love."

"More than ever?" he asked.

"More than ever," she said. "You know it to be true, don't you?"

For a good while, he looked at her, saw the hint of a grimace at the corners of her mouth, took note of the pleading in her eyes, urging him to say yes, to please say yes, understood that she was afraid he might turn away from her.

"Yes," he said, "I do."

She threw her arms around his neck, and he held onto her, held her there while the last of the daylight faded, pressed his face into her hair and breathed in the scent of her Aqua Net, held her while she cried a little, and he said, "Shh, shh, shh. There's nothing to cry about. Everything will be just fine."

24

GRINNY WASN'T SO SURE, EVEN though he and Mr. Heath had come to an agreement. Millie would have the baby, and the Heaths would adopt it. They'd allow Millie and Grinny and Peg the opportunity to visit and to be a part of the child's life. They'd take care of all of Millie's doctors' bills.

"But the baby will be yours," Grinny said. He sat in Mr. Heath's den in a club chair of tufted leather. Mr. Heath paced back and forth behind his desk. He picked up a glass paperweight the size of a softball—crystal, Grinny decided—and tossed it into the air and let it smack against his waiting palm. The ease with which he did that shamed Grinny. An object so fine and surely expensive, tossed and caught with confidence, no thought at all that it might drop and shatter. Grinny understood that he'd never know what it was like to have that kind of hold on things.

"It's only right," said Mr. Heath. "My wife and I are younger…" Then his voice trailed off, and he looked down at his feet for just a split second before lifting his head and smiling at Grinny. "Well, you see what I'm saying, don't you?"

Grinny knew exactly what he was saying—that he and Mrs. Heath would give the child a better home than a cab driver and his aging wife. Grinny bristled now over all he'd agreed to when he'd accepted Mr. Heath's offer. Not only had he given over Millie's baby, he'd admitted, in so doing, that his life had always been the wrong kind of life, not the kind of life that gave them a right to the child.

Mr. Heath was right. Already, they were stretched thin. What sort of life would they be able to give that baby?

One of love. That was something that Grinny knew for sure, and it was what kept him going back to the moment he'd shaken Mr. Heath's hand and said, "All right, then."

He wished he could go back and change his mind. He wished he'd never given Millie's baby away. He knew, no matter how willing the Heaths were to share the child, he and Peg and Millie would never be able to give him or her the advantages that the Heaths could. Grinny imagined he and Peg and Millie showing up at their grand house for a visit: Peg in her plain cotton dress or the wool coat with the frayed sleeve and the worn lapels, Millie looking so tiny and afraid, and him with his porkpie hat in his hands and his toothless grin. What could they offer that would ever be enough? How would they ever avoid seeming poor and wanting?

Still, the arrangement was one that would save the child. Grinny was looking forward to returning the five hundred dollars to Raymond Hardy, along with the interest he requested—provided, of course, by Mr. Heath, but still, it would give Grinny great satisfaction to know he'd resisted that sin, to be able to tell Raymond that he wouldn't be needing Dr. Claridge's help after all.

"You're going to have the baby," Grinny said to Millie when he came back from Lawrenceville that evening.

She was curled up on her bed, her cheeks still wet with tears. "You mean…"

Grinny didn't want to hear her say the word, so he cut her off. "Mr. Heath and I struck a deal."

He went on to explain that the Heaths would raise the child, but that Millie would be able to be a part of its life.

"I don't want to have to see him," she said.

"Him?"

"Tom. I don't ever want to see him again."

Grinny nodded. "I'll see what I can do about that." He went to her then, and sat on the edge of her bed and laid his hand to her face, the way he'd done so many times when she'd been a child herself. "It's the best I could do," he said to her. "If I had the money, I'd give you and the baby the moon and the stars."

"I know you would, Papa," she said, and then she put her hand on top of his, and like that they went on.

It was a Monday when Grinny came home from work and found the envelope from the Lawrence County state's attorney waiting for him.

"I didn't dare open it," Peg said.

She was peeling potatoes at the kitchen sink. The envelope was on the table. Grinny looked at it for a long time. He was afraid to open it, too.

"You have to," Peg said.

So he took a pen knife from his pocket and slit the envelope and took out the paper inside and handed it to Peg. "You read it," he said.

She dried her hands on her apron. She held the paper under the fluorescent ring above the sink.

"It's a subpoena," she finally said. "You have to appear on November 12."

"Charlie Camplain," he said.

Peg nodded.

"I'm going to have to tell them what I know. I'm going to have to live that day all over."

That was the day he'd found out that Millie was pregnant.

Peg said, "I know it's been hard, Bert, but we're going to get through everything just fine. You're a good man. You've proven that. You're looking out for our little girl."

That was what broke him: Peg's forgiveness for what he'd almost done, her trust in him to do better, his awareness that he'd never be able to do enough. His voice wavered when he finally spoke. Tears filled his eyes.

"Peg, old girl," he said. "I wish I could do more."

She came to him and held him to her. "She knows that, Bert," she said. "Millie knows that."

And they stood there until they heard Millie coming down the stairs, calling out, "When's supper? Golly, I'm starved."

25

Norville told the state's attorney all that he remembered, and Grinny did the same, as did Tom Heath, and Robbie, and Mary Ellen. One by one, they climbed the steps to the courthouse, and sat in the state's attorney's office and recalled the events of the morning of September 3.

"It was a beautiful day," Norville said, consulting his ledger. "The high temperature was 83 degrees. The first day of school." Then he told the story of Charlie Camplain checking out of the Grand Hotel that morning and needing a cab to take him to Lawrenceville, where, so he claimed, he was going to propose to Miss Jean De Belle. "I thought he had the world on a string," Norville said. "How marvelous. It was such a lovely day. It seemed like a day made for new beginnings."

"He was spiffy," Grinny said. "Looked like a million bucks. I picked him up at the Grand, and I thought maybe my luck was going to change. I didn't know it then, but he told me later, and mister, I believed him. He said, 'I'm a dangerous man.' I wish I could have stopped him. I wish I'd never taken him where he wanted to go."

Tom Heath was so nervous he had a hard time keeping his voice steady. "He was crazy all right, that man, that Charlie Camplain. He had a gun." Tom told the story of driving Camplain to Westport and how he played Russian roulette as Tom drove. Then at the Showboat, Camplain made him get out of the car, and he kept that gun on him until the cab driver, Mr. Haines, made it so he could get away. "I thought someone was going to die," Tom said. "I didn't know what he'd done to Miss De Belle. It makes you think, doesn't it?" About what? the state's attorney wanted to know. "About all of it, I guess," Tom said. "Everything we do and where it takes us."

Robbie was waiting in the outer office when the frosted glass door to the state's attorney's office opened, and out walked Tom Heath. All the color was gone from his face. He was wearing a shirt and a tie, and his face was almost as white as that shirt. "Robbie," he said, and she would think later it was like he thought there might still be a chance for them, and who was to say that there wouldn't be.

"I've decided to go to college," she told him.

"That's good," he said, but she could tell he didn't mean it. He knew that once she was gone from Lawrenceville, she'd likely be gone for good, and there he'd be with whatever life he'd already started to make, that night with Millie Haines. "That's good," he said again. And then there was nothing else to say. The state's attorney was standing in the open door, and he was calling Robbie's name, and she had to go inside and leave Tom behind her.

Mary Ellen had just come into the outer office after visiting the ladies' room to try to compose herself.

"Mrs. McVeigh," Tom said. "I'm so sorry."

She could barely bring herself to look at him. "About what?" she asked.

"So much," he said. "About everything."

She stood there, letting the boy feel what he did, letting him get familiar with regret. She wouldn't let him know this, but she was trying to get familiar with it, too. The regret she felt over how she had let herself fall in love with Jean De Belle and given her heart over to what she imagined might be theirs. The lines from that poem, that kiss on the cheek, and here she was for the first time in over twenty years with no classes to teach, no students to instruct.

Later on that Monday evening, her phone rang, and on the other end of the line was Mr. Pomeroy, and he said, "Mary Ellen." And of course she knew what the board had decided from the somber tone of his voice, and she said, "Well, what did I expect?" Her contract was to be terminated immediately. A substitute would be in place for the next day's classes. Mr. Pomeroy suggested that she wait until the next evening to come to the school, and the custodian would let her in so she could gather any personal items. "It's a small town, Mary Ellen. Parents talk. It was that kiss. If it hadn't been for that, I might have been able to defend you. If only you'd denied that…"

She didn't respond. She laid the receiver back onto its cradle and stood there a long, long time, trying to imagine what life would be like for her now. Then she heard Robbie at the top of the stairs. "Mother?" she said in a tremulous voice.

Mary Ellen wouldn't turn around. She straightened her back. "It's done," she said, and she waited until she heard Robbie's footsteps coming down the stairs, and she let her come up behind her and put her arms around her waist the way she had when she'd been a little girl.

"Maybe it won't be so bad," Mary Ellen said. Then she turned and took Robbie into her arms, and Robbie said, "It's my fault." And Mary Ellen said, "Things happen, and we don't know why right away. We have to be patient. We have to wait and see. Sometimes it can seem like the end, when really it's a brand-new start."

Now, she said to Tom, "Nothing to be sorry about. People do what they do, and then life goes on. That's what you'll find out when you're older. Life goes on until it doesn't anymore, and then there you are."

He gave her a puzzled look. "Where?" he asked.

She said it as kindly as she could. "At the end, of course. At the very end."

26

So it came to pass, in the months to follow, that the days stretched on from autumn to winter to spring.

Charlie Camplain's trial took place in December. He'd confessed to the murder at the time of his arrest in September, but since that time, he'd changed his plea from guilty to innocent.

"They made me say I did it," he said. "The sheriff and his boys. They roughed me up pretty good. I never would've hurt Jean. I loved her, and she loved me. She was going to be my wife."

His attorney argued that Sheriff Malone had coerced the confession, so the court seated a jury, and the trial began.

And again, one by one, Norville and Grinny and Tom and Robbie and Mary Ellen took the stand and said what they knew about that day in September.

Camplain's attorney, a Mr. Tucker, tried to discredit each witness, and in this way, things they wished might never be spoken of again were announced in court, reported in the newspaper, and entered onto the trial transcripts that anyone, years in the future, could read.

Mr. Tucker was a man without sentiment—a shark, someone said, who feasted off blood in the water. He had silver hair that he wore in a flattop, the bristles atop his head stiff with butch wax, and he was dressed impeccably, as was his client. Crisp white shirts, dark neckties, dark suits.

Charlie Camplain's father was there. He sat staring straight ahead, his jaw set, his fedora resting on his knee.

And Jean De Belle's parents were there offering testimony about Charlie's Camplain's drinking and temper. They gave their testimony on the final day of the trial and were gone before the verdict came down.

How Mr. Tucker knew what he knew, no one could say. It was as if he'd somehow been listening in on their conversations and following their comings and goings all that autumn. Snow was falling outside the courthouse, and the pine flocking and the lighted stars on the street lamps were tossing about in the wind. Inside the courtroom, the light grew dim, and everyone listened to Mr. Tucker's cross-examination of the State's witnesses, and by the end of the three days, everyone in Lawrenceville and all the parts there around knew that Norville Rich was to marry Lorene Devereux in spite of her rather checkered past, a past that included sexual liaisons with various men, at least one of which—"Isn't it true, Mr. Rich?"—ended in an illegal termination of a pregnancy.

And wasn't it true that Mr. Haines had been distracted on the morning of September 3, distraught over the news he'd received that morning that his sixteen-year-old daughter was with child? And wasn't it true that Tom Heath was the boy who'd fathered that child?

Which of course unsettled Miss McVeigh and her mother, since Tom was Miss McVeigh's boyfriend.

And when it came to Mrs. McVeigh and the victim, Miss De Belle—"Well, isn't it true, Mrs. McVeigh, that you were relieved of your teaching duties out of a suspicion that you and Miss De Belle were involved in, shall we say, an unnatural relationship?"

Even though the state's attorney voiced his objections and sometimes succeeded in having certain testimony stricken from the record, it all got said, and enough of it stuck to make each of the witnesses regret the things they'd done.

"Seems to me," Mr. Tucker finally said, "there was a good deal of upset going on that morning. How in the world could any of you be sure of what you saw and heard?"

Finally, Mr. Tucker put Charlie Camplain on the stand, and asked him to describe his military service, the injury to his hearing, his time at Walter Reed Hospital, his experiences at Eastern Illinois University. Camplain cupped his hand to his ear and leaned forward in the chair on the stand. He had to ask Mr. Tucker to repeat himself, and he fiddled with the volume on his hearing aid until it squealed, and he pulled the wire from his ear, and tears came down his cheeks, and he said, "This is my life. This has always been my life—a life of being on the outside— ever since I served my country in the war."

Then he told the story of how the boys in his rooming house at Eastern called him "Dummy" and made fun of him behind his back because of his hearing.

"Jean was the only thing good in my life," he said. "She was my light."

It was a good performance, and the people who sat in that courtroom and watched it couldn't help but feel sorry for him, but still, facts were facts, and Mr. Tucker knew he had to construct an alibi for Charlie Camplain. He couldn't very well deny that Camplain had come to the high school that morning. Witnesses had provided a trail for him all the way up to the moment when he approached Jean De Belle in the hallway and took her inside that empty classroom, where they disappeared into what would always be only theirs, until Mary Ellen heard the shots and came running down the stairs to find Jean slumped in the chair.

At that time, Mr. Tucker tried to argue, Charlie Camplain was walking out of the school, on top of the world, because Miss De Belle had accepted his engagement ring, had said she would indeed marry him.

"And you got a ride with Tom Heath, and you were playing the fool with that gun because you were giddy with excitement, and you were having yourself some fun. Isn't that right, Mr. Camplain?"

At that point, the charade broke down. Charlie Camplain wasn't able to keep it up.

"She was my light," he said in a choked voice. "If she wouldn't have me." Here, his voice trailed off, and he sat bent over in his chair, staring at his hands. "When she refused me," he finally said. "Well, I had that gun. When she said no, what else was I to do?"

And like that, it came to an end. All Mr. Tucker was able to do for his client was to successfully argue for a second-degree murder conviction, and a few weeks later, Charlie Camplain was sentenced to twenty years in prison for the shooting death of Miss Jean De Belle.

He would end up serving fifteen years of that sentence. A model prisoner, he was able to successfully petition for early parole. Where he went upon his release, no one in Lawrenceville or Vincennes ever knew, although on occasion someone would report seeing a man with a hearing aid that looked very much like Charlie Camplain.

In those fifteen years, Norville Rich married Lorene Devereaux, and the two of them took great delight and comfort from each other's company. They went for walks along the river beside the Old Cathedral and came home to share a quiet supper. They watched the wrestling matches on Saturday night, each of them with a glass of Schlitz beer, and when they lay down to sleep, they gave each other a tender kiss, and Norville said, "Goodnight, sweet girl." And like that, they were happy.

Millie Haines had her baby in the early spring of 1953. It was a boy, and she named him Bert, after her father. "He looks just like you," she said. "Same bald head and not a tooth in his mouth." Lord, how that baby could make Grinny grin!

As the years went on, and he and Peg found themselves alone in the house, Millie on her own after getting her cosmetologist's license from the Vincennes Beauty College, baby Bert growing up healthy and happy with the Heaths, Grinny would say to Peg, "Sometimes I think of what I almost let happen, and my heart nearly stops. How in the world could I have ever considered giving up this precious boy?"

And he was precious, their Bert. He was smart in school and good with his scout work, and the Heaths and Grinny and Peg watched him go off to high school, where, like his father, he ran track and worked on the *Toma Talk*.

"We get mixed up sometimes," Peg said to Grinny one night in bed. She reached out and snapped off the lamp, and the moonlight came in through the window. They heard the clock sound the hour at the Old Cathedral. She said. "We get mixed up, and then we find our way home."

Robbie went away to school and found out she was good at art. "Ain't that a hoot?" she said to her old friend Dixie Dale, who was the one who was supposed to follow in her father's footsteps and become an artist.

"Spread your wings," Dixie told her. "Robbie, spread your wings."

And she did. Bit by bit she tried to forget all that had transpired in the autumn of 1952. She tried to paint it out of her.

As the years went on, Mary Ellen heard from people who had seen Robbie's paintings hanging in galleries in New York, and she'd say, with great pride, "Yes, Robbie has had quite a bit of success. Not bad for a Lawrenceville girl. I always knew she'd go places."

Mary Ellen, in the winter after she'd lost her teaching job, stubbornly refused to leave town, no matter that she was the object of gossip. She wouldn't give people that pleasure. She wouldn't run and hide. No, she'd go uptown just as big as you please. She'd even go to basketball games at the high school. She'd visit the stores and businesses of every man on that school board and make them look her straight in the eye.

"Shame on you," she said one day to Mr. Piper at the radio station. "Shame."

She took a job as a sales clerk at Delzell's, and it gave her great pleasure to know that the wives of those men had to shop there, had to make small talk with her, had to rely on her for help, no matter how uncomfortable it made them. Dixie Dale worked there, too.

"You give it to them, Mrs. M.," she said one day. "All those old biddies. You let them know you're not going anywhere."

"I'm just doing my job," Mary Ellen said.

"Everyone knew it wasn't true," said Dixie. "You were the best teacher I ever had."

Small moments of grace like that were enough to sustain Mary Ellen. She watched the years come and go until she'd settled into a life alone. She saw Tom Heath marry Lola Malone, the sheriff's daughter, and then take over his father's paint store when Mr. Heath took ill with a cancer in his stomach and died. Mary Ellen took no great pleasure from that fact. She focused, instead, on what a good mother Lola was to the little boy, Bert. Mary Ellen watched that young family grow up. She sometimes saw Grinny and Peg walking with them on the square. The boy was beautiful—dark hair and big round dark eyes, and a blush to his fair cheeks—and Mary Ellen could tell that both Tom and Lola, as well as Grinny and Peg, were so very, very proud.

From time to time, Mary Ellen would write Robbie letters telling her about the people in the town, but Robbie, when she wrote back, never made mention of any of the news that she'd passed along. Robbie's letters were full of stories about her life in New York, her visits to Paris. She'd fallen in love with a man who was running for the U.S. Senate. "I'm happy, Mother," she wrote. "I'm very, very happy."

How could Mary Ellen not be happy for her? Though she missed her terribly, her heart thrilled to each letter, each photograph, each phone call.

One Sunday night, in 1968, the phone rang, and Mary Ellen rushed to answer it, thinking that it must be Robbie calling as was her habit.

But the voice on the other end of the line was a man's voice, and what he said, without a word of greeting, was, "You loved her, too, didn't you?"

Mary Ellen knew she was talking to Charlie Camplain. With an unsettling swoon she felt herself transported back to the autumn of 1952.

"How did you find me?" she asked.

He ignored her question. "What was she like that morning? That last morning?"

Mary Ellen remembered that first day of school, and how Jean rose early. Mary Ellen heard the bath water running. In the kitchen, she cooked breakfast. It was such a glorious morning, summer still hanging on. The window above the sink was open and a light breeze was stirring the curtains. Outside, the birds were singing. A glorious, sunny day. The first day of school.

Then Jean came down the stairs, and Mary Ellen said, "Oh, my."
What a picture she was in her new clothes. What a smile on her face.
She looked like a bright new penny.

It was all so clear to Mary Ellen, even after sixteen years, that she
couldn't help herself. She began to speak, and what she told Charlie
Camplain was that Jean had been happy—very, very happy. She'd been
nervous, yes, but also excited.

"Like she knew something grand was waiting for her," Mary Ellen
said.

Charlie Camplain didn't say a thing. She heard him breathing on
the other end of the line, and she wondered whether he hadn't heard
her.

So she said, "Yes, I loved her, too."

She was embarrassed to say this thing to Charlie Camplain. She
had no idea what he might be thinking as the silence went on, but she
wondered if he, too, were going back in time to the first days of his
love for Jean—days that no one but the two of them would ever know.

"Mr. Camplain?" she said, after the silence got too much for her.

She heard the line go dead. She stood there with the receiver pressed
to her ear, ashamed that she half wished he'd come back on the line.

Mary Ellen thought she'd put Jean away from her for good, but
now here she was. She was standing in the library. They were about
to go to the auditorium for the assembly. Mary Ellen could tell Jean
was just a little frightened. Mary Ellen would be an old lady before
any of this would make sense to her. You could think the worst thing
had happened, but it hadn't. It was somewhere in the future, just like
Charlie Camplain was that morning in September, but you didn't dare
think about it. You didn't want to give it size or shape. You didn't want
to give it power.

The rest of her life, Mary Ellen would remember Jean that
morning in the library. Her fingers were trembling. Mary Ellen kissed
her on the cheek. She squeezed her hand. Oh, the look on her face—
that smile, that spark in her eyes—as if she knew that all that she'd
ever hoped was almost there. It was in the way the books smelled, and

the freshly waxed floors, and the locker doors slamming shut, and the footsteps in the hall, and the students' bright voices. Such a glorious day in September. Everything she'd dreamed. She could hardly wait to begin.

ACKNOWLEDGMENTS

I WANT TO THANK MY agent, Susan Cohen, for her support of my work and her efforts on my behalf. Many thanks also go to Allison Cohen for her insightful readings of this book when it was in manuscript, and to Michelle Dotter for her excellent edits. Thank you, too, to Dzanc Books for giving me a home.

I wrote a good portion of this book in Lawrenceville, IL, where the crime took place. The crime is true; the rest is pure imagination. I wrote on my laptop in the genealogy room at the same public library I used when I was a high school student in neighboring Sumner. I so appreciate this library and the days I spent reconnecting with the people of my native Lawrence County. I especially want to thank the librarian, Dianne Dehner Brumley, for giving me this quiet place to write.

Above all, I thank my wife, Cathy, for her love and encouragement. Cath, I feel your strength every step along the way. I'm a better person and a better writer because of you.